Beach Blanket Bad Boys

Beach Blanket Bad Boys

LINDA LAEL MILLER

ALISON KENT

LUCY MONROE

JILL SHALVIS

SUSANNA CARR

MORGAN LEIGH

BRAVA

KENSINGTON PUBLISHING CORP.
http://www.kensingtonbooks.com

BRAVA BOOKS are published by

Kensington Publishing Corp.
850 Third Avenue
New York, NY 10022

ISBN 0-7582-1094-9

First Kensington Trade Paperback Printing: June 2005
10 9 8 7 6 5 4 3 2 1

CONTENTS

BATTERIES NOT REQUIRED

Linda Lael Miller

The last thing I wanted was a man to complicate my life. I came to that conclusion, on the commuter flight between Phoenix and Helena, Montana, because my best friend Lucy and I had been discussing the topic, online and via our Black-Berrys, for days. Maybe the fact that I was bound to encounter Tristan McCullough during my brief sojourn in my home-town of Parable had something to do with the decision.

Tristan and I had a history, one of those angst-filled sum-mer romances between high school graduation and college. Sure, it had been over for ten years, but I still felt bruised whenever I thought of him, which was more often than I should have, even with all that time to insulate me from the experience.

My few romantic encounters in between had done nothing to dissuade me from my original opinion.

Resolved: Men lie. They cheat—usually with your room-mate, your best friend, or somebody you're going to have to face at the office every day. They forget birthdays, dump you the day of the big date, and leave the toilet seat up.

Who needed it? I had B.O.B., after all. My battery-operated boyfriend.

Just as I was thinking those thoughts, my purse tumbled out of the overhead compartment and hit me on the head. I should have realized that the universe was putting me on notice. Cosmic e-mail. Subject: *Pay attention, Gayle.*

Hastily, avoiding the flight attendant's tolerant glance, which I knew would be disapproving because I'd asked for extra peanuts during the flight and gotten up to use the rest room when the seat belt sign was on, I shoved the bag under the seat in front of mine. Then I gripped the arms of 4B as the aircraft gave an apocalyptic shudder and nose-dived for the landing strip.

I squeezed my eyes shut.

The plane bumped to the ground, and I would have sworn before a hostile jury that the thing was about to flip from wingtip to wingtip before crumpling into a fiery ball.

My stomach surged into my throat, and I pictured smoldering wreckage on the six o'clock news in Phoenix, even heard the voice-over. *"Recently fired paralegal, Gayle Hayes, perished today in a plane crash outside the small Montana town of Parable. She was twenty-seven, a hard-won size 6 with two hundred dollars' worth of highlights in her shoulder-length brown hair, and was accompanied by her long-standing boyfriend, Bob—"*

As if my untimely and tragic death would rate a sound bite. And *as if* I'd brought Bob along on this trip. All I would have needed to complete my humiliation, on top of losing my job and having to make an appearance in Parable, was for some security guard to search my suitcase and wave my vibrator in the air.

But, hey, when you think you're about to die, you need *somebody*, even if he's made of pink plastic and runs on four 'C' batteries.

When it became apparent that the Grim Reaper was otherwise occupied, I lifted the lids and took a look around. The flight attendant, who was old enough to have served cocktails on Wright Brothers Air, smiled thinly. Like I said, we hadn't exactly bonded.

Despite my aversion to flying, I sat there wondering if they'd let me go home if I simply refused to get off the plane.

The cabin door whooshed open, and my fellow passengers—half a dozen in all—rose from their seats, gathered their belongings, and clogged the aisle at the front of the airplane. I'd scrutinized them—surreptitiously, of course—during the flight, in case I recognized somebody, but none of them were familiar, which was a relief.

Before the Tristan fiasco, I'd been ordinary, studious Gayle Hayes, daughter of Josie Hayes, manager and part owner of the Bucking Bronco Tavern. *After* our dramatic breakup, Tristan was still the golden boy, the insider, but I was Typhoid Mary. He'd grown up in Parable, as had his father and grandfather. His family had land and money, and in ranch country, or anywhere else, that adds up to credibility. I, on the other hand, had blown into town with my recently divorced mother, when I was thirteen, and remained an unknown quantity. I didn't miss the latest stepfather—he was one in a long line—and I loved Mom deeply.

I just didn't want to be like her, that was all. I wanted to go to college, marry one man, and raise a flock of kids. It might not be politically correct to admit it, but I wasn't really interested in a career.

When the Tristan-and-me thing bit the dust, I pulled my savings out of the bank and caught the first bus out of town.

Mom had long since moved on from Parable, but she still had a financial interest in the Bronco, and the other partners wanted to sell. I'm a paralegal, not a lawyer, but my mother saw that as a technicality. She'd hooked up with a new boyfriend—not the kind that requires batteries—and as of that moment, she was somewhere in New Mexico, on the back of a Harley. A week ago, on the same day I was notified that I'd been downsized, she called me from a borrowed cell phone and talked me into representing her at the negotiations.

In a weak moment, I'd agreed. She overnighted me an airline ticket and her power of attorney, and wired travel expenses into my checking account, and here I was—back in Parable, Montana, the place I'd sworn I would never think about, let alone visit, again.

"Miss?" The flight attendant's voice jolted me back to the present. From the expression on her face, I would be carried off bodily if I didn't disembark on my own. I unsnapped my seat belt, hauled my purse out from under 3B, and deplaned with as much dignity as I could summon.

I had forgotten why they call Montana the Big Sky Country. It's like being under a vast, inverted bowl of the purest blue, stretching from horizon to horizon.

The airport at Helena was small, and the land around the city is relatively flat, but the trees and mountains were visible in the distance, and I felt a little quiver of nostalgia as I took it all in. Living in Phoenix for the decade since I'd fled, working my way through vocational school and making a life for myself, I'd had plenty of occasion to miss the terrain, but I hadn't consciously allowed myself the indulgence.

I made my way carefully down the steps to the tarmac, and crossed to the entrance, trailing well behind the other passengers. Mom had arranged for a rental car, so all I had to do was pick up my suitcase at the baggage claim, sign the appropriate papers at Avis, and boogie for Parable.

I stopped at a McDonald's on the way through town, since I hadn't had breakfast and twenty-six peanuts don't count as nourishment. Frankly, I would have preferred a stiff drink, but you can't get arrested for driving under the influence of French fries and a Big Mac.

I switched on the radio, in a futile effort to keep memories of Tristan at bay, and the first thing I heard was Our Song.

I switched it off again.

My cell phone rang, inside my purse, and I fumbled for it.

It was Lucy.

"Where are you?" she demanded.

I pushed the speaker button on the phone, so I could finish my fries and still keep one hand on the wheel. "In the trunk of a car," I answered. "I've been kidnapped by the mob. Think I should kick out one of the taillights and wave my hand through the hole?"

Lucy hesitated. "Smart-ass," she said. "Where are you really?"

I sighed. Lucy is my best friend, and I love her, but she's the mistress of rhetorical questions. We met at school in Phoenix, but now she's a clerk in an actuary's office, in Santa Barbara. I guess they pay her to second-guess everything. "On my way to Parable. You know, that place we've been talking about via BlackBerry?"

"Oh," said Lucy.

I folded another fry into my mouth, gum-stick style. "Do you have some reason for calling?" I prompted. I didn't mean to sound impatient, but I probably did. My brain kept racing ahead to Parable, wondering how long it would take to get my business done and leave.

Lucy perked right up. "Yes," she said. "The law firm across the hall from our offices is hiring paralegals. You can get an application online."

I softened. It wasn't Lucy's fault, after all, that I had to go back to Parable and maybe come face to face with Tristan. I was jobless, and she was trying to help. "Thanks, Luce," I said. "I'll look into it when I have access to a computer. Right now, I'm in a rental car."

"I'll forward the application," she replied.

"Thanks," I repeated. The familiar road was winding higher and higher into the timber country. I rolled the window partway down, to take in the green smell of pine and fir trees.

"I wish I could be there to lend moral support," Lucy said.

"Me, too," I sighed. She didn't know about the Tristan debacle. Yes, she was my closest friend, but the subject was too painful to broach, even with her. Only my mother knew, and she probably thought I was over it.

Lucy's voice brightened. "Maybe you'll meet a cowboy."

I felt the word "cowboy" like a punch to the solar plexus. Tristan was a cowboy. And he'd gotten on his metaphorical horse and trampled my heart to a pulp. "Maybe," I said, to throw her a bone.

"Boss alert," Lucy whispered, apparently picking up an authority figure on the radar. "I'd better get back to my charts."

"Good idea," I said, relieved, and disconnected. I tossed the phone back into my purse.

I passed a couple of ranches, and a gas station with bears and fish and horses on display in the parking lot, the kind carved out of a tree stump with a chain saw. Yep, I was getting close to Parable.

I braced myself. Two more bends in the road.

On the first bend, I almost crashed into a deer.

On the second bend, I braked within two feet of a loaded cattle truck, jackknifed in the middle of the highway. I had already suspected that fate wasn't on my side. I knew it for a fact when Tristan McCullough stormed around one end of the semi-trailer, ready for a fight.

My heart surged up into my sinuses and got stuck there.

The decade since I'd seen him last had hardened his frame and chiseled his features, at least his mouth and lower jaw. I couldn't see the upper part of his face because of the shadow cast by the brim of his beat-up cowboy hat.

What does Tristan look like? Take Brad Pitt and multiply by a factor of ten, and you've got a rough idea.

"Didn't you see the flares?" he demanded, in that one quivering moment before he recognized me. "How fast were you going, anyway?" It clicked, and he stiffened, stopped in his tracks, a few feet from my car door.

"No, I didn't see any flares," I said, and I must have sounded lame, as well as defensive. "And I don't think I was speeding." My voice echoed in my head.

He recovered quickly, but that was Tristan. While I was pining, he'd probably been dating rodeo groupies, cocktail waitresses, and tourists. While I was waiting tables to get through school, he was winning fancy belt buckles for the school team and getting straight A's at the University of Montana without wasting time on such pedantic matters as studying and earning a living. "Back around the bend and put your flashers on. Otherwise, this situation might get a whole lot worse."

I just sat there.

"Hello?" he snarled.

I still didn't move.

Tristan opened the door of the rental and leaned in. "Get out of the car, Gayle," he said. "I'll do the rest."

My knees were watery, but I unsnapped the seat belt and de-carred. Four stumpy French fries fell off my lap, in seeming slow motion. It's strange, the things you notice when the earth topples off its axis.

Tristan climbed behind the wheel and backed the compact around the bend. When he returned, I was still standing in the road, listening to the cattle bawl inside the truck trailer. I felt like joining them.

"Are they hurt?" I asked.

"The cattle?" Tristan countered. "No. Just annoyed." He did that cowboy thing, taking off his hat, putting it on again in almost the same motion. "What are you doing here?"

For a moment, I was stumped for an answer. His eyes were so blue. His butternut hair still too long. Everything inside me seized up into a fetal ball.

"Gayle?" he prompted, none too kindly.

"The Bucking Bronco is up for sale, as you probably know. My mom sent me to protect her interests."

The azure gaze drifted over me, slowly and thoughtfully, leaving a trail of fire in its wake. "I see," he drawled, and it sounded like more than an acknowledgement of my reasons for returning to Parable, as if he'd developed x-ray vision and could see the lace panties and matching bra under my linen slacks and white cotton blouse. My blood heated, and my nipples went hard. When we were together, Tristan had had a way of undressing me with his eyes, and he hadn't lost the knack.

I flushed. "How long until you get this truck out of the way?" I asked. "I'd like to get my business done and get out of here."

"I'll just bet you would," he said, and a corner of his mouth quirked up in an insolent ghost of a grin. He leaned in, and I felt his breath against my face. More heat. "You're real good at running away."

My temper flared. "Whatever," I snapped. If he wanted to

make the whole thing my fault, fine. I wouldn't try to change his mind.

His gaze glided to my left hand, then back to my face. "No wedding ring," he said. "I figured you would have married some poor sucker, out of spite. Maybe even had a couple of kids."

"Well," I said, "you figured wrong."

"No boyfriend?" There was a note of disbelief in his voice, as though he thought I couldn't go five minutes without a man, let alone ten years.

I straightened my spine. The pitiable state of my love life was nobody's business, least of all Tristan McCullough's. "I'm in a committed relationship," I said. "His name is Bob."

Tristan's mouth twitched. "Bob," he repeated.

"He's in electronics," I said.

Something sparked in Tristan's eyes—humor, I thought—and I hoped he hadn't guessed that Bob was a vibrator.

Get a grip, I told myself. Tristan might have known where all my erotic zones were, but he wasn't psychic.

Feeling bolder, now that I knew I wouldn't spontaneously combust just by being in Tristan's presence—provided he didn't *touch* me, that is—I cast a disgusted glance toward the trailer, full of unhappy cows. "So, how long did you say it will take to get this truck off the road?"

"You already asked me that."

"Yes, but you didn't answer."

He looked irritated. "I called for some help. There's a wrecker on the way. Guess you're just going to have to be patient."

I approached the trailer—the cattle smelled even worse than they sounded—and noticed that a set of double wheels at the front had slipped partway into the ditch. Beyond it was a drop-off of several hundred feet.

My stomach quivered. "I really hope they don't all decide to stand on one side of the trailer," I said.

Tristan was right beside me. He looked pale under his rancher's tan. "Me, too," he said.

"What happened? I thought you were this great driver."

He scowled, did the hat thing again. Before he had to answer, we heard revving engines on the other side of the truck. We ducked between the trailer and the cab and watched as a wrecker and about fourteen pickup trucks rolled up.

An older man—I recognized him immediately as Tristan's grandfather—leaped out of a beat-up vehicle and hurried toward us. "We gotta get those cows out of that rig before they trample each other," he called. He squinted at me, but quickly lost interest. Story of my life. Sometimes, I think I'm invisible. "Jim and Roy are up on the ridge road, unloading the horses. We're gonna need 'em to keep the cattle from scattering all over the county."

Tristan nodded, and I looked up, trying to locate the aforementioned ridge road. High above, I saw two long horse trailers, pulled by more pickup trucks, perched on what looked like an impossibly narrow strip of land. I counted two riders and some dozen horses making their careful way down the hillside.

"What's she doing here?" the wrecker guy asked Tristan, after cocking a thumb at me.

I didn't hear Tristan's answer over all the ruckus. Oh, well. I probably wouldn't have liked it anyway.

"Get out of the way," Tristan told me, as he and the guys from the flotilla of pickup trucks up ahead got ready to unload the cattle. I retreated a ways, and watched as he climbed onto the back of the semi-trailer, threw the heavy steel bolts that held the doors closed, and climbed inside.

An image came to my mind, of the whole shebang rolling over the cliff, with Tristan inside, and I almost threw up the twenty-six peanuts, along with the Big Mac and the fries.

The horsemen arrived, and several of the men on the ground immediately mounted up. Tristan threw down a ramp from inside.

"Watch out them cattle don't trample you!" the grandfather called. He'd gone back to his truck for a lasso, and he looked ready to rope.

Over the uproar, I distinctly heard Tristan laugh.

A couple of cows came down the ramp, looking surprised to find themselves on a mountain road. The noise increased as the animals came down the metal ramp. The trailer rocked with the shifting weight, and the wheels slipped slightly.

"Easy!" Grampa yelled.

"I'm doing the best I can, old man!" Tristan yelled back.

The trailer was big. Just the same, I would never have guessed it could hold that many cattle. They just kept coming, like the critters bailing out of Noah's Ark after the flood, except that they didn't travel two by two.

Before long, the road was choked with them. There was dust, and a lot of cowboys on horseback, yelling "Hyaww!" I concentrated on staying out of the way, and wished I hadn't worn linen pants and a white blouse. On the other hand, how do you dress for something like that?

Tristan came down the ramp, at long last, and I let out my breath.

He wasn't going to plunge to his death in a cattle truck.

I found a tree stump and sat down on it.

I lost track of Tristan in all the fuss. The cattle were trying to get away, fanning out over the road, trying to climb the hillside, even heading for the steep drop on the other side of the road. The cowboys yelled and whistled and rode in every direction.

All of a sudden, Tristan was right in front of me, mounted on a big bay gelding. A grin flashed on his dusty face. "Come on," he said, leaning down to offer me a hand. "I'll take you into town. It'll be a while before the road's clear."

I cupped my hands around my mouth to be heard over the din. "What about my car?"

"One of the men will bring it to you later."

I hadn't ridden a horse since the summer of my American Cowboy, but I knew I'd get trampled if I tried to walk through the milling herd. I went to stand up, but my butt was stuck to the stump.

Tristan threw back his head and laughed.

"What?" I shouted, mortified and still struggling.

"Pitch," he said. "You might have to take off your pants."

"In your dreams," I retorted, and struggled some more, with equal futility.

Grinning, Tristan swung down out of the saddle, took a grip on the waistband of my slacks at either side, and wrenched me to my feet. I felt the linen tear away at the back, and my derriere blowing in the breeze. If I'd had my purse, I'd have used it to cover myself, but it was still in the rental car.

My predicament struck Tristan as funny, of course. While I was trying to hold my pants together, he hurled me bodily onto the horse, and mounted behind me. That stirred some visceral memories, ones I would have preferred to ignore, but it was difficult, under the circumstances.

"I need my purse," I said.

"Later," he replied, close to my ear.

"And my suitcase." I'm nothing if not persistent.

"Like I'm going to ride into town with a *suitcase*," Tristan said. "It could spook Samson."

"Why can't we just borrow one of these trucks?"

"We've got a horse." I guess he considered that a reasonable answer.

Tears of frustration burned behind my eyes. I'd hoped to slip in and out of Parable unnoticed. Now, I'd be arriving on horseback, with the back of my pants torn away. Shades of Lady Godiva.

"Hold on," Tristan said, sending another hot shiver through my system as the words brushed, warm and husky, past my ear.

He didn't have to tell me twice. When he steered that horse down into the ditch—one false step and we'd have been in free fall, Tristan, the gelding, and me—I gripped the saddle horn with both hands and held on for dear life. I would have closed my eyes, but between clinging for dear life and controlling my bladder, I'd exhausted my physical resources.

We bumped up on the other side of the trailer and, once we were clear of the pickup trucks, Tristan nudged the horse into a trot.

I bounced ignobly against a part of his anatomy I would have preferred not to think about, and by that time I'd given up on trying to hold the seat of my slacks together. He was rock-hard under those faded jeans of his, and I sincerely hoped he was suffering as grievously as I was.

Parable hadn't changed much since I'd left, except for the addition of a huge discount store at one end of town. People honked and waved as we rode down the main drag, and Tristan, the show-off, occasionally tipped his hat.

We passed the Bucking Bronco Tavern, now closed, with its windows boarded up, and I felt a pang of nostalgia. Mom and I weren't real close, but I couldn't help remembering happy times in our little apartment behind the bar, with its linoleum floors and shabby furniture. My tiny bedroom was butt up against the back wall of the tavern, and I used to go to sleep to the click of pool balls and the wail of the jukebox. I felt safe, knowing my mother was close by, even if she *was* refereeing brawls, topping off draft beers, and flirting for tips.

Behind the stores, huge pines jutted toward the supersized sky, and I caught glimmers of Preacher Lake. In the winter, Parable looks like a vintage postcard. In fact, it's so 1950s that I half expected to blink and see everything in black and white.

I had reservations at the Lakeside Motel, since that was the only hostelry in town, besides Mamie Sweet's Bed and Breakfast. Mom wouldn't have booked me a room there, since she and Mamie had once had a hair-pulling match over a farm implement salesman from Billings. Turned out he was married anyway, but as far as I knew, the feud was still on.

Tristan brought the horse to a stop in front of the Lakeside, with nary a mention of the B&B, another sign that Mom and Mamie had never had that Hallmark moment. He dismounted and reached up to help me down.

I didn't want to flash downtown Parable, but my choices were limited. As soon as I was on the ground, I closed the gap in my slacks. Tristan grinned as I backed toward the motel office, my face the same raspberry shade as my lace underpants.

The woman behind the registration desk was a stranger, but from the way she looked me over, she one, knew who I was, and two, had heard an unflattering version of my hasty departure on the four o'clock bus.

I bit my lower lip.

"You must be Gayle," she said. She was tall and thin, with short dark hair. I pegged her for one of those people who live on granola and will risk their lives to protect owls and old-growth timber.

I nodded. I had no purse, and no luggage. I'd just ridden into town on a horse, and I was trying to hold my clothing together. I didn't feel talkative.

Suddenly, she smiled and put out a hand in greeting. "Natalie Beeks," she said. "Welcome to the Lakeside." She ruffled through some papers and slapped a form down on the counter, along with one of those giveaway pens that run out of ink when you write the third item on a grocery list. "You're in Room 7. It overlooks the lake."

After glancing back over my shoulder to make sure no one was about to step into the office and get a good look at Victoria's Secret, I took a risk and signed the form. "My stuff will be arriving shortly," I said, in an offhand attempt to sound normal.

"Sure," Nancy said. Then she frowned. "What happened to your pants?"

She'd probably seen me on the front of Tristan's horse, and I didn't want her jumping to any conclusions. "I—sat in something," I said.

She nodded sagely, as though people in her immediate circle of friends sat in things all the time. Maybe they did. Country life can be messy. "I could lend you something," she offered.

I flushed with relief, claiming the key to Room 7 with my free hand. "I would really appreciate that," I said. There was no telling how long it would be before my car was delivered, along with the suitcase.

"Hold on a second." Nancy left the desk, and disappeared

into a back room. I heard her feet pounding on a set of stairs, and she returned, handing me a pair of black polyester shorts, just as a minivan pulled into the gravel parking lot out front.

I practically snatched them out of her hand. "Thanks."

A husband, a wife, and four little kids in swimming suits got out of the van, stampeding for the front door. I eased to one side, careful to keep my butt toward the wall. Out of the corner of my eye, I thought I saw Nancy grin.

"Heck of a mess out on the highway," the husband announced, as he stepped over the threshold. He was balding, clad in plaid Bermuda shorts and a muscle shirt. The effect of the outfit was brave but unfortunate. "Cattle all over the place. We had to wait at least twenty minutes before the road was clear."

"Where's the pool?" one of the kids yelled. All four of them looked ready to thumb their noses and jump in.

Their mother, a harried-looking woman in a saggy sundress, brushed mouse-brown bangs back from her forehead. "There isn't a pool," she told the children, eyeing me curiously as I sidestepped it toward the door, still keeping my back to the wall. "You can swim in the lake."

"Excuse me," I said, and edged past her to make a break for it, the borrowed shorts clutched in one hand.

Room 7 was around back, with the promised view of the lake, but I didn't bother to admire the scenery until I'd slammed the door behind me, peeled off my ruined slacks, and wriggled into the shorts.

Only then did I take a look around. Tile floors, plain double bed, lamps with wooden bases carved to resemble the chain-saw bears I'd seen in the gas station parking lot. There was a battered dresser along one wall, holding up a TV that still had a channel dial. The bathroom was roughly the size of a phone booth, but it was clean, and that was all that mattered. I wouldn't be in Parable long. Sit in on the negotiations, sign the papers, and I'd be out of there.

I splashed my face with cold water and held my hair up off my neck for a few seconds, wishing for a rubber band.

Going to the window, I pulled the cord and the drapes swished open to reveal the lake, sparkling with June sunlight. There was a long dock, and I could see the four little kids from the office jumping into the shallow end, with shouts of glee, while their mother watched attentively.

I felt a twinge of yearning. The Bronco backed up to the lake, too, and Mom and I used to skinny-dip back there on Sunday nights, when the tavern was closed and the faithful were all at evening services.

I was tempted to call her, just to let her know I'd arrived, but I decided against it. There would be a charge for using the phone in the room, and my budget was severely limited; better to wait until my stuff arrived and I could use my cell. I had un-limited minutes, after all, and besides, she probably wouldn't hear the ring over the roar of the Harley engine. My mother, the biker chick.

The lake was really calling to me by then. I would have loved to wander down to the dock, kick off my sandals, and dangle my feet in that blue, blue water, but I couldn't bring myself to intrude on the swimming party. Anyway, I figured being at the fringe of that happy little family would have made me feel lonelier, instead of lifting my spirits.

I was sitting on the end of my double bed, leafing through an outdated issue of *Field & Stream,* when the telephone jan-gled and nearly scared me out of my skin.

"Hello?" I said uncertainly.

"Just thought I'd let you know your car is here," Nancy told me. "It's parked in the lot, and I have the keys here in the office."

I thanked her and rushed to reclaim my suitcase and purse.

When I got back to the room, I took a shower, scrubbing the pitch off my backside, and put on clean jeans and a tank top. My cell phone, nestled in the bottom of my bag, was on its last legs, making an irritating bleep-bleep sound.

I turned it off, plugged it in for a charge, and peered out the window again. The minivan family was still in the water. The dad had joined them by then, but the mom still sat on the dock, smiling and shading her eyes with one hand.

I grabbed my purse, locked up the room, and stopped by the office to return Nancy's shorts. I suppose I should have washed them first, but that seemed a little over the top, considering I'd worn them for half an hour at the outside.

Leaving the rental car in the lot, I set out on foot for the Bucking Bronco. I was hoping for a peek inside, though I don't know what I expected to see.

Passing cars slowed, so the driver and passengers could gawk, as I walked toward the tavern. Strangers always get noticed in towns like Parable—if I could be considered a stranger. Most likely, people remembered me as the poor girl who thought someone like Tristan McCullough could really be interested in her.

I waved cheerfully and picked up my pace.

Reaching the Bronco, I noted, without surprise, that the front doors were padlocked. I tried looking through the cracks between the boards covering the windows, but to no avail. I went around back, hoping for better luck.

Here, there were no boards and no padlocks. I turned to scan the sparkling lake for watching boaters, but there were none to be seen, so I tried the door.

It creaked open, and I stopped on the threshold. I thought I heard music, soft and distant. The jukebox? Impossible. The Bronco had been closed for several years, according to Mom, and the electricity must have been shut off long ago.

Still, my breath quickened. I stood still, listening. Yes, there was music. And the familiar click of pool balls.

Ghosts? The only people who would have haunted the Bronco were Mom and I, and we weren't dead.

I stepped inside, hesitantly, my heart hammering. I wasn't scared, exactly, but something out of the ordinary was definitely going on. My curiosity won out over good sense, and I followed the sounds, swimming through a swell of memories as I passed through the little apartment. Mom at the stove, stirring a canned supper and humming a Dolly Parton song. Me, curled up on the ancient sofa, studying.

The door between the apartment and the bar stood open.

The music brought tears to my eyes. Tristan and I used to dance under the stars to the song that was playing. For a moment, I was transported back to our favorite spot, high on a ridge overlooking his family's ranch, with that old, sentimental tune pouring out of the CD player in Tristan's truck. I felt his arms around me. I remembered how he'd lay me down so gently in the tall, sweet-scented grass, and make love to me until I lost myself.

I took another step, even though everything inside me screamed, *Run!*

There was a portable boombox on the dusty bar, and Tristan stood next to the pool table, leaning on his cue stick. He was wearing the same dusty clothes he'd had on before, and his hat rested on one of the bar stools.

"I knew you'd show up," he said.

My throat felt tight and raw. I couldn't think of anything to say, and couldn't have gotten the words out even if I had.

He hung the cue stick on the wall rack and walked toward me.

I was frozen in place, temporarily speechless, just the way I'd been on the road outside of town an hour or so earlier.

Tristan pushed a button on the boombox, and our song began to play. "Dance with me," he said, and pulled me into his arms.

I stumbled along with him. He used the pad of one thumb to brush away my tears.

I finally found my voice. "I didn't see your horse outside," I said.

He laughed. For all that he'd been herding cattle, he smelled of laundry detergent and that green grass we used to lie down in, together. "Gramps took him back to the ranch," he said. "I walked over here from the office. Left my truck there."

"How did you know I'd come here?"

"Easy," he said. "This was home. I knew you couldn't stay away." He kissed me, a light, nibbling, tasting kiss.

I should have resisted, but the best I could do was ask, "What do you want?"

"We have some unfinished business, you and I," he said, and caught my right earlobe lightly between his teeth.

A thrill of need went through me. "We don't," I argued, but weakly.

I felt the edge of the pool table pressing against my rear end. That was nothing compared to what was pressing against my front. "You cheated on me," I murmured.

He kissed me again, deeply this time, with tongue. The floor of the tavern seemed to pitch to one side, like the deck of a ship too small for the waves it was riding.

"You cheated on *me*," he countered.

We'd had that argument just before I left Parable, ten years before, but the circumstances had changed. There had been a lot of yelling then, and I'd thrown things.

Tristan slid a hand up under my tank top, and I didn't stop him. I don't know why. I just didn't. I groaned inside.

He pushed my bra up, cupped my breast, chafing the nipple with the side of his thumb, and kissed me once more.

I am not a loose woman, but you'd never have known it by the way I responded to Tristan's kisses and the way he caressed my breast. I was wet between the legs, and I could already feel myself opening to take him inside, even though I had no intention of letting him get into my jeans.

He unsnapped them, pushed the zipper down, then tugged my tank top down to bare my breast. When he took my nipple into his mouth, I cried out, buried my hands in his hair, and held him close.

I felt his chuckle of triumph reverberate through my breast, but I still didn't stop him. *Just a minute more,* I remember thinking. *Just a minute more, and then I'll push him away and slap his face for him.*

"Oh, God," I said instead.

He hooked a thumb in the waistband of my jeans and panties and pulled them down, in one move. Without releasing my breast, he hoisted me onto the pool table, eased me back onto the felt top, and reached inside to find my sweet spot.

I gasped his name.

He pushed up my top, and my bra, took his time enjoying my breasts.

My vision blurred. *Just a minute more . . .*

"Remember how it was with us?" Tristan asked throatily, kissing my belly now. My jeans and panties were around my ankles by then. "Remember?"

I'd tried to shut the memory out of my mind for ten years, but I remembered, all right. At a cellular level.

Tristan stopped long enough to pull off my shoes and toss my pants aside. Then he was nibbling at my navel again, and I felt his fingers glide inside me.

I wish I could blame him, but I was the one who lifted my heels to the edge of the pool table and parted my legs.

I held my breath, waiting. There was a debate going on inside my head.

Tell him to stop.

Just a minute more . . .

The debate was nothing, compared to the riot in my senses. The weather was mild, but my skin burned as the passion grew.

Tristan parted me, took me into his mouth.

I moaned.

He teased me with the tip of his tongue. Made me beg.

He sucked again, then went back to flicking at me.

I bucked on that old pool table, and when he knew I was ready to come, he slipped both hands under my buttocks, raised me high, and ate me until I exploded. I had one orgasm, then another, deeper and harder. I lost count before he finally eased me down onto the felt again, and even though I was dazed with satisfaction, I knew it wasn't over.

I sensed that he was unbuttoning his jeans, unwrapping a condom, putting it on.

He moved sleekly into me, and that was when I caught fire again. He'd worked me over so well that I wouldn't have thought I had another orgasm in me, but I did.

Tristan put his hands behind my shoulders and lifted me up, so I was sitting on him. I wrapped my bare legs around his hips and held on tight. I knew from experience that this ride would be wilder than anything the rodeo had to offer.

"God, you feel good," Tristan rasped, kissing me again. "So good."

He raised me, then lowered me slowly along his shaft. I gave a sob, tilted my head back, and closed my eyes.

"Look at me," he said.

I was under a spell by then, rummy with need. I did as he asked.

I had three more orgasms before Tristan laid me down again, on the pool table, and thrust hard, one, twice, a third time. We came together, me sobbing and clinging, drenched in perspiration, Tristan with his head flung back like a stallion taking a mare. He gave a muffled shout, and stiffened against me, driving deeper than ever.

When it was over, he braced both hands against the side of the table, on either side of my hips, breathing heavily.

"Is it like that with Bob?" he asked.

That was when I slapped him, hard.

He stepped back, grinning, but the look in his eyes was hard. He handed me my jeans and panties and stepped back, after pulling me to my feet. I scrambled into my clothes, jammed on my shoes. I wanted to slap him again, but a part of me was ashamed of doing it once, let alone a second time. I'm not a violent person, and I don't believe in hitting people.

"You bastard," I said. Then I fled, across the tavern, through the apartment, out into the backyard, letting the screen door slam hard behind me. The lake was right there, shimmering with azure blue beauty, and I wanted to drown myself in it.

Behind me, the door hinges squeaked.

"Gayle." Tristan's voice. I knew without looking that he was in the doorway.

I wasn't planning to turn around, but I did. Hadn't planned on letting an old boyfriend screw me on a pool table, either. Did that, too.

Tristan was leaning against the door jamb, just as I'd imagined, rumple-haired and too damned attractive, even then. "I'm sorry," he said.

I stared at him. I'd expected something else, I don't know what. Mockery, maybe. More seduction. But certainly not an apology.

"I shouldn't have mentioned your boyfriend."

I almost defended Bob, before I remembered he was a vibrator. "You proved you could still make me lose control. Let's leave it at that, okay."

"Is he going to be mad?"

I suddenly saw the humor in the situation, even though I knew there were fresh tears on my face. "There'll be a buzz," I said.

Tristan looked confused, which was fine by me. "You're planning to tell him?"

I nodded. I was on a roll. "He'll be rigid about it."

"Did it ever occur to you that he might not be the right man for you, if it was that easy to get hot with me?"

So much for nonviolence. I would have slapped him again if he hadn't been well out of reach. "Maybe it's not a great relationship," I said, "but at least Bob doesn't cheat on me."

Tristan shoved a hand through his hair, and his jawline hardened. But, then, he wasn't in on the joke. "No, but you cheat on him. Some things never change."

I tightened my fists. "No," I snapped. "Some things never do."

With that, I headed for the rocky beach that runs along the edge of the lake. I was both relieved and disappointed that Tristan didn't follow.

The motel was a half-mile hike, but I was so distracted that I hardly noticed. Fortunately, the Fun Family had left the swimming area, so I didn't have to worry about anybody seeing me with my hair messed up and my eyes puffy from crying furious tears.

I pulled my key from the hip pocket of my jeans, let myself into the room, and immediately took another shower.

I wanted to hibernate, but the Big Mac had worn off, and I knew the Lakeside didn't offer room service. I dressed carefully in the only other set of clothes I had, besides the prim business suit I planned to wear to the meeting with the other owners of the Bronco and the new buyers, a cotton sundress. I'd briefly scanned the papers, and knew the gathering was scheduled for ten the next morning; I would worry about the where part later.

Determined to restore some semblance of dignity, I put on makeup, styled my hair, and left the motel again.

There was still only one restaurant in Parable, a hole-in-the-wall diner on Main Street, across from the library. I had to pause on the sidewalk out front and brace myself to go in.

I was the girl who had done Tristan McCullough wrong, and I knew the locals remembered. By now, some of them might even know that I'd just done a pool-table mambo with the golden boy, though I didn't think Tristan would stoop so low as to screw and tell. Just the same, I'd be lucky if they didn't throw me out bodily.

I was starved, and the only other place I could get food was the supermarket. That would mean going back to the motel for my rental car, shopping for cold cuts and chips, and huddling in my room to eat.

No way I had the strength to do all that.

I needed protein. Immediately.

So I forced myself to go in.

The diner hadn't changed much since the last time I'd been there. Red vinyl booths, a long counter, a revolving pie case. There was no hostess, and all the tables were full.

I took a stool at the counter and reached for a menu. I could feel people staring at me, but I pretended I had the restaurant to myself. Oh, I was a cool one, all right. Unless you counted a tendency to boink Tristan McCullough on a pool table with little or no provocation.

"Help you, honey?"

I looked up from the menu and met the kindly eyes of an aging waitress. She seemed vaguely familiar, but I didn't recog-

nize her name, even when I read it off the little tag on her uni-
form.

Florence.

"I'll take the meat loaf special," I said, looking neither to
the left nor right. "And a diet cola. Large."

"Comin' right up," Florence assured me, and smiled again.

I relaxed a little. At least there was one person in Parable
who didn't think I ought to be tarred, feathered and run out of
town on a rail. Make that two—Nancy Beeks, over at the
Lakeside, had been friendly enough.

The little bell over the door tinkled as someone entered,
and the diner chatter died an instant death. I knew without
turning around that Tristan had just walked in, because every
nerve in my body leaped to instinctual attention.

Damn him. He wasn't going to leave me alone. He'd gotten
past my well-maintained defenses without breaking a sweat.
He'd made love to me in an empty tavern. What more did he
have to prove?

He took the stool next to mine, reached casually for a
menu. He'd showered, too, I saw out of the corner of my eye,
and put on fresh clothes—Levi's and a blue chambray shirt.
"Fancy meeting you here," he said, without looking my way.

"Like it's a surprise," I retorted.

Florence set my diet cola down, along with clean silverware. "That special will be ready in a minute, sweetie," she
told me, before turning her attention to Tristan. "Hey, there,
handsome. You stepping out on me, all slicked up like that?"
she teased.

To my satisfaction, color pulsed in Tristan's neck. "Would I
do that to you, Flo?"

She laughed. "Probably," she said. "Who's the lucky gal?"

"You wouldn't know her," he replied, smooth as could be.
"The meat loaf sounds good. I'll have that, and a chocolate
milk shake."

Flo glanced at me, then looked at Tristan again. Somehow,
she'd connected the dots. She smiled broadly and went off to
give the order to the fry cook.

"How long are you going to be in town?" Tristan still wasn't looking at me, but I figured he wasn't asking the customer on the other side of him. The man had the look of a long-time resident.

"As long as it takes to finalize the sale of the Bronco," I answered, because I knew he wouldn't leave me alone until I did. Tristan was a hard man to ignore. The reference to the tavern made me squirm, though, because I couldn't help remembering how many orgasms I'd had, and how fiercely intense they'd been. I hadn't exactly kept them to myself.

"Shouldn't be long," he said, still staring straight ahead, as if he'd taken a deep interest in the milk shake machine, already churning up his order. "The other owners are eager to sell, and the buyer is ready to make out a check."

"Good," I replied, and took a sip of my diet cola. At the moment, I wished it would turn into a double martini. I could have used the anesthetic effect.

He turned his stool ever so slightly in my direction, but there was still no eye contact. Like everybody in the diner didn't know we were talking. "I suppose you've talked to Bob by now," he said.

Bob was in my dresser drawer, under four pairs of panties. "Of course," I said lightly. "Bob and I are honest with each other."

"Right. By now, he's probably on his way here to punch me in the mouth."

"Bob isn't that sort of man." Bob, of course, wasn't *any* sort of man.

"I'd do it, if I were him."

I smiled to myself, though I was shaken, and there was that peculiar tightening in the pit of my stomach again. "He's not the violent type," I said.

Flo set my plate of meat loaf down in front of me. Hunger had driven me to that diner, but now I had no appetite at all. Because I knew Tristan and everybody else in the place would make something of it if I paid my bill and left without taking a bite, I picked up my fork.

"And I am?" Tristan asked tersely.

"You said it yourself," I replied, with a lightness I didn't feel. I put a piece of meat loaf into my mouth, chewed and swallowed, before going on. "If you were in Bob's place, you'd punch him in the mouth."

"What does he do for a living?"

"I told you," I answered smoothly. "He's in electronics. Mostly, though, he just concentrates on keeping me happy."

"I'll just bet he does."

I wanted to laugh. I ate more meat loaf instead.

Tristan looked annoyed. His voice was an edgy whisper. "What kind of man doesn't mind when somebody else boinks his woman?"

"Bob gets a charge out of things like that," I said. It wasn't the complete truth. I didn't have to plug him into the wall like I did my cell phone. He ran on Duracells.

"I can't believe you'd settle for a man like that," Tristan snarled. He glowered at Flo when she brought his milk shake and silverware, and she retreated quickly, though she was grinning a little. "Don't you have any pride?"

The meat loaf turned to cardboard, and stuck in my throat. I took a gulp of cola to avert any necessity of the Heimlich maneuver. "Funny you should ask," I replied quietly, "after what just happened at the Bronco."

At last, Tristan turned far enough to face me. He looked straight into my eyes. "You don't love this Bob bozo," he said bluntly. "If you did—"

At my panicked look, he stopped. For all I knew, the people on both sides of us were listening to every word we said.

Flo came back with his meat loaf, but he pulled some bills out of his Levi pocket and tossed them on the counter without even looking at her or the food. "Come on," he said. Then he grabbed my hand and dragged me out of the diner.

I dug in my heels when we hit the sidewalk. "I wanted to finish my dinner," I lied.

"I'll fix you an omelet at my place," he said. There was a big, shiny SUV parked at the curb. He opened the passenger door and practically tossed me inside.

"I am not going to your place," I told him. But I didn't try to escape, either. Not that I could have. He was blocking my way. "What we did at the Bronco was a lapse of judgment on my part. It's over, and I'd just as soon forget it."

"We need to talk."

"Why? We had sex, it was good, and now it's history. What is there to talk about?" Was this me talking? Miss Traditional Love and Marriage, hoping for a husband, two point two children and a dog?

Tristan stepped back, slammed the car door, stormed around to the other side, and got in. His right temple was throbbing.

"Maybe that's all it means to you," he bit out, jamming the rig into gear and screeching away from the curb, "but to me, it was more than sex. *Way* more."

My mouth dropped open. We were hovering on the brink of something I'd fantasized about, with and without Bob—or were we? Maybe I was out there alone, like always, and Tristan was leading me on. It didn't take a software wizard to work out that he wanted more sex.

"Like what?" I said.

He turned onto a side street, and brought the SUV to a stop in front of a two-story house I used to dream about living in, as a kid. It was white, with green shutters on the windows and a fenced, grassy yard. There were flowerbeds, too, all blooming.

And the sign swinging by the gate read, "Tristan McCullough, Attorney at Law."

"Never mind like what," he snapped, while I was still getting over the fact that he was a lawyer. "Things didn't end right between us, and I'm not letting this go till we talk it out!"

I was a beat or two behind. Last I'd heard, Tristan was planning to major in Agriculture and Animal Husbandry. Instead, he'd gone on to law school.

Sheesh. A lot can happen in ten years.

I'd been into survival. He'd been making something of his life.

The contrast hurt, big-time. I sat there in the passenger seat like a lump, staring at the sign.

Tristan shut off the engine, thrust out a sigh, and turned to face me squarely. His blue eyes were narrow, and shooting little golden sparks.

"Impressed?" he asked bitterly.

I flinched. "What?"

"Isn't that why you left Parable? Because you thought I'd turn out to be a saddle bum, following the rodeo?"

"I thought," I said evenly, "that you would work on the ranch. Family tradition, and all that."

He sighed again, rubbed his chin with one hand. He'd showered and changed clothes between the Bronco and the diner, but he hadn't shaved. An attractive stubble was beginning to gleam on the lower part of his face.

"I keep getting this wrong," he muttered, sounding almost despondent. I wasn't sure if he was talking to me, or to himself.

I wanted to cry, for a variety of reasons, both simple and complicated, but I smiled instead. "It's okay, Tristan," I heard myself say. My voice came out sounding gentle, and a little raw. "We never did get along. Let's just agree to disagree, as they say, and get on with our lives."

"As I recall, we got along just fine," he said. I could tell he didn't want to smile back, but he did. "Until one of us said something, anyway."

I laughed, but my sinuses were clogged with tears I wouldn't shed until I was alone in Room 7, with a lake view. "Right."

"How's Josie?"

The question took me off guard. "Fine," I said.

"She was a kick."

"Still is," I said lightly. "She's into bikers these days."

Tristan brushed my cheek with the backs of his fingers, and I had the usual cattle-prod reaction, though I think I hid it pretty well. "Got to be better than Bob," he said.

I felt a flash of guilt. "Listen, about Bob—"

Tristan raised an eyebrow, waiting.

I couldn't do it. I just couldn't bring myself to admit that Bob was a vibrator. It was too pathetic. "Forget it," I said.

"Like hell," Tristan replied.

A stray thought broadsided me, out of nowhere. Tristan was a lawyer, and most likely the only one in Parable, given the size of the place. Which probably meant he was involved in the negotiations for the Bucking Bronco.

"Who's buying the tavern?" I asked.

It was his turn to look blank, though he recovered quickly. "A bunch of investors from California. Real estate types. They're putting in a restaurant and a marina, and building a golf course across the lake."

"Damn," I muttered.

"What do you care?" he asked.

"You're representing them, and my mother knew it."

"Well, yeah," Tristan said, in a puzzled, so-what tone of voice.

"She *knew* I would have done anything to avoid seeing you."

"Gee, thanks."

"Well, it's true. You broke my heart!"

"That's not the way I remember it," Tristan said.

I unfastened my seat belt, got out of the SUV, and started for the Lakeside Motel. By now, my phone would be charged. I intended to dial my mother's number and hit redial until she answered, if it took all night.

I had a few things to say to her. We were about to have a Dr. Phil moment, Mom and I.

Tristan caught up in a few strides. "Where are you going?"

"None of your damn business."

"I did *not* break your heart," he insisted.

"Whatever," I answered, because I knew it would piss him off, and if he got mad enough, he'd leave me alone.

He caught hold of my arm and turned me around to face him. "Damn it, Gayle, I'm not letting you walk away again. Not without an explanation."

"An explanation for what?" I demanded, wrenching free.

Tristan looked up and down the street. Except for one guy mowing his lawn, we might have been alone on an abandoned movie set. Pleasantville, USA. "You know damned well *what*!"

I did know, regrettably. I'd been holding the memories at bay ever since I got on the first plane in Phoenix—even before that, in fact—but now the dam broke and it all flooded back, in Technicolor and Dolby sound.

I'd gone to the post office, that bright summer morning a decade ago, to pick up the mail. There was a letter from the University of Montana—I'd been accepted, on a partial scholarship.

My feet didn't touch the ground all the way back to the Bronco.

Mom stood behind the bar, humming that Garth Brooks song about having friends in low places and polishing glasses. The place was empty, except for the two of us, since it was only about 9:30, and the place didn't open until 10.

I waved the letter, almost incoherent with excitement. I was going to college!

Mom had looked up, smiling, when I banged through the door from the apartment, but as she caught on, the smile fell away. She went a little pale, under her perfect makeup, and as I handed her the letter, I noticed that her lower lip wobbled.

She read it. "You can't go," she said.

"But there's a scholarship—and I can work—"

Best of all, I'd be near Tristan. He'd been accepted weeks ago, courted by the coach of the rodeo team. For him, it was a full ride, in more ways than one.

Mom shook her head, and her eyes gleamed suspiciously. I'd never seen her cry before, so I discounted the possibility. "Even with the scholarship and a minimum-wage job, there wouldn't be enough money."

For years, she'd been telling me to study, so I could get into college. She'd even hinted that my dad, a man I didn't remember, would help out when the time came. Granted, he hadn't paid child support, but he usually sent a card at Christmas, with a twenty-dollar bill inside. Back then, that was my idea of fatherly devotion, I guess.

"Maybe Dad—"

"He's got another family, Gayle. Two kids in college."

"You never said—"

"He was married," Mom told me, for the first time. "I was the other woman. He made a lot of promises, but he wasn't interested in keeping them, and I doubt if that's changed. Twenty dollars at Christmas is one thing, and four years of college are another. It would be a tough thing to explain to the wife."

The disappointment ran deep, and it was more than not being able to go to college. "You led me to believe he was going to help," I whispered, stricken.

"I thought I could come up with the money, between then and now," Mom said. She looked worse than I felt, but I can't say I was sympathetic. "I wanted you to think he cared."

I turned on my heel and fled.

"Gayle!" Mom called after me. "Come back!"

But I didn't go back. I needed to find Tristan. Tell him what had happened. And I'd found him, all right. He was standing in front of the feed and grain, with his arms around Miss Wild West Montana of 1995.

I came back to the here and now with a soul-jarring crash, glaring up at Tristan, who was watching me curiously. He'd probably guessed that I'd just had an out-of-body experience. "You were making out with a rodeo queen!" I cried.

Tristan looked startled. "What the hell—?"

"The day I left Parable," I burst out. "I came looking for you, to tell you I couldn't go to college like we planned, and there you were, climbing all over some other girl in broad daylight!"

"*That's* why you left? Your letter said you met somebody else—"

"I lied, okay? I wanted to get back at you for cheating on me!"

"I *wasn't* cheating on you."

"I *saw* you with Miss Rodeo!"

"You *saw* me with an old friend. Cindy Robbins. We went

to kindergarten together. The vet had just put her horse down, and she was pretty shook up."

It was just ridiculous enough to be true.

I *really* got mad then. Mad at myself, not Tristan. I'd been upset, that long ago day, because I'd just learned my dad was a married man and my mother was his lover, and because I wasn't going to college. I hadn't stopped to think, or to ask questions. Instead, I'd gone to the bank, withdrawn my paltry savings, dashed off a brief, vengeful letter to Tristan, explaining my passion for a made-up guy, and caught the four o'clock bus out of town, without so much as packing a suitcase, let alone saying good-bye to my mother.

Rash, yes. But I was only seventeen, and once I'd made my dramatic exit, my pride wouldn't let me go home.

"Hey," Tristan said, with a gruff tenderness that undid me even further. "You okay?"

"No," I replied. "I'm *not* okay."

"There wasn't any other guy, was there?"

I shook my head.

He grinned. I was falling apart, on the street, and he *grinned*.

"Bob's not a guy, either," I said.

"What?" Tristan did the thumb thing again, wiping away my tears.

"He's a vibrator."

Tristan threw back his head and laughed, then he pulled me close, right there in front of God and everybody. "Hallelujah," he whispered, and squeezed me even more tightly.

He walked me back to the Lakeside Motel, and I might have invited him in, if the minivan family hadn't been there, swimming again. They smiled and waved, like we were old friends.

"Later," Tristan said, and kissed me lightly.

With that, he walked away, leaving me standing there with my room key in one hand, feeling like a fool.

I finally let myself in, locked the door, and took a cold shower.

When I got out, I wrapped myself in a towel, turned on my cell phone, and dialed my mother's number. I was expecting the usual redial marathon, but she answered on the second ring. I heard a motorcycle engine purring in the background.

"Hello?"

"Mom? It's me. Gayle."

She chuckled. "I remember you," she said. "Are you in Parable?"

"Yes, and you set me up."

"Sure did," she replied, without a glimmer of guilt. "The meeting's tomorrow, at Tristan's office. Ten o'clock."

"Thanks for telling me."

"If you'd bothered to read the documents, you would have known from the first."

"It was a sneaky thing to do!"

"I'm a mother. I get to do sneaky things. It's in the contract."

I paused. My mother is no June Cleaver, but I love her.

"How are you?" I asked, after a couple of breaths. My voice had gone soft.

"Happy. How about you?"

"Beginning to think it's possible."

"That's progress," Mom said, and I knew she was smiling. The Harley engine began to rev. Biker impatience.

"Gotta go," Mom told me. "I love you, kiddo."

"I love you, too," I said, but she had already disconnected.

I shut off the phone, curled up in a fetal position in the middle of the bed, and dropped off to sleep.

When I woke up, it was dark and somebody was rapping on my door.

I dragged myself up from a drugged slumber, rubbing my eyes. "Who is it?"

"Guess." Tristan's voice.

I hesitated, then padded over and opened the door. "What do you want?"

He grinned. "Hot, slick, sweaty sex—among other things."

His eyes drifted over my towel-draped body, and something sparked in them. He let out a low whistle. "Lake's all ours," he drawled. "Wanna go skinny-dipping?"

My nipples hardened, and my skin went all goose-bumpy. "Yep," I said.

He scooped me up, just like that, and headed for the lake, leaving my room door wide open. I scanned the windows of the motel as he carried me along the dock, glad to see they were all dark.

I'm all for hot, slick, sweaty sex, but I'm no exhibitionist.

The lake was black velvet, and splashed with starlight, but the moon was in hiding. Tristan set me on my feet, pulled off the towel, and admired me for a few moments before shedding his own clothes.

Then he took my hand, and we jumped into the water together.

When we both surfaced, we kissed. The whole lake rose to a simmer.

He led me deeper into the shadows, where the water was shallow, over smooth sand, and laid me down.

We kissed again, and Tristan parted my legs, let me feel his erection. This time, there was no condom. He slid down far enough to taste my breasts, slick with lake water, and I squirmed with anticipation.

I knew he'd make me wait, and I was right.

He turned onto his back, half on the beach and half in the water, and arranged me for the first of several mustache rides. Each time I came, I came harder, and he put a hand over my mouth so the whole world wouldn't know what we were doing.

Finally, weak with satisfaction, I went down on him in earnest.

He gave himself up to me, but at the edge of climax, he stopped me, hauled me back up onto his chest, rolled me under him. He entered me, but only partially, and the muscles in his shoulders and back quivered under my hands as he strained to hold himself in check.

I lifted my head and caught his right earlobe between my teeth, and he broke. The thrust was so deep and so powerful that it took my breath away.

I'd thought I was exhausted, spent, with nothing more to give, but he soon proved me wrong. Half a dozen strokes, each one harder than the last, and I was coming apart again. That was when he let himself go.

I don't know how long we laid there, with the lake tide splashing over us, but we finally got out of the water, as new and naked as if we'd just been created. Tristan tossed me the towel, and pulled on his jeans. We slipped into my room without a word, made love again under a hot shower, and banged the headboard against the wall twice more before we both fell asleep.

When I woke up the next morning, he was gone, but there was a note on his pillow.

"My office. Ten o'clock sharp. After the meeting, expect another mustache ride."

Heat washed through me. The man certainly had style.

I skipped breakfast, too excited to eat, and at ten straight up, I was knocking on Tristan's office door. The buyers and other owners had already arrived, and were seated around the conference table. Tristan looked downright edible in his slick three-piece suit, and even though he was all business, his eyes promised sweet mayhem the moment we were alone.

The crotch of my pantyhose felt damp.

The negotiations went smoothly, and when the deposit checks were passed around, I glanced down and noticed my own name on the pay line, instead of Mom's.

"There's been a mistake," I told Tristan, in a baffled whisper.

"No mistake," he whispered back. "Josie signed the whole shooting match over to you."

I stared at him in disbelief.

The meeting concluded amiably, and in good time. Everybody shook hands and left. Everybody but Tristan and me, that is.

Tristan loosened his tie.

I quivered in some very vulnerable places.

"Ever made love on a conference table?" he asked. He locked the door and pulled the shades.

"Not recently," I admitted.

"Not even with Bob?"

I laughed. "Not even with Bob."

Tristan took the check out of my hand, damp from my clutching it, and drew me close. He felt so strong, and so warm. "If you plan on having your way with me," he said, "you're going to have to make a concession first."

"What kind of concession?"

"Agree to stay in Parable."

I loosened his tie further, undid the top button of his shirt. "What's in it for me?" I teased. I thought I knew what his answer would be—after all, it was burning against my abdomen, practically scorching through our clothes—but he surprised me.

"A wedding ring," he said.

I tried to step back, but he pulled me close again.

"It seems a little soon—" I protested, but my heart felt like it was trying to beat its way out from behind my Wonder bra.

"I've been waiting ten years," he answered. "I don't think it's all that soon." He caught my face in his hands. "I loved you then, I love you now, and I've loved you every day in between. The engagement can be as long or as short as you want, but I'm not letting you go."

My vision blurred. My throat was so constricted that I had to squeeze out my "Yes."

"Yes, you'll marry me?"

I nodded. The words still felt like a major risk, but they were true, so I said them. "I love you, Tristan."

He gave me a leisurely, knee-melting kiss. "Time we celebrated," he said.

I took the lead. Forget foreplay. I wanted him inside me.

I unfastened his belt and opened his pants and took his shaft, already hot and hard, in my hand. And suddenly, I laughed.

Tristan blinked. Laughter and penises don't mix, I guess.

"I was just thinking of Bob," I explained.

He groaned as I began to work him with long, slow strokes. "Great," he growled. "I've got a hard-on like a concrete post, and you're comparing me to a vibrator."

I teased him a little more, making a circle with the pad of my thumb. "Ummm," I said, easing him into one of the fancy leather chairs surrounding the conference table and kneeling between his legs.

"Oh, God," he rasped.

"Payback time," I said.

He moaned my name.

I got down to business, so to speak.

Tristan took it as long as he dared, then pulled me astraddle of his lap, hiked up my skirt, ripped my pantyhose apart, and slammed into me. I was coming before the second thrust.

That's the thing about a flesh-and-blood man.

They never need batteries.

Sara Smiles

Alison Kent

Chapter One

Sara Wade stood on her suite's balcony overlooking the villa's private beach of tropical white sand, and stared unsmiling across miles of blue Pacific at the horizon awash with the first rays of the sun. She'd been up long before dawn.

Sleeping in an unfamiliar bed, an unfamiliar room, no matter how comfortably lush, never came easy. But last night's insomnia had another name.

Jax Stacey.

The man she'd been seeing for three years, in love with for two, living with for one.

The man who, six months ago, had proposed.

The man to whom she'd said no.

He'd taken her refusal better than she had. She'd wanted immediately to call back the word, retract the shake of her head. What she had not wanted was to replace it with a nod, or to say yes.

She'd only wanted not to hurt Jax.

He'd told her that she hadn't, that he understood her reticence—hell, he'd known her long enough, loved her long enough, to get where she was coming from, especially considering the circumstances.

It was hard for both of them to watch marriages of friends and family disintegrate around them and want to risk their own status quo. Why mess with a relationship that was perfect by putting matching rings on their fingers?

They didn't need an outward symbol, a document, a ceremony to prove to anyone what they already knew.

That their love was meant for a lifetime.

She'd felt even worse after that. His steadfastness meant everything to her; her refusal reduced his needs to nothing. And he was arriving today. Any moment, in fact. Her stomach fluttered madly at the thought.

It had been a spur of the moment decision that had her booking the long weekend at the plush resort nestled into Mexico's Pacific coastline. A decision as right as the reason behind it. A reason that, right or not, had her as nervous as did the wait for Jax.

She'd spent a tidy sum from her savings—money earned billing clients for a Houston law firm—after he'd assured her he'd have no problem getting free. He and his partner often traded weekends; their auto body shop was closed half days on Saturdays as it was, and going in late Monday would be no big deal.

The sun now sparkling on the rippling ocean water, Sara breathed deeply of the salty air, of the chlorine rising from the private pool on the suite's first floor, of the tropical blooms turning a kaleidoscope around hovering butterflies. She had come a day early to make certain the place was as wonderful as her travel agent promised.

It was more than wonderful. It was perfect. The service, the food, the facilities made for the perfect getaway. The ambience made for the perfect lovers' tryst. All she could do now was hope it also made for the perfect magic she needed to pull together her full-circle plan.

Oh, but wasn't Jax going to be surprised.

She curled her fingers over the balcony's dark green railing and leaned forward, eyes closed, absorbing the tingle of the ocean cooling the breeze. The sun hadn't yet risen fully to heat the surf and the sand.

It would be a good time to walk down and enjoy the secluded beach, to get a grip on her emotions, to organize her thoughts so he wouldn't see her anxiousness and worry.

Because he would worry. He would.

And she loved that about him. The way he was so perceptive of her moods. How he knew when to coddle, when to protect, when to back off because she needed to step up to her own plate and swing.

Sighing, she wrapped her arms around her middle and silently shook her head, wondering what in the world she had done to deserve him.

Here was this big gorgeous man who worked with his hands, who could crush a skull if he had to, yet understood her so well he seemed to be capable of reading her mind.

She'd never find anyone else to compare, had never known anyone else like him. She never wanted to imagine her days spent without him. He was the love of her life. He had been since the moment they'd met.

"Sara?"

She startled. Surprise skittered the length of her spine, settled at the base, and spread deep into her bones. Her body resonated with his voice as it would from his embrace. She inhaled slowly and turned.

Jax Stacey was a beautiful man, and her stomach clenched so hard she ached with it. He stood in the rectangle of the open French door, one forearm braced shoulder-high on the frame. He wore indigo jeans and biker boots, his waistband dipping low due to the hand shoved down deep in his pocket.

His hair was short and dark and tousled, as if he'd tried to sleep on the early morning flight but had managed to do no more than muss himself up. She liked him mussed up. Liked the sleepy look in his dark gold eyes. Liked the way his thick lashes drooped down and fanned out to shadow his cheeks.

He made her hungry. He made her knees weak. He made her wonder what she was going to do if this time he turned her down. Her lips trembled. It was almost a smile. Almost, but not quite. She wasn't quite ready for that.

"You were so quiet. I didn't even hear the door."

He stared at her for another long moment, searching, seeking, studying . . . then finally shoving away from his perch to join her. He came closer, moving the way he always did, his steps purposeful yet unhurried, his body fluid and loose and built to make her think about sex.

She tilted up her chin as he drew near, holding his gaze, which simmered. The one time she opened her mouth, he simply shook his head to shush her. She swallowed hard and took a step in reverse.

When her backside contacted the railing, she reached back with both hands to hold on. And when he reached her, he cupped her arms just above her elbows and pulled her hands forward. He wanted her to hold onto him.

It made so much sense to do so. He had never let her down. He had never turned her away. She knew, as well, that he would never hurt her. He would *never* hurt her the way she had surely hurt him. His denial all those months ago had only been halfway convincing.

And so much had changed since then.

She sighed as he held her, moving her hands to the small of his back, pressing her face to his chest and breathing him in. He smelled of clean air and woods, grasses and Ivory soap. "You feel so good. You smell so good."

He cupped the back of her head with one big palm. "You're not too lumpy or stinky either."

She rolled her eyes, pushed back far enough to look up into his face. "You flew all this way to tell me I'm not lumpy or stinky?"

"No, Sara." He shook his head, reached up to brush stray wisps of hair from her face. "I flew all this way to tell you this."

She closed her eyes as his head descended, parting her lips to accept his kiss. He was gentle, and he tasted like home and like heaven. Like her life and her future. Like the Jax she knew and loved so very much.

He caught her bottom lip between both of his and tugged, sucking it into his mouth briefly, then letting her go. She returned the show of affection, and so it began, that way they had of speaking without speaking, of turning a kiss into an act that said everything neither of them needed words to say.

When his tongue pressed for entrance, she opened up and let him inside, melting at his touch, at the way he filled her mouth even as he filled her soul, at the way his hand moved from the center of her back to the base of her spine and lower still, until he cupped her bottom, squeezed and drew her flush.

She felt him against her belly; he was thick and hard already. Thick and hard and so very tempting, yet he wouldn't push or press or insist. He would wait until she was ready. And oh, how easily he made her that way.

Even now she responded, splaying her palms between his shoulder blades, absorbing his body's heat as well as the tension tightening his muscles.

She loved how he held back, hated how he held back, wondered where he found the control when she had next to none. She wanted so much from him. She wanted it all. Things that surprised her with their insistence. Things that never before had seemed so right. Things that had always been a dream, one from which she was slowly waking up.

She wanted everything.

Everything.

And she wanted it with Jax.

The reminder brought her back to the truth of why they were here. She slipped out of the kiss, eased her mouth away, her body away, sighed in his arms, and turned. He continued to hold her; she leaned back into his chest.

In the near distance, the shadow of the villa had retreated, leaving a long stretch of white sand to welcome the sun. "Jax, we need to talk."

"I'm listening." He said it as he would were they discussing replacing the refrigerator or the habit his shepherd mix, Bongo, had of burying Milk-Bones. And then he did what he always did, what he was so good at doing.

He nuzzled the skin beneath her ear, rubbing his coarse two-day-old beard against her until she shivered and her nipples tightened. "Maybe so, but I can't think when you do that, much less talk."

Instead of backing away, he dipped his knees, fitting his lower body into the curve of hers. His hands found their way to her waist and slipped beneath the loose Indian cotton of her sleeveless shell to her bare middle. "I like it when you're speechless."

She tucked her head back into the crook of his shoulder, closed her eyes, lifted her chin. "You like shutting me up, you mean." Even though she could hardly care that he had.

He shook his head. "No, baby. I like this."

He brought up his hands, skated his palms over her gumdrop nipples, teasing her, only just touching her. The link between them tugged at the tightrope strung from that barest point of contact into her womb.

"I like the way you always respond. I like making you breathless."

"You like making me horny." Though that had never required much effort on his part at all.

"What I like is making love to the woman I love," he murmured close to her ear, his hips grinding into hers, one hand now kneading the breast he held, his other hand busily gathering up the loosely woven fabric of her madras print skirt.

When his fingertips grazed her thigh, teased the elastic edge of her plain white panties, she shivered. "We really need to talk, Jax. I need to tell you something."

"So, tell me." His hand left her breast and moved to her other hip. The breeze whispering through the balcony's bougainvillea whispered over the backs of her thighs, bared completely now that he'd lifted her skirt to her waist.

"How am I supposed to put anything into words when you're doing that?" This time she was the one who whispered, her voice hardly louder than the sound of her cotton panties being pulled down.

"And I thought I was the one with the one-track mind," he teased, his fingers teasing, too, sliding beneath the curves of her ass, slipping between her legs.

She spread them, she opened—how could she not? "Jax, please."

"Please stop? Please don't stop? Tell me, Sara. Tell me what you want."

What she wanted was to tell him how their lives were about to change. How nothing about their world would ever be the same. How much she loved him, wanted him.

How he would always come first in her life.

Of that one thing she had to convince him. That one thing he had to know. That she would never push away his needs or wants. "Don't stop, Jax. Don't ever stop. Touching me. Loving me."

She turned in his arms, saw the clear and raw, unshuttered emotion welling in his eyes before he did that guy thing he was so good at and masked his feelings with a smile that was all about sex.

"Are you kidding?" He laced his fingers in the small of her back, rocked their bodies in a gentle side-to-side sway. "You're everything I could ever want. I don't know many guys as damn lucky as I am. But then, I've always been about getting lucky."

That killer smile again. White teeth and dimples in a shadow of a dark sexy beard. She slid her hands from his chest to his shoulders. "You, Jax Stacey, are such a man."

"Do something for me, Sara?" he asked softly.

"Anything," she said, and meant it.

"Undo my pants."

Chapter Two

Jax would get back to worrying about what was up with Sara later.

Soon.

When the blood returned to his brain.

Right now, he was too caught up in what being with her did to his body to think. The way his arousal turned her on amazed him. He'd never known another woman this incredibly hot, and had no idea what the hell he'd done right in his screwed-up life to have her love him.

Her fingers worked deftly at his button fly. He loosened his hold on her, moving his hands from her back to her waist, and followed the direction of her gaze down to where she watched her hands at work, watched the band of his boxers come into view.

Then he watched her thumb the damp circle he'd left on the cotton, a dark spot of the clear fluid that had seeped from the slit in the head of his cock.

"I love it when you do that," she said, and he echoed the sentiment once he'd found his voice. Then he added, "There's a whole lot more where that came from."

She laughed softly. "How well I know."

He wanted her clothes off. His clothes off. He wanted to bury himself in her mouth, to feel her tongue and her suction. He wanted to slide into the warmth between her legs, to feel her milk him, to spread her slick juices and use them to ease his way inside.

He wanted to come, but not before bringing her off.

He glanced behind him, decided the balcony's lounger would do, and backed up, bringing her with him. When his calves hit the chair, he released her only long enough to shuck down his boxers and jeans.

One hand at her waist, the other brushing back loose wisps of her short blond hair, he watched her raise a questioning brow. He waggled both of his as he sat, then reached for her wrist and tugged her into his lap.

She shifted around, pulled off her panties, and hiked up her skirt to straddle him. Her knees sank into the cushion on either side of his hips. Then she poked the center of his chest. "After this, we talk."

"If you still have the energy, sure."

"Awfully confident in your abilities, aren't you?"

He shook his head, tried not to choke on what he was feeling. "I'm confident in what we have, Sara. Of how well I know you. That's all."

"Oh, Jax," she said, her words nearly inaudible. "I hope so."

Again he found himself pushing away a strange niggling of something being wrong. Out of sorts. But he lost it when she lifted her hem, settling the yards of material up around her belly so he could see all the good stuff between her legs.

"God, Sara. What are you doing to me?"

"I haven't done much yet at all," she said, cupping her palm over the tight, blood-filled head of his cock.

"Keep telling yourself that, baby." He pulled in a sharp hissing breath. "Keep telling yourself that."

She wrapped her fingers lower on his shaft, opened the lips of her sex, and rubbed him between them. When he shuddered, she asked, "You like?" and he shuddered again.

For several long seconds, she played him like that, teasing them both, arousing them both. He grew harder. She grew wetter. Moisture seeped from her entrance to run between his legs and dampen his balls, and he gripped her thighs more roughly than he meant to do.

"Sara, you are making me nuts here."

"Losing your confidence?"

"Only my patience."

When he growled, she spread out her fingers, pressed the heel of her palm into his abs. "Did you know I can feel you vibrate inside when you do that?"

All he knew was the ache in his balls. "Put me there, Sara. Put me inside you."

Her flesh was sweet and pink around the nearly purple head of his erection. He couldn't tear his gaze away as she swallowed him whole, her juices slick and thick on his cock. His eyes rolled back, and he closed them, grinding his jaw as he throbbed, pulsed, threatened to blow.

"I can feel that, too." Her whole body shuddered. "I love when you do that. And I love feeling you come."

"You're going to be feeling it sooner than later if you don't sit still for a minute."

"Mmm, good. It's sexy when you lose control."

"I never lose control," he lied, shoving his hips upward. "I just lose patience."

"So you said." She raised her hips, rotated them, settled herself in his lap again.

He pushed down on her thighs to still her, but she wouldn't be stilled. "Do something for me, Sara."

"Anything." She was riding him like a trick pony, up and down and around on his shaft, her hands braced behind her on his knees. "What do you want me to do?"

"Sit. Don't move."

She did as he ordered. "That's all?"

Hell, no. He just needed that before he could breathe to ask for anything else. "Take off your top."

Her lips came together in a sly little bow. "Unbutton yours."

It took him mere seconds, and then he sat there clenching and clutching, gritting and grinding, doing his best to hold still while she parted the sides of his shirt just enough to bare a long strip of skin from his throat to the thatch of hair at his crotch.

That done, she stripped her top over her head and off, then slipped her hands beneath his shirt to knead his pecs. The movement plumped her breasts together between her upper arms. And the massaging motion of her fingers plumped the extension of his erection all the way to his ass.

That was it. No more being sweet Sara's plaything. It was time for her to come so he could get off watching as she did.

The second he took hold of her nipples between his fore-fingers and thumbs, her eyes closed, her hands on his chest stopped moving. She sighed, then moaned. He increased the tweaking pressure, and she brought up her hands to cover his, holding him in place.

"That feels so good," she whispered, an almost reverent sound.

"I'll make it better," he said, pulling one hand from beneath hers and applying the same attention to her clit. She leaned back, dug her fingertips into the muscles of his bare thighs.

She shuddered, quivered, panted. The walls of her pussy grabbed him, and he ground up against her, thrusting until he felt her spasms break, felt the milking pull of her muscles, and then he let go.

Crying out, he surged upward, spilling himself inside of her, feeling nothing beyond the rush of fluid and that of the blood in his veins.

It took longer than he'd known he could last to finish, longer than usual for Sara to come down. Even that connec-tion was one they shared, a thought that amazed him once he was able to get any thoughts straight in his head.

When Sara sighed, he opened his arms and she leaned against him, holding him inside for another few moments before slip-ping her body from his and cuddling up to his side in the cushy lounger.

"Welcome to Puerto Vallarta," she said with a little bit of a laugh. "I'd actually thought we might take a walk on the beach when you got here."

"That was a hell of a lot more relaxing than a walk on the beach."

She raised up to look into his face. "Oh no, you don't, Jax Stacey. You are not going to fall asleep on me now."

He grinned, tucked her close again. "Just a nap. I got up too damn early catching that flight."

She sighed again, but settled, slipping her hand beneath the tangled material of her skirt and his shirt to find his skin and tug at the hair growing low on his belly. "We still need to talk."

"I'm still listening." He may have shot his wad physically, but he was good for listening.

She took a deep breath, expelled it slowly, shook her head as if talking herself out of saying anything at all. That definitely got his attention.

Sara was never short on words, never hesitant—or reticent—to speak her mind.

It was one thing he enjoyed so much about her. Her honesty. Her convictions. The way she made his life complete. "Baby? What is it?"

"I've changed my mind, Jax." She paused, breathed deeply; her fingers tugging at his short hairs stilled. "If you haven't changed yours, then yes. I'll marry you. I want to marry you. I want to be your wife."

His nap would have to wait. He wasn't the least bit sleepy. In fact, he wasn't sure if he'd ever been so wide awake. "Sara? What's going on?"

She snuggled up into the curve of his shoulder, her head tucked beneath his chin. "I love you. I've loved you for so long. And I haven't stopped asking myself why I originally told you no."

"We talked about this then, Sara." He stroked her bare shoulder, teased his way into the pit of her arm. "I understood your fear of things getting messed up."

"It was a stupid fear. Nothing between us is ever going to get messed up. How could it?"

"Well, I know I said you could do Russell Crowe if you got the chance, but I'd rather you not. That might mess things up." He laughed when she laughed, then went on to say, "But something tells me this isn't about Russell Crowe."

She shook her head. "This is about us, Jax. About us and the baby we're going to have."

Chapter Three

By the time Sara made it out of the shower, out of the suite, out of the biggest part of the funk left by Jax's silence, and down to the beach, the sand was just this side of being too hot to walk on barefooted. She hadn't been thinking clearly enough to slip on her thongs.

Hey, if Jax could deal with it, she could, too. After all, they were in this together—whether he liked it or not.

She still could not believe he hadn't responded to her news. Of all the reactions she'd braced for, that wasn't one. Shock, excitement, uncertainty, even fear. Those she'd been ready to deal with. But not his silence. Never his silence.

She'd screwed up, telling him like she had, blurting it out when it was so much more important than that, and she wasn't sure she knew where to begin fixing round two in her big fat ongoing mistake.

Up ahead, Jax stood in knee-deep water, staring out beyond the villa's private inlet toward the open sea. He wore tropical print board shorts, and his arms hung limp at his sides.

Limp, as if he didn't see any use in fighting against something so completely out of his control.

His shoulders gleamed, the sun glinting off the droplets of water clinging to his skin. He'd been swimming, working off the frustration of the weight she'd thrown on him.

She wanted to walk up behind him, to wrap her arms

around his middle, to rest her cheek in the center of his back and show him with no more than that how much she loved him, how she wished she could fix all the things she'd done wrong.

Instead, she dropped to the dry sand above the tide line from where he stood, tucked her sarong beneath her, her arms around her shins, her chin into the cradle of her knees, and watched him, wondering what thoughts were going through his mind.

He was like most men in that he didn't talk much about feelings. Not about the sort that he didn't want to share. He wasn't the least bit bothered about spreading the wealth of his joy when the Astros played a good game. And he'd never had an issue demonstrating his feelings for steak and potatoes, Harley-Davidson bikes, or for her.

This was different. This tested that control he was so proud of. This put him at the mercy of what was happening in her body. And put her at the mercy of whatever decision he made. She didn't like that. Didn't like that at all.

But there wasn't a hell of a lot she could do until he accepted the fact that they had to talk.

She knew when he sensed her behind him because of the way he stiffened before he turned. Stiffened, and hung his head. Defeated. Dejected. Resolved.

She almost got up and left. The beach, the villa, the country. She'd raise this baby on her own. She didn't need anything from Jax—a lie that lasted only long enough for her to sigh and admit the truth.

She needed him as surely as she needed air to breathe, water to drink, her cushy feather pillow on which to fall asleep. She dropped her forehead to her knees and closed her eyes. Her heart raced; her breathing remained uneven. All she could do was wait him out. He couldn't keep her locked out forever.

Only a few minutes passed before she felt the fall of his shadow, smelled the salt and sun on his skin, sensed him dropping down to sit beside her, near enough to touch her if he reached out. He didn't, and neither did she.

But he did speak, and for that, for his willingness to break their awkward silence, she was happy.

"Do you remember Tim and Tania?" he asked. "How much fun they were to be around?"

Before Tania got pregnant, he meant. Before the couple got married, he might as well have added. She turned her head to the side and glanced over. "Sure. They were great fun. I miss seeing them."

Jax leaned back on his elbows, crossed one ankle over the other. "It's so weird to think they broke up. They seemed so perfect together."

Until they screwed up the good thing that they had. "We're not Tim and Tania, Jax."

"I know."

She didn't like the track onto which his train of thought had jumped. She didn't like the way her heart pounded to stay ahead. "And they were only perfect together as far as was outwardly visible."

He shrugged, his sunglasses shading his expression along with his eyes. "Do you really believe that? That they could fake out everyone for that long?"

God. Oh, God. Her head thudded so hard she thought she would vomit. "What do you think?"

"That they made for a hell of an acting team." He paused, leaned back to watch a lone gull circle. "Or else everything went to hell when they got hitched."

It wasn't the hitched part bothering him. About that much she was certain. If it were, he would never have originally proposed. No, this was about the baby. Their baby, not the other couple's.

She turned away, rested her chin on her knees, stared at the ocean, which was calmer than she thought she'd ever be again. "For all we know, the baby was just the final straw on a broken down camel."

A huff. A snort. "Like I said. Hell of an acting couple."

He was blaming Tania's pregnancy and her subsequent marriage to Tim on the couple's breakup. He wasn't considering other issues that might have been in play. "Do you remember Molly Ryan's barbecue last Labor Day?"

Jax laughed. "Are you kidding? I remember all of Molly's barbecues. Weren't the Astros playing that day?"

Molly had given her husband his freedom in exchange for their house, complete with the detached garage he'd converted into a sports bar before he began watching *Monday Night Football* naked in his secretary's bed. "I wouldn't know. I spent most of the afternoon with Molly in her bedroom."

Jax glanced over. "Did I miss out on some hot chick-on-chick action?"

Sara rolled her eyes, straightened her legs out in front of her, leaned back on her palms in the sand. "You missed out on me and Molly doing our best to convince Tania that Tim's getting drunk when he came home every night didn't mean he didn't want to be there with her."

"Huh," was all Jax said. At first. But after she remained silent and he'd had time, he added, "He did get pretty wasted that day. I remember pouring him into their truck and Tania driving home."

"I can't imagine bringing a baby into that situation helped either of them."

"Yeah. Tim was probably too much the life of the party for his own good."

"And Tania was probably thinking of her baby's future when she left." Sara stared off into the distance, seeing little with her vision blurred by her tears. "We're not Tim and Tania, Jax. I don't believe for a minute that it was getting married or having the baby that broke them up."

"Maybe," he said, and then he fell silent. A silence that mirrored the one he'd fallen into earlier on the balcony, the one which had brought her out here.

One she didn't like because it wasn't the comfortable sort between two people who had no need to talk.

And she and Jax needed to talk. Desperately. "Here's the thing, Jax. What we have works. Hell, it seems to have done just fine by Goldie Hawn and Kurt Russell. Or Tim Robbins and Susan Sarandon. We can go on just as we've been doing."

"Wait a minute." He shook his head as if settling a thought still floating loose. "You said on the balcony that you'd changed your mind. That you want to get married."

She dropped her gaze to her lap. "I do."

"You're not making any sense here, Sara," he said, his voice tight. "Either you do or you don't."

God, this was so hard to explain when it hardly made sense. "What I want is to be with you, Jax. Forever. However it works for us. But, yes. The idea of this baby has made me realize that I want it all. The ceremony. The ring. The white picket fence."

"So now you're willing to risk what we have. Because of the baby. But six months ago you weren't willing to risk it for me."

What was she supposed to say to counter his hurt and anger? She barely understood her feelings herself. She only knew they existed. "I was stupid. A coward."

"And now all of a sudden you're goddamn Martha Stewart maternal," he fairly growled.

Her hackles came up. "I'm not sure how maternal Martha Stewart is."

"Betty Crocker, then. Aunt Jemima. Mrs. Paul. Who the hell ever."

She closed her eyes, then got to her feet. She didn't know where she was going, just away from here before she told him what an ass he was being. Even if he did have a right to lash out at what was a discomfiting upheaval.

She stepped over his legs. He reached up and grabbed her hand, stopping her, holding her. He stood, then he released her. But he remained where he was, blocking her path. "Listen, Sara. I asked you to marry me because I love you. Because I want a life with you."

"And I want the same thing," she whispered, brushing back blowing strands of her hair from her face.

"No, you don't." He shook his head slowly, regretfully. "You want legitimacy and security for the baby."

The baby. Not *our* baby. "That's part of it, yes."

"I want to marry you because it's right for us." A vein pulsed in his temple. "Not because of a baby. It needs to be about us."

"Oh, Jax. It is about us." How could he think otherwise?

And then, his dimples deep in the shadow of his beard as he smiled a humorless smile, he said the words women everywhere hated to hear. "Prove it."

Chapter Four

He hated letting her go. He wanted to draw her close, hold her. He wanted everything to be the way it had been when he'd boarded the plane at Hobby Airport this morning.

But it wasn't. And it never would be again.

Because he was going to be a father.

He sure as hell hadn't started out as much of one.

He hadn't even said a thing about what he was feeling about it to Sara. He'd been too caught up in her changing her mind about marrying him—and then realizing why she had.

"Daddy." He said the word aloud, then chuckled. His hands at his hips, water lapping at his ankles, the sun beating down on his shoulders and back, he chuckled.

And then he laughed so loudly he imagined Sara in the villa stopping in her tracks to check on the crazy man wading in the water.

He was crazy. About her. About the idea of being a father. About the two of them raising a child, their child, and doing so within the structure of a traditional family.

But he'd be goddamned if he'd marry the woman simply because she was pregnant. And if she didn't get that, she didn't know him as well as he thought.

The Tim and Tania thing, he'd thrown that out to get Sara's

reaction without realizing the extent of the other couple's issues. Sara had known because that's how she was.

He didn't think he'd ever met a kinder, more generous or empathetic woman. One who should've been applying those same observation skills to him over the last two years.

Or had she even noticed that he hadn't introduced her to any of his family?

She had, of course, and he was being stupid.

Because he was the one who'd never told her why he wasn't close to his family, the one who'd never found the words to explain his childhood, how he'd been raised in a home with parents who'd stayed married for the sake of the kids.

Talk about one screwed-up reason for a couple not to split. It might look good to observers and sit well with Dr. Phil. But it sure as hell didn't give the kids involved much credit for seeing through the bullshit.

Because that's what it had been. A crapfest of a marriage. A big fat stinkin' lie of a family life. One to which he would never subject a child of his own.

And that was what he needed Sara to understand. That was what he needed to tell her. Now, before things between them shot any further off course. Before he never again saw her smile.

Because the way she'd looked at him earlier? The way she walked away and left him alone? He was afraid that was exactly what would happen.

That his pride, his lame-ass challenge, and his hard fuckin' head had just ruined the very best thing in his life.

"There you are," Sara said, turning as Jax came through their suite's door.

She'd been on the balcony while the masseuses had been setting up their tables, watching him walk along the water's edge, sensing the weight on his shoulders, the thoughts he was surely mulling over.

She'd almost sent the masseuses away. She'd scheduled

them as part of the getaway package, but after talking to Jax on the beach, she doubted he was much in the mood to relax on a table beside her.

And then she'd heard him laugh.

Not for a minute had she thought she was imagining the sound; she knew it too well. Jax's laugh had been the reason they'd met. The reason she'd turned and glanced toward the pool tables in Sherlock's Pub. The reason she'd walked away from her girlfriends and asked him to buy her a beer.

Hearing it now, seeing him now . . .

She wrapped the white terry robe she wore tighter and waved him out onto the balcony to join her, her encompassing gesture taking in the villa's two employees. "Surprise."

He glanced from table to table, masseuse to masseuse, then settled his sunglasses back in place to shade his eyes. "What's this?"

"I told you I planned to spoil you this weekend," she said, wondering how long he'd feel the need to hide.

He waited long enough for her heart to begin to flutter before saying, "You certainly work fast."

She knew what he was getting at. That she arranged this because of their . . . situation. She couldn't quite call it a fight. It wasn't a fight. A fight put them on opposite sides, and she refused to believe that was happening.

"Actually, I don't," she said with a shrug that was much more nonchalant than she was feeling. "The travel agent made the arrangements for me when she booked the weekend."

"Hmm." He leaned a forearm overhead on the door frame, the hair in the pit of his arm damp from the swim he'd taken. "I thought you might've cooked this up as proof."

The flutter in her belly turned into a throttle of the outboard motor sort. "All this proves is that I want to spend the weekend relaxing. And would very much like you to do the same."

His head nodded almost imperceptibly. "I can deal with that."

"Good." God, but she'd never thought this would be so

hard. "There's a robe on the bed. Just strip out of your shorts and put it on."

His mouth tightened in what felt like a dare. "Just the robe?"

She met it, nodded. "Just the robe."

"Sure thing," he said, and disappeared into the room.

She watched him go and remained unmoving, not breathing, hardly daring to think until the masseuse nearest to where she stood, a beautiful Hispanic woman who spoke very little English, patted the table and encouraged Sara to climb on.

Loosening the sash on her robe and opening it beneath her, she lay on her stomach and shrugged the garment from her shoulders. The masseuse replaced the robe with a soft sheet and did so without ever baring more than Sara's back.

She told herself to relax, an admonition that served to tighten her muscles further. At this point, she doubted the massage would do her any good at all.

She'd walked off the beach earlier and left things too unsettled with Jax. And nothing would be right until she made it all better. Until together they worked it all out.

She'd closed her eyes as the masseuse began kneading her neck and shoulders, but at the creak of the second table taking on weight, Sara looked over—and did so in time to see Jax shedding his robe.

As long as she'd known him, as well as she knew him, the sight of his body never failed to cause a hitch in her chest. She blew out her sigh slowly as he lay down.

His skin was smooth, lightly tanned, kissed warmly today by the morning's sun. The dusting of soft dark hair in the center of his chest narrowed mid-abdomen, traveled down to his groin and blossomed, creating a wiry thatch to cradle his penis and balls.

She shivered with the thought, with the desire to thread her fingers there, to cup him, enclose him in the glove of her hand and measure his heaviness while at rest. She loved touching him intimately, learning his body, how he wanted her touch.

She followed the line of his hips and legs, smiling to herself at the nicely rounded rise of his ass beneath the masseuse's sheet. He teased her about her fetish, but she'd always been a butt girl and Jax had the best. Toned and taut and perfect to pinch and to kiss and even nibble on when he let her.

He often didn't let her because of how ticklish he was—a thought that had a grin teasing her mouth, had her gaze crawling back up to his face where she found him watching her.

"See something you like?" he asked, his eyes sharp and flashing, the masseuse working the muscles and tissue connected to his shoulder blades.

"Your cute hiney," Sara said with a wink, sensing him tighten the object of her affection.

He rolled his eyes, closed them, his expression one of physical pleasure as he relaxed beneath the masseuse's hands. "If I'd known when I met you that you were a butt girl . . ."

"Hey, it's no worse than you being a breast man." A preference that had always been a curiosity since she wasn't overly well-endowed. At least for now . . .

A thought Jax picked up as if reading her mind. "I guess you'll be getting some, uh, big ones here soon, huh?"

Getting some *big ones*? Men. Always about the big ones. "All the better to wear low-cut tops and tempt you with."

"Hmm." He closed his eyes again, his lips caught in a hint of a prurient smile. "The lower the better."

She waited several minutes before responding, lost in the sensation of her body turning limp and lethargically liquid. Scheduling a regular massage once she returned home had just become a priority.

She idly wondered if the baby would benefit. If not from the actual touch of another's hands, then from her own relaxed state of bliss. And then she wondered how long it would be before she'd be able to feel the baby when lying like this on her belly.

So many changes to anticipate. "Jax?"

"Hmm?"

"You know it's not just my breasts that will balloon. My ass is also going to be spreading far and wide."

He didn't even open his eyes. "Just more to hold onto."

She thought of riding him, of the way he gripped her hips to guide her. She thought of lying beneath him, of how he would slide his hands under her bottom and squeeze.

Then she wondered why they were both focusing on her body's changes in relationship to sex instead of the reason for the swelling expansion.

"There's also going to be a whole lot more of me taking up space in the recliner." They always sat in the big cushy chair together when watching TV, her legs usually draped sideways over his. "And I won't have a lap to hold the popcorn bowl much longer."

His eyes opened, and he met her gaze squarely. "What's your due date?"

"February fourteenth." Valentine's Day. The day he'd proposed. "An interesting bit of irony."

"The day I'd thought about being a husband is the day I might become a father instead."

At least he hadn't said it would be a day that lived in infamy. Her stomach rolled wildly when she offered, "You could be both."

"True."

The admission didn't sound as halfhearted as she'd expected. She took a deep breath, took the next step. The white-caps in her belly dipped and soared in proportion. "It would be nice, you know. To be married by then. To have the baby after we're married rather than before."

A moment later, a moment following the one during which she'd forgotten to breathe, he shifted onto his side, bracing himself on his elbow, then just as quickly swinging his legs over the side of the table to sit.

"*No mas. Gracias, no mas,*" he said to the masseuse as he hopped down, completely in the buff.

He grabbed up his robe and shrugged into it while heading into the room. Almost immediately, he returned, a hefty tip in his hand.

The women quickly packed their oils, broke down their tables, and left. Sara, having donned her robe as well, did nothing but perch on the edge of the lounger and wait to see what he had on his mind.

Whatever it was, she couldn't believe it would be good.

Chapter Five

Having returned to the suite to find the balcony set up like the spa at his health club had surprised Jax and thrown him for a bit of a loop.

It wasn't that he'd minded—hell, getting naked and getting rubbed down, who would?—except that he'd arrived ready to talk. Willing to talk. Wanting to talk.

Any or all of the above was so unlike him that Sara could never have anticipated his mood.

He'd tried to relax, to enjoy her gift, to hold in the words that were making him antsy, but he kept picturing her body changing, growing, becoming ripe and lush and full.

He couldn't wait to see her carrying his child. Their child. But this marriage thing . . . it had to be settled. And it wasn't going to be settled here with Sara looking like he was more her executioner than the man she wanted to marry.

Besides, he had sand in the crack of his ass that was making him nuts.

He held out a hand. "C'mon," he said, and pulled her to her feet.

He led her through the suite's main room of Mexican tiled floors, bamboo and rattan accents, woven fabrics in bright south-of-the-border colors, and into the bedroom's huge master bath. Once there, he turned on the water in the deep marble tub built for two.

He added bath salts from the jar Sara handed him, gauging the amount—what did he know about bath salts?—by the shake of her head, then her nod. That done, he turned to face her, sliding his hands beneath the lapels of her robe and pushing it off her shoulders.

Her skin was soft and warm, and the terry cloth puddled at her feet, leaving her standing there naked, uninhibited, and his blood began to stir.

"God, you're beautiful."

"And you're wearing way too many clothes," she responded shyly.

He was out of everything he was wearing in nanoseconds, his Good Time Charlie bobbing a bit as, being a penis, he was prone to do.

Sara noticed, as she was prone to do, which had Jax wishing he'd run a cold bath instead.

Having her wet and naked was enough of a distraction. He didn't need to see that look in her eyes. The one he'd never seen in another woman. The one that was all about how much Sara loved sex.

He climbed into the tub, settled back so that the scented blue-green water lapped chest-high. Then he waggled his brows. "If you want, I'll let you wash off the sand that's made its way into my no-man's-land."

"Hmm." She followed him into the water, slid down against the deep curve of the tub to face him. "And here I thought you were pitching in to romanticize our weekend. I should have known you had ulterior motives."

He stretched out his legs, his feet on either side of her hips, his arms along the wide lip of the tub. She seemed strangely small and fragile, an awareness no doubt based in his own dread of what he needed to say.

In the words that might hurt her when he wanted to do nothing of the kind. "So, you brought me here to romance me?"

She tilted her head. "Isn't that what I told you originally?"

"You did, yeah." He gave her a pointed look. "But you hadn't laid out all the facts then."

"The baby wasn't a factor. This weekend was supposed to be"—she paused, drew up her knees—"*is* supposed to be all about you and me."

He shook his head slowly. "It can't be. Not now. Not anymore."

"Of course it can be, silly." She slapped lightly at the water, splashing him. The motion reflected the sunbeams shimmering through the skylight overhead. "Second honeymoons. Weekend getaways. Couples vacationing without their children. It's not exactly unheard of."

She was right, he supposed. It just wasn't in his realm of experience. His own parents needed their kids around at all times as buffers. They had never gone anywhere alone, and rarely with Jax and his siblings in tow.

If they stayed home and gave up family vacations, they had a better chance of having somewhere to go when the other came into the room.

That was Jax's experience. What he needed Sara to see.

He shrugged. "I guess not," he said, sounding anything but convincing.

He sure as hell hadn't convinced her as evidenced by her questioning, "Jax? What is it? What's wrong?"

He pulled his arms in off the tub's edge, swirled his hands through the water, finding Sara's feet and pulling them into his lap.

He started with her toes, rubbing his way from the balls to the arches. "I don't want our child to ever think his parents had to get married. Or that his parents stayed married for his sake."

"His parents. Jax." She chewed at her lip. "You're talking about us. Not about some random couple."

"My parents aren't a random couple either, Sara. And that's exactly what they did."

She hesitated before responding, then responded with a

shiver. He stilled his hands on her feet, waiting, and damn anxiously, while she cleared her throat.

"Why haven't you ever told me that before?" she asked, her voice unsteady, shaken, tight with the emotion caught in her chest.

"Because it hasn't really mattered." He tried to sound as if he spoke the truth. Instead, he sounded like a man frightened by the thought of losing what he had. He was frightened. He was fucking scared to death.

"Of course it matters," Sara said breathlessly. "Anything . . . *everything* about you matters to me. How can you think otherwise?"

Because it had been easier all this time to live in the present? To avoid the past, and for the most part, the future? To avoid admitting he knew nothing about making a family work? "We never really talked about having kids."

"No, but that shouldn't have stopped you from telling me about you." Tears welled in her eyes, threatened to spill, turned her expression into one of liquid longing. "You, Jax. You're the reason I'm here."

He didn't know what to say, couldn't find any words, even the ones he'd been ready to say to her when he'd first come back to the room. Right now, it hurt to even figure out where to go from here.

The thought of losing this woman, the only woman he'd ever loved, stabbed and twisted like a sharp blade in his belly.

And so he said the only thing around which he could wrap his very male mind. "If I'm the reason you're here, then why are you still on that side of the tub?"

He didn't have to ask twice.

She scooted across the tub, water swirling, splashing, and settled in at his side, draping a knee over his thigh, loving the feel of his hair softened by water.

She rested her head on his shoulder, rested her hand in the center of his chest. Her gaze lazily skimmed the surface of the bath where the sunlight twinkled like starbursts on the blue-green foam.

"Mmm. That's better," he murmured, shifting so that his leg wedged up further beneath hers.

"All you had to do was ask." Not that she wouldn't have eventually ended up right here anyway. She loved too much the feel of being close to him to stay away long.

He wrapped his arm around her, stroked his fingertips up and down the outer curve of her breast. "I didn't know if you'd be in the mood."

"For what? Snuggling?" That wasn't what he meant, of course, being the two-headed man that he was, but she wasn't letting him off that easily.

"Not snuggling, no." He nuzzled the top of her head with his chin, sweetly kissed her hair. "For sticking around."

Sticking around? That wasn't at all what she'd expected to hear. Not at all. "Do you listen to anything I tell you? Or do you just not believe me?"

"About me being the reason you're here?"

"Yes. About that." There were times she could understand the advantage of remaining single. Especially when it came to the oil and water mixture of men and emotions.

She sat up a bit straighter, angled herself to better see his face, his brow, which was so strong, his eyes so beautifully golden beneath lashes so beautifully long that her throat tightened.

He made it hard to think, much less speak. "Let me ask you something, Jax. The trip to New Orleans for Mardi Gras you surprised me with. What was that all about?"

His grin left no question. "Getting you drunk and naked?"

"Besides that." She toyed with his nipple until it peaked and his heart raced beneath her hand.

"Getting away," he said, his voice husky, throaty. "Partying."

"Uh-huh." She tweaked the hair on his chest.

"Being with you."

"Exactly. It works both ways. Really it does." She knew that he knew that. They'd been together long enough, shared a connection that was soul deep and rare in its depth. "I planned this weekend because I wanted the time away with you. Yes, I wanted to talk, to tell you about the baby, but it was always about being with you."

He shifted his hips, pumped them upward in a slow languid motion that caused a corresponding urge to thrust deep in her belly. "Weren't you going to do something about proving that?"

"No," she said firmly, because even the impressive size of his erection wasn't going to deter her. "You wanted me to prove that wanting to marry you wasn't about being pregnant."

"Hmm," he murmured, relaxing deeper into the water. "So how did this whole baby thing happen anyway?"

She slid her hand down to his belly. "In the usual way."

"Uh-huh. But you're on the pill. And we sheathed the beast when you were taking meds for your strep throat."

"We did, yes. Except for that one time." She closed her fingers around the base of his shaft. He was hot and hard. So very much of both. "In the kitchen. When we were making sundaes."

Jax groaned. "I can't believe how amazing you were. All those things you let me do."

The ice cream had been about easing the fire in her throat. In the end, the heat in her throat hadn't melted a thing. It had been all about her body. His body. Even now, with no more than the memory, her sex began to swell and to ache.

She shivered, sent her hand deeper between his legs, cupping his balls, which were loose and warm, sliding a finger along the extended ridge of his erection to his ass. "I didn't think we'd ever get the table clean."

His chest rose and fell heavily, his breathing having taken on the rasp of sandpaper. "Not to mention the chairs. And the floor."

It had taken days before either one of them had stopped finding dried smears of whipped cream. The thought of what they'd done with the chocolate syrup, with the cherries . . . and the banana.

Oh, God, the banana. She swallowed the thought, clenched her thighs. "Jax?"

"Don't make me talk, Sara," he said with a grunt. "Not right now."

"I don't want you to talk." She pulled her hand from his body, crawled over him on her hands and knees, water sloshing onto the floor, her breasts hanging to brush through the hair on his chest.

His nostrils flared, then his eyes, sparks of embers and bright shooting stars. "What?"

"Sit." She reached behind him, patted the warm tiled ledge surrounding the tub. "Up here."

"Why?"

She ran her tongue around her lips, then leaned forward, one hand on the tub ledge, one wrapped around his erection, and whispered against his mouth, "Because you wouldn't want the mother of your firstborn to drown giving you a blow job."

Chapter Six

Without another word, Jax did as Sara asked, using his palms to boost himself up to sit where she wanted him. She eased back onto her heels, placed her palms on his knees, pushed open his legs, and marveled yet again.

The night they'd eaten the ice cream, he'd been the one to feast on her. He'd used his fingers and eaten her up with his lips, teeth, and tongue. It was her turn now. And she let him know with her eyes exactly how hungry she was.

Starving, she moved closer, sliding her hands up the inside of his thighs. Drops of water clung to the hair on his legs and that surrounding his penis, which was thick and jutted boldly. Fortunately, Jax had never been the least bit shy about letting her look her fill.

And so she did, taking in a deep breath along with the beauty of his erect length, his thickness, which had often made her wonder how they fit together at all, his skin stretched taut and tinted purple, which she knew would feel like silk on her tongue.

She leaned forward, slid the ring of her fingers from the head of his cock down the length of his shaft, where she held him and squeezed. And then, lips parted, she leaned forward, opened her mouth, and took him inside.

The moan that rolled out of his throat filled her mouth. She felt the rumble in the ring of her fingers, in the cup of her tongue, in her heart. She closed her lips tightly and sucked, easing away and pulling him with her.

He hissed and shuddered. "Jesus, Sara. I hope like hell you're ready for this."

She was ready. She was always ready. She loved loving him this way, the pleasure it gave him, the pleasure she took at offering him what only she gave. He leaned back, bracing his weight on his elbows, sliding his lower half forward to give her better access to the places he loved her to touch.

His sac had drawn tight, the puckered skin holding his balls protectively close to his body. She cupped and caressed him, sliding an index finger over the swollen ridge behind, sliding her tongue along his shaft and the dark ropey veins bulging there.

He hardened further, pulsing in her mouth, and the beat of her heart thundered wildly. She tasted the salty smear of clear fluid he released and lapped it up, the flat of her tongue teasing the rim of his glans, the seam beneath, the slit in the tip of his cock.

He let out a groan then, one that echoed through her body and the water that splashed around her shoulders as he shifted to sit straighter, shifted his hips away, and covered her fingers on his cock. With a long, low hiss of desperate breath, he pulled himself out of her mouth.

She knew he was ready to come, had felt it with her fingers, tasted it with her tongue. And so she licked her lips and scooted to the far end of the tub, pulling her knees to her chest, her heels to her hips. She rubbed a finger in circles around her engorged clit, wanting him inside of her, wanting him filling her, wanting him so very much.

From where he sat, Jax stared into the water where she'd exposed herself fully, slowly stroking his cock until the skin appeared ready to burst. Then he smiled and reached down to trip the lever keeping the water in the tub.

She sat there and closed her eyes, feeling the water creep down her torso, her arms, her legs. Gooseflesh pebbled her wet skin as the air breathed over her, and then Jax was there on his knees, nuzzling her neck and shoulder, finally helping her to her feet and out of the tub.

"Where are we going?" she asked, and all he said was, "To bed."

She shivered as she padded behind him from warm tile to cool, letting him lead her into the airy bedroom where the balcony's French doors stood open and the warm summer breeze blew through.

The look in his eyes when he laid her back on the bed, when he climbed over her, his body so large, so powerful, so beautifully sculptured, muscled, and male . . . the look in his eyes might have frightened her had she not known him and trusted him. Had she not loved him as fiercely as she did.

Fierce. That was it. Hungry and nearly feral. That was how he was looking at her. That was the predatory truth she saw in his eyes, wide and focused, that she sensed in his body, taut with holding back.

She reached up a hand, stroked it over his cheek, his forehead, brushing back the dark fall of hair from his brow. Her throat tightened, her chest welled with all that she was feeling, with the ways she needed him, the ways she adored him. The ways he made her feel safe and secure, and so much a part of his life that he would never let her go.

She couldn't help it. Her breath hitched, and silent tears rolled from the corners of her eyes and into her hair. "I love you, Jax. I love you so much."

He lowered his body, covering her, slipping an arm beneath her as she wrapped hers around his back as tightly as she could. He held her close, held her as if letting her go meant losing an essential part of who he was. And that above everything gave her hope.

"I need you, baby." His voice was a rough whisper near her ear. He wedged a knee between her legs. "Please, Sara. I need you."

She opened for him, held him to her, gasping as he entered her, sighing with the joy of being filled.

Of being one.

They moved together slowly, silently, the only sounds in the room that of their labored and heavy breath, the tinkle of the balcony's wind chimes, the rush of the ocean's waves, the shared dampness between their legs and the sticky suction as they moved.

And then Jax stopped, rolling to the side just enough to slip one hand between their bodies and spread his warm palm low on her belly. "I love you, Sara. I want us to always be as perfect as we are now."

"Oh, Jax." She sobbed, hating being female and emotional when he needed her assurance, not her tears. "We will be. Forever."

"The baby. I don't want the baby to change you and me." His eyes grew red, watery. "You're the best thing that's ever happened to me. You make me a better man."

He choked on the words, and Sara cried. "What we have, Jax? It's everything to me. You are everything to me. My life, my hope, my future. That's why I want us to be married. I want to belong to you. I want to be your wife."

She felt his penis throb and swell, felt the burn low in her belly flame higher. Felt the great heaving weight of his chest as he expelled a shuddering breath and began to move over her again.

She hooked her heels around his knees, using the leverage to meet his slow downward thrusts. With one hand, she caressed his back, his ribs, his shoulder blades. His head lay in the crook of her elbow, and with her other hand, she stroked his jaw, his neck, the shell of his ear and his cheek.

When he came, it was a shuddering, silent release. His entire body shook, and she felt the warmth of his semen filling her, a sensation that triggered her own climax. He rocked against her tenderly and took her apart.

And when she came down from the high of being loved by him, she fell asleep in his arms.

*   *   *

This time, Sara was the one to pass out after sex instead of him. The reversal of their routine wasn't that much of a surprise when Jax thought about it.

He was wired to the gills and wide awake with the day's happenings, while all afternoon he'd expected her to snap from the emotional tension. The fact that she'd let go and relaxed long enough to come put a bit of a grin on his mouth.

He loved making her come.

Today had been one of the wildest days of his life and it was only half over. Sara had shared a mammoth secret, an announcement she knew would turn their lives upside down. Yet she hadn't hesitated. She'd held nothing back. She'd wanted him to be part of the changes from the beginning.

Her trust, her love, her belief in him humbled him to his knees. As did her insistence that he was her life—as she was his.

With all the truth in the open now, all the cards on the table, where they went from here was up to him. It was a huge responsibility, but then that's what parenting was. That's what loving her was.

Breathing a bit shakily, he spooned closer to her, covered them both with the bed's soft sheet. He'd wake her soon. The sun was on its afternoon slide into the sea. He could see the long streaks of yellow light on the water through the balcony's doors.

And he was starving. A man could only survive on sand, surf, and sex for so long. Even having this big ball in his court wasn't enough to take away his appetite. A steak, that's what he needed. A big juicy steak, and broiled shrimp with garlic butter for Sara.

He knew what he was going to do. It had really never been a question. Sara was his world, after all. Having a baby with her was not going to change his feelings for her. Unless, perhaps, they grew stronger since she would be the mother of his child.

God, he was going to be a father. He was going to have a

little bambino underfoot. A baby he'd made with Sara. His chest expanded with the joy until he could barely breathe.

He eased away from Sara, tucking the sheet around her and slipping quietly into the bathroom. He shrugged into the robe he'd left there and headed for the main room to make the phone calls he needed to make.

Chapter Seven

Sara sat up in bed, shaking off the sheet and the sense of lost time. The last thing she remembered was making love with Jax, and that had been just after noon. Gauging by the sun on the horizon, it had to be close to six.

Argh, she was going to strangle him for letting her sleep away their weekend. This was supposed to be their time together, not his to brood. Think, yes. But she didn't want to be left out in the cold—or in this case left sleeping—while he did his man-alone thing.

She crawled out of bed and made her way to the stand where she'd propped open her suitcase last night. But her suitcase was gone. In its place lay her laciest panty and bra set. That was all.

Frowning, she checked the closet. Her white slides were on the floor inside and the one dressy dress she'd brought hung alone on the rod. Jax had packed the rest of her things. They were leaving.

She hurried to the bathroom where she found her makeup case and robe. She shrugged into the garment, fumbling for the belt on her way into the suite's main room. Jax wasn't there, but her suitcase was. By the front door. As was his.

She wasn't going to panic. She refused to panic. Panic wasn't going to get her anywhere or do anyone any good. But she couldn't help it. Her heart thundered. Her hands shook. Her head pounded as if the top was a volcano ready to blow.

He was canceling the weekend she'd looked so very forward to sharing with him. He was making *their* decision, and damn if she was going to go down without a fight. And then she stopped and frowned because she swore she smelled food.

Following her nose, she found him on the balcony pouring two glasses of wine, one red and one white. Two covered dishes sat on the glass-topped table now covered with a white linen cloth.

A good-bye dinner?

A been-fun-see-ya-later *adios*?

Oh, no. This wasn't happening. It couldn't be happening now.

When she stepped through the door, pushing back hair she knew was a tousled mess and doing her best not to scowl, he looked over and smiled in that way he had of melting her down to her toes.

"What's going on?" she asked, even more confused, even more uncertain, and definitely lacking any appetite.

He gestured for her to sit. "Eat up. We've got a flight to catch."

She settled into her chair with a bit of trepidation, took the glass of chardonnay he offered, though she wasn't sure she could swallow a drop. "A flight? Tonight? Where are we going?"

He sat across from her, lifted away the cover from his plate to reveal a gorgeous steak along with a football-sized baked potato. For her, he'd ordered broiled shrimp and a fluffy rice pilaf in a halved avocado that normally would have tempted her to dive right in.

But answers first before she made any attempt to eat. "Jax?"

He didn't even look up from his steak. "Eat, Sara. The car will be here in an hour."

She set her wine on the table, folded her hands in her lap. "I'm not eating until you tell me what's going on."

He finally glanced up, his eyes sparkling with a mischief that should've set her at ease. Instead, the flutters in her stomach launched a thousand ships.

"I took you to New Orleans in February," he offered.

"Uh-huh."

"And you brought me here."

"Uh-huh."

"So"—he gestured with his fork and knife—"now it's my turn."

This was making no sense. "Jax, we both have to work on Tuesday. We don't have time for another trip. And I only packed for the beach."

"You're fine, Sara," he said with a smile, adding, "You've got everything you need." Except then he hesitated, frowning as he cocked his head and considered her. "Unless you don't want to do this now."

"Do what?" How could she give him an answer when she had no idea what he was talking about?

"Get married."

The roar in her head drowned out that of the waves in the distance. Her fingers, clenched tightly together, went numb. "Married? You want to get married."

He nodded. "I do, Sara."

"You want to get married now?" She couldn't even think of anything else to ask.

He nodded again, pushed back from the table, came around and dropped to one knee at her side. "If you'll have me, Sara Wade, I want to be your husband. A father to our child. I want you to be my wife."

She couldn't breathe. She couldn't feel her fingers or her toes. "Just like that? You've changed your mind?"

He shook his head, held onto the back of her chair with one hand, opened his other in her lap, holding hers. "I never changed my mind. I proposed to you, remember?"

"Yes, but earlier today you didn't want anything to do with getting married."

"No, Sara." He shook his head slowly. "I didn't want us to get married for the wrong reasons."

"The baby, you mean." When he nodded, she asked, "So now you think the reasons are right?"

"I do."

"Why? What's the difference now?"

"You."

"But I haven't changed at all."

"No. But you reminded me of exactly what we have, what I never expected to have with any woman." He wrapped his fingers around hers, looked down at their joined hands. "But to have it with you? God, Sara. I can't imagine not having you in my life. And to have a baby with you?"

"Oh, Jax," she whispered, moving her hands to cradle his face. "Are you sure?"

He looked back up, his eyes bright. "Yes, baby. I'm sure." And then he winked. "Now, let's go to Vegas."

Sara wore white Mephisto slides, a sleeveless white dress with a deep V neckline, and her laciest bra and panty set to her wedding. Jax, being in charge of wardrobe, wore jeans, biker boots, and a white oxford shirt.

He bought her pink roses after they left the Clark County Courthouse at midnight, and they cuddled in the backseat of the limo on their way to the chapel. Jax had arranged everything. The flight, the car, the reservations for the chapel, the two-day Mandalay Bay honeymoon.

It was the closest he could get her to a beach in Las Vegas, he'd said on the flight. She hadn't cared about the beach. She'd had a fantasy day in Puerto Vallarta, running through a full spectrum of emotions, from anxiety to fear to anger to joy. What she'd remember most was the joy.

What she'd always remember most was the joy.

And now here she was, standing on a deep burgundy carpet at the front of a room filled with empty wooden chairs painted white. Overhead hung a chandelier bedecked with ribbons and cherubs and doves in the same white and deep wine color as the rest of the room, along with touches of gold.

The minister wore white clerical robes. His wife, serving as their witness, wore the same color scheme used throughout the chapel. Soft organ music played in the background, and it took very little imagination to believe they weren't being married in a tiny church on their own private island.

She listened to his words, registering little of what he said, focused instead on Jax at her side. He stood perfectly still, a statue, and she wanted to press her cheek to his chest to see if he was even breathing. Instead, she squeezed his fingers where they hung laced with hers. He squeezed back, and then at the minister's instructions, he turned.

Taking both of her hands and folding them in his, Jax took a deep breath. His head hung low, his chin at his chest, he softly began to speak.

"Sara, I vow to be your faithful husband and promise to walk by your side. To love, help, and encourage you. To listen and to care. I will share your laughter and your tears. I will be your partner and your friend. I promise to always respect you, to always honor you. I give myself to you as I am, and as I will be for all of my life."

She stared into his eyes, which brimmed with the same tears through which she could barely see. "Jax, you are my greatest love." She sniffed, started again. "I struggle desperately to find the words to tell you how much I love you. How I adore you. I pledge myself to you now. I give you my mind, my body, and my heart, and I promise to love you and cherish you for as long as we both shall live."

The minister placed his hand over their joined ones. "By the power vested in me by the State of Nevada, I now pronounce you husband and wife. You, Jax Stacey, may kiss Sara Stacey, your beautiful bride and wife."

And, at that, Sara smiled.

Chapter One

"*Secret Service? Really?*"

"Jane said her dad said he heard it from Tom Crane, the realtor."

"Well, Patty Lane said her mother heard from her hair dresser that he's nobility, like an earl or something."

"Maybe he's *both*."

Tabby's friends spoke in low undertones laced with breathless curiosity. Wearing identical expressions of titillated speculation, the only two women in Port Diamond shyer than she was turned to face Tabby.

"Do you know anything?" asked one.

"He's got a boat docked here at the marina," the other added. "A luxury cruiser."

"My dad runs the marina, not me," Tabby reminded them.

"But you've got to have heard *something*."

Tabby had spent most of her adult life being pumped for information about her gorgeous, *thin* sister, Helene. So, this was nothing new. She was adept at sidestepping answers she did not want to give, but at least when it came to Helene, she *could* answer the inquiries when she wanted to.

However, Tabby knew nothing more than the other women about the mysterious Englishman who had so recently moved to Port Diamond.

Nothing except that, despite the fact she'd never said more

than ten words to Calder Maxwell, he sparked a desire in her that fried her nerve endings and froze her vocal chords. She'd woken up pulsing from a dream-induced climax for the first time in her life the night she'd met him.

"I can tell you he's not Secret Service. He's from England, not Washington."

"Well, you know what I mean. He looks like he could give James Bond a run for his money."

Tabby looked across the room at the gorgeous man standing with her dad and Helene, and had to agree. A cross between Timothy Dalton and Cary Grant, he was every fantasy she'd ever had rolled into one perfect package—the only flaw being his obvious interest in Helene.

Just like every other male who came into contact with the Payton sisters, he found Helene's sweet nature and gorgeous looks irresistible. Tabby had seen them talking on the pier near his boathouse a couple of times, but hadn't been able to nerve herself up enough to join them. Helene wouldn't have minded. She was always happy to see her sister.

Tabby doubted Calder would have been as appreciative, which is why she'd stayed away—no matter how much she'd longed to simply stand close enough to hear his voice.

Noticing her gaze still fixed on Calder, Tabby's friend gave a theatrical sigh. "He's yummy, isn't he?"

"Yes."

At that moment, the object of their speculation turned and caught the trio of women gawking at him. One corner of his mouth tilted, but it couldn't quite be called a smile, and his dark gaze assessed them with cool regard.

"Oh, my gosh, he's looking this way. Quick, turn around and pretend to be getting food at the buffet."

Tabby rolled her eyes. "He's already seen us. I don't think he'll be fooled." And she didn't particularly want him thinking she was interested in the buffet.

A throwback to her paternal great-grandmother, she didn't have the willowy figure of her mom and sister, or anything approaching her dad's athletic build. Nope, she was a little too round, a lot too curved, and slightly too short for that.

"He's headed this way!"

And suddenly she was alone, deserted by her gossiping friends.

He stopped in front of her, his tall frame towering over her own five feet, five inches. He would fit in with the rest of her family just fine. *In fact, he and Helene make a striking couple*, she thought with an inner twinge.

"Good evening, Miss Payton."

Her heart fluttered at the smooth English accent and her lungs refused to issue forth enough air to power words of greeting. It had felt like this the first time they met in her bookstore, too. He'd come in looking for a book on home improvement, of all things, and she'd barely said six words to him between recommending a title and ringing up his purchase.

Feeling crowded by his proximity, although he wasn't standing all that close, she took an involuntary step backward and ran into one of the buffet tables. She grabbed for the edge to steady herself and got a handful of crab salad instead.

Turning to look, she stared in horrified stupefaction at the mess covering her hand. Mom was going to have a hissy fit. The salad required a two-day prep and was her most recent culinary pride and joy. Now an entire buffet-size bowl of it was good only for the garbage disposal.

"I can't believe I just did that," she muttered.

"Can I help you?"

She looked up at him then, too upset by her predicament to be her usual tongue-tied self around him. "Do you have any suggestions for hiding the evidence?"

"Perhaps we could take the bowl to the kitchen?"

"And leave a gap on the table?"

He took hold of her wrist and lifted her hand away from the bowl, careful not to let the crab salad anywhere near his dinner suit or her dress. "Go clean up and I will take care of our small disaster."

In spite of her embarrassed chagrin, the feel of his fingers curled around her wrist was surprisingly nice.

"It's not your disaster." She sighed in self-deprecation. "It's mine and I can't leave it to you." Even if she wished she could.

"Of course, I'm at fault. I startled you." She opened her mouth to argue, but he shook his head. "Don't let it concern you. I have some experience in this sort of thing."

"Rescuing women from the wrath of their temperamental chef mothers?"

He smiled, even white teeth flashing all too briefly. "Hiding the evidence."

Her eyes widened in mock horror. "Oh, my gosh, you're a member of the British mafia and here everyone was thinking you were some sort of displaced nobleman or spy or something."

That made him laugh, and she felt the sound all the way to her toes.

"You have a nice laugh." She couldn't believe she'd said that. Trust her to go from mute to uttering inanities. What an improvement.

"And you have a charming sense of humor, but you also have a hand that is about to drip crab salad on your lovely dress."

She extended her arm further from her body, having no desire to ruin the dress it had taken four hours of shopping in San Diego to find. "I'll just go wash this off."

She took as long as she could in the ladies' room, washing her hands, tidying her appearance, and wishing she could fall through a hole in the floor rather than go back out and face Calder Maxwell.

She got a moment alone with the focus of her fantasies and what did she do?

Go diving in a buffet bowl.

She never had been all that handy in the kitchen.

When she came out of the softly lit alcove, Calder was waiting for her. He gave her a look that made her go tight in some really interesting places. "Are you all right, Miss Payton?"

"Fine. Uh . . . call me Tabby. Everyone else does."

"Tabby, then." He drew her name out as if he were savoring it on his tongue.

What a ridiculous thought.

She peeked around him at the buffet table and saw that the bowl was gone and things had been rearranged so no one could tell it had been there to begin with. "Thank you for hiding the evidence, although she's going to know something happened when she finds the salad in the kitchen."

"I emptied it into a trash bag and tossed it in the dumpster outside. Unless she's watching closely, she'll assume it all got eaten."

"You really are good at this sort of thing."

"Thank you."

"You're fast, too."

"So I've been told." The chill in his voice, despite the humor in his eyes, made her wonder by whom.

"Enjoying the party?" she asked by rote.

Technically, the Port Diamond Yacht Club hosted the annual summer gala, but her parents owned the marina and restaurant where it was held, making them the unofficial hosts of the evening and her their not-so-willing accomplice.

She wasn't overly fond of large crowds.

"Everyone has been quite nice."

Which wasn't an answer to her question. In fact, it sounded like one of her own sidestepping comments, the kind that got her out of trouble with her mother for not trying hard enough to be social without having to lie. She found herself smiling.

"Obsessively interested, you mean."

His smile short-circuited her brain receptors. "There does seem to be a great deal of speculation about me."

"Well, as I said, rumor has it you're former secret government something, or maybe a member of the English nobility, but you've shown your true colors to me," she said in a teasing tone usually reserved for close friends and family. People she trusted.

His willingness to shoulder responsibility for something

that had been entirely her fault, and then rescue her from the consequences, had gone a long way toward relaxing her with him.

"Is that your subtle way of fishing for the truth?"

"Not if you don't want to tell me." So far, so good. Her tongue wasn't tied in knots yet and she hadn't made an inane comment in five minutes.

"The truth would no doubt bore you," he said dismissively.

"You're very good at that."

"What?"

"Sidestepping."

"And you are more observant than most."

She shrugged. She'd had a lot of practice.

Just then her sister walked by on her way to the deck with one of her many boyfriends and waved at Tabby.

Tabby waved back and smiled.

"She's quite effervescent, isn't she?"

With a sinking heart, Tabby nodded. The inquest had begun. Would he be as good at seeking out information as he was at avoiding giving it?

For once, she really wished one of her sister's admirers had gone to someone else for insights into Helene.

"She's very bubbly," Tabby said, answering his question. "One of the nicest people I know."

"Your family is very close, aren't they?"

"Yes, we are."

His gaze was focused on the dancers on the deck, probably watching Helene charm her partner. "You are lucky."

"Blessed. My parents are both good people and they raised Helene and me to value the bonds of family."

He turned to face her again. "Would you care to dance?"

The question hit her like a brick upside the head. No. Not that. The pumping was bad enough, but to have to dance with him, being held in close proximity to a body that made hers go haywire while he did it? That would be cruel and unusual punishment. Besides, he didn't want to dance with her. Not really. She'd had this ploy played many times before.

A man asked her to dance and then made some excuse for her to switch partners with Helene. Calder was just the type of man to handle that sort of thing with aplomb, but she didn't want to be handled. Not that way, anyway.

"I'm not much of a dancer," she lied, and hated herself for doing so. She put a lot of stock in honesty and even white lies bugged her.

"Your father said differently."

Darn it, Dad had ratted her out. "Did he?"

"Yes."

She barely refrained from rolling her eyes. He'd probably told Calder all about the lessons she'd taken as a kid. She'd danced in competitions until she was thirteen and sprouted breasts and hips overnight. "Um . . ."

"Don't you want to dance with me?" he asked, sounding amused.

And well he should be. He had to know that half the women present tonight were panting for a chance to be held by the gorgeous Englishman. She should be thrilled he'd picked her to partner, even if it was with ulterior motives. What woman wouldn't be, knowing they got to dance with their idea of male perfection?

One smart enough to realize it would be pure torture, she thought. However, he was looking at her expectantly and she let out a huff of frustration.

Better to get this over with and then go back to lusting after him from afar.

"Sure, I'll dance with you." She grimaced inside at her lack of savoir faire.

Charm, thy name is not Tabitha Payton.

He put his hand out and she took it, pretending for this short space in time that it was her he was interested in, and knowing as she did so how dangerous such inner pretence could be.

Chapter Two

He led her to an outdoor dance floor lit by nothing more than several strands of twinkling lights and the full moon. He drew her to him as a bluesy ballad filled the night air. The atmosphere surrounding the dancers was one of romantic intimacy, something she could do without if she wanted to keep her mental faculties together.

He pulled her into shocking full body contact before she realized his intention. Okay, maybe there was an inch or so between them, but she'd seen him dance earlier with Helene and he had held *her* at arm's length. Tabby had expected the same.

She'd been wrong, so utterly, beautifully wrong.

A riot of sensations exploded through her and it was all she could do to stay vertical and breathing as her body reacted to his nearness. He started them swaying to the soft beat and her hands went of their own volition around his neck. His skin was warm and his black hair silky against her fingers.

And he smelled delectable. His expensive aftershave was subtle and did not mask his personal scent, which teased her senses.

"You're a good dancer."

"I'm not exactly doing anything," she said, no hope of tact anywhere on the horizon. She was too busy trying to focus on not jumping his bones.

But, *man*, how she wanted to. She *ached* to rub certain

body parts against his hard masculine form, and her mouth watered at the thought of tasting the smooth jawline so temptingly close.

"You're doing enough." His voice sounded funny, but she couldn't concentrate on what that meant, not with her brain on meltdown.

Suddenly it occurred to her that while it might feel more incredible than anything she'd ever known, if she didn't get out of his arms very soon, she was going to do something that would lead to her utter humiliation. Like grab his face and kiss him stupid, or close the inch of distance between them and press hardened nipples against his sculpted pecs.

Oh, yeah, that would feel good. Too good.

"She looks eighteen, but she's twenty-four. She teaches kindergarten because she loves children, but she hasn't gotten married because she's never been in love." The words came tumbling out in a torrent of jittery need to get this over with. "She's not dating anyone special at the moment, but she does date. A lot," she couldn't help inserting. Tabby was a much better relationship bet, not that Calder would see it that way, of course.

No more than she wanted to date the guy who came in every Wednesday to ask if she had any new Earl Stanley Gardner books in the shop. Even if he didn't have that little quirk, she wasn't attracted to the mystery fan. Couldn't help it. Neither could Calder wanting Helene.

"Her favorite color is yellow, her favorite candy is peanut butter fudge. There's a place up the beach that makes some she cannot resist. She looks great in evening wear, but her preferred date is a trip to the San Diego Zoo, or even Sea World. She's a sucker for cotton candy and despite the fact we were raised on the beach, she's not all that enamored of the ocean and hates getting sand in her shoes."

"What?" He stared down at her, but she ducked her head so he couldn't see her eyes. "If I might be so bold as to ask, who the bloody hell are you talking about, Tabby?"

"As if you don't know. Who else would I be yammering on

about while dancing with the sexiest man in the room?" she mumbled at his chest. "My sister, Helene."

She didn't mind the information seeking, but she hated the protestations of innocence, which was why she rarely let on she knew what was happening. She hated being lied to more than she hated lying. Only, she couldn't believe what her frustration had led her into saying this time. *The sexiest man in the room?*

Oh, man.

"And you've shared this wealth of information with me because why?" he asked, his precise English accent laced with inexplicable amusement.

Not appreciating being laughed at on top of everything else, she tipped her head back and glared up at him. "You want to know. I don't want to spend all evening fencing with you verbally so I can feed the information in such a way as to preserve your illusions or my pride."

"You believe I am dancing with you because I want information from you about your sister?" he asked in a voice that implied he doubted her sanity.

"Are you trying to tell me you aren't?"

"Why do you believe this?" he asked instead of giving her a direct answer again.

"You really are a master at conversational misdirection."

He smiled, the latent amusement still there in his dark eyes, but a surprising determination was evident, as well. "I am also quite adept at procuring the information I require. Why do you believe I am dancing with you in order to draw particulars about your sister from you?"

"That's what men do. Since I was eighteen and she was a precocious, gorgeous fourteen-year-old with more friendliness and native grace than I will have when I'm ninety."

"You believe men approach you only to get closer to your sister?"

"Yes."

"You are wrong."

"I made the mistake of believing that a few times, but after ten years I'm no longer that naive." She took a deep breath, wishing things could be different. Knowing they weren't. "It's always about Helene. Always."

"Yet you two are very close."

"I adore her as much as everyone else does."

His fingers locked at the small of her back, while one thumb caressed a lazy pattern against her spine. "You aren't jealous at all."

"No. Why should I be? I don't want to be her. I'm a lot more private. I'd hate a gaggle of boyfriends following my every move."

"Your father said you were shy."

"I don't like meeting new people. It makes me nervous."

"You do not appear nervous right now."

That's because she was too busy trying not to drool or rub against him like a cat in heat. "No," was all she said.

"She is twenty-eight and rather shy. She is not overly fond of candy, but she adores ice cream, especially coconut macadamia."

All the air whooshed out of Tabby and she stopped dancing in shock.

Calder didn't seem to mind. In fact, now that she realized it, he'd danced her off the deck and into a secluded spot away from the other party guests. She could hear the ocean, and the sound of wind on the waves stirred her already stimulated senses.

"I'm the one who likes coconut macadamia ice cream."

"Yes. You also love the beach and will spend hours walking in your bare feet right at the tide line."

"I don't understand."

"You are not dating anyone special and you haven't in a long time. You own a small bookshop on the pier, which you bought with a trust fund left you by a great-aunt. You quit university after getting a two-year degree instead of a bachelor of arts like your parents wanted you to."

"They've gotten over that."

"No, they have not, but they respect your right to make your own choices."

"Oh."

"Shall I go on?"

"About what?"

The sound he made was one hundred percent masculine irritation, all of his humor seemingly having taken a vacation.

"Very well. You are quite blunt with people you know, kind to strangers even if they intimidate you, and your favorite color is sea green. Oh, yes, and you love the opera and theater. You adore yellow roses, but I personally think you should consider the beauty of the scarlet blooms."

"Red is for passion, yellow is for everlasting love," she said in a dazed voice.

"Ahh . . . that explains it. You are a romantic."

"I'm . . ." She had no idea what to say. It sounded as if he'd been pumping someone else for information on her.

"Your father is very proud of you, if a bit exasperated at times, and is more than willing to wax poetic on the subject of his eldest daughter."

"You asked him . . . about me?"

"Yes. I have also discussed you at length with Helene, who thinks as highly of you as you do of her."

"Why?" she asked, stupidly maybe, but with a genuine need to know.

"I should think that was obvious. I want you, Tabitha Payton, and I intend to have you." His Cary Grant eyes glittered down at her, the words coming out in his precise English accent, somehow making them even more sexy.

She shook her head, trying to clear it, convinced she couldn't have heard him say what she'd thought he'd said.

"Oh, yes . . . and I think you want me, too, in spite of your rather blatant attempt to toss your sister in my path."

Calder watched in fascination as multiple emotions chased across Tabby's expressive features.

Shock. Disbelief. Hope. Pleasure. Desire.

It was the desire he reacted to.

He pulled her into his body, pressing her soft curves against flesh hungry for the feel of her. He had wanted the little darling since the first time he saw her walking along the beach close to sunset. He'd been sitting on the deck of his recently inherited house, trying to determine what he wanted his future to hold, when she came into his line of vision.

His first thought had been the foolishness of a woman walking alone on an almost deserted beach; his second thought had been both carnal and imaginative.

The red glow from the fading sun had outlined her luscious form while a gentle wind stirred her dark blond hair around her shoulders and face. She had looked both ethereal and incredibly sensual. Simply watching her had made him hard.

Although her body had called to him like a siren, it had been the sense of solitude surrounding her that did not smack of loneliness, which had cemented his ache to possess her. Her words tonight had only fueled that fiery need.

She'd spent her adult life fending off her sister's boyfriends and yet did not resent the other woman.

Tabitha Payton was a very special woman.

However, she was oblivious to her uniqueness and appeal. While he found that refreshing, it was also frustrating. Seducing her body would be quite easy. It was something he was very good at. However, making her believe she was the woman he wanted above all others might turn out to be bloody difficult.

"I want you." He brushed her lips with his, a mere whisper of touching, nothing too passionate. Not yet. "Tell me you want me, too."

She quivered against him, her lips full and soft in preparation for the kiss her feminine instincts knew was coming even if her mind did not. "I . . ."

"I do not want Helene."

She licked her lips and stared at him, big green eyes begging reassurance while her mouth remained stubbornly mute.

"Believe me."

"But everyone wants her," she said, sounding bemused and disbelieving.

"Not everyone. I want *you*. Now tell me you want me."

She'd pulled her hair up in a sleek French twist and it

framed a heart-shaped face creased in doubt. "If I tell you I want you, you could hurt me."

"Never."

"Not physically, I know that . . . but if I say it, you'll know . . . and then you could turn away and say you never meant me to take you seriously."

He didn't think she knew what she was saying. She sounded dazed and her words came out in disjointed bursts.

"Has that happened before?"

"Yes."

Bloody idiotic men she'd known. "I mean what I say. There is no mistake. I am quite serious when I say you are the one woman I want."

"The *one* woman?" She laughed like it was a joke.

With a suddenness that shocked him, his patience gave out and he kissed her, claiming her mouth with hot passion and a lot less finesse than a man of his talents should exercise. However, there was no room for refinement in this kiss. She belonged to him in a way he neither understood nor would deny, and he felt a remarkably savage need to imprint that truth on her body.

The only option available to him at the moment was a kiss, and so he took it.

Her mouth remained impassive in surprise for several seconds, and then she kissed him back so hard his teeth ground against his inner lip. He opened his mouth and licked the seam of her ardent mouth with his tongue. She jerked in his arms and went completely still, like a fawn drinking from a stream for the first time.

Only he was the one doing the sipping.

The kiss changed as he revered sweetly compliant lips that assured him of the desire she had been incapable of voicing. Deliciously female, her mouth was unconsciously sensuous in its startled immobility, and yet temptingly pliable.

Perfect.

But not nearly enough.

He needed more than her lips. He wanted all of her, and he would have her soon or he would go mad.

He undid her hair, pulling out pins and fingering through the silken strands because he needed to touch her this way. He massaged her head and she moaned against his lips, pressing her body intimately to his. That small sound, coupled with background noise that had suddenly grown louder, brought him back to his senses.

They could not do what he wanted to do with her out here, and regardless of how much his body craved hers, it was too soon. He did not want to spook her.

He pulled away, gently removing her hold on him. She stood there looking shell-shocked, her lips swollen from his kisses. He wanted nothing more than to pull her back into his arms, but he forced himself to refrain. Now was not the time.

The music had been turned up. Playing at a much faster tempo than it had been, it filled the silence between them.

She bit her lip and then looked at him as if he were a species alien to her experience. "Why did you do that?"

Chapter Three

O f all the questions he might have anticipated at that moment, why he'd kissed her was not one of them.

"Because I wanted to, though I can appreciate now might not have been the best time."

"You wanted to kiss me?" She needn't sound so surprised.

"I did say I meant to have you. Kissing is the normal prelude to what is to come."

"Is there something wrong with you? I mean, maybe your family sent you over here because you're their big embarrassment. Do you howl at the moon during lunar eclipses, or get so drunk on your birthday you dance on tabletops?"

"I assure you, I am no one's big embarrassment." He would have been offended by her suppositions if she weren't so charmingly confused by his attentions. "You really are used to men trying to get to Helene through you."

"Well, um, duh . . . yes. I did say so, didn't I?"

He laughed. He couldn't help himself. He couldn't remember the last time a woman reacted to him with such refreshing honesty.

"I suppose it's going to take some getting used to you having me around."

"You're going to be around?"

"Love, you're not exactly tracking tonight, are you?"

"I hear what your mouth is saying, but the words don't make any sense in my world."

"I guess it's a good thing I'm in your world now because they make perfect sense to me."

"You want to date me?" she asked, as if she were trying to get it absolutely straight.

"Yes." And more, but he'd already told her that.

"You don't want to date Helene?"

"No."

"Why not?" she asked, her tone just the tiniest bit aggrieved.

"Because I am not attracted to her."

"And you are attracted to me?" She peered at him through her lashes, this time as if she were trying to see into his head.

"Yes. Very," he added for good measure.

"You did notice I'm the one with a figure from a bygone era? The shy one . . . not a tinkling laugh in my repertoire?"

"I noticed everything about you and I find it quite a potent package, if you must know."

"You're not over here de-stressing from some over-the-top job are you? I mean, that would explain your aberrant behavior."

"There is nothing aberrant in my behavior." Well, not much. Or at least not what she was thinking.

He had never had a relationship of the type he wanted to have with her. Purely personal, possibly permanent, and definitely passionate.

"Right."

He couldn't decide if he wanted to laugh again or shake her. The woman was annoyingly stubborn and fixated. "I'm thirty years old. I know my own mind."

"What size was your last girlfriend?"

"What?"

"Dress size. What did she wear?"

"I don't know the American equivalent."

Her lips twisted. "Uh-huh. Just show me with your hands how big around her waist was."

He did.

Tabby nodded, her expression gleaming with triumph. "Exactly. Probably a size six."

"What the hell does that have to do with us?"

"You normally date women like my sister. Men like you do."

"According to you, all men prefer women like your sister."

She bit her lip. "They do."

"I don't, and do not start yammering about dress sizes again. You are perfect as you are." In fact, she was luscious. "I don't want you to be any different."

"This is really weird for me."

"Let's spend the rest of the evening together and see if we can't get you used to it."

"All right." She said it grudgingly, but he could have sworn her green eyes reflected the same yearning that made it so impossible for him to leave her alone.

The next morning, Tabby awoke to the strident ring of the telephone. She fumbled for the receiver from underneath the light comforter on her bed.

"Hello?"

"Did I wake you, dear?"

"Hi, Mom. Yes, you woke me."

"Sorry, you're usually up early on Sunday, but I couldn't help noticing you missed church."

"I slept through my alarm."

"Up late?"

"You know I was."

"Later than I think?"

Tabby sat up and fluffed the pillows behind her as a backrest. "I did not bring him home with me!"

Not that she would have turned him down—she didn't think—but he hadn't asked, which made her protestation sort of overdone.

"I see. So, is he nobility, former spy, what?"

"What do you *see*?"

"Nothing in particular. It's a phrase we mothers use. I'm sure you'll find yourself saying it someday, too. It means we're thinking over what our child just told us. Now answer my question."

"The answer is: I don't know. We didn't talk about his past." He'd managed to neatly sidestep any conversational byways in that direction.

"You spent the whole evening so wrapped up in each other's company, you barely noticed when everyone else had left and you didn't talk about his past? What *did* you talk about?"

"Everything. It was wonderful, Mom."

It had been like talking to a really good friend, one she'd known forever . . . which had been as worrisome as his strange fixation on her instead of Helene. She could really fall for this guy. That would leave her open to major pain when he figured out that James Bond was supposed to date Octopussy, not Anne of Green Gables.

"Everything including why he's in Port Diamond?" her mother probed.

"He inherited his house from an uncle on his mother's side. She was American."

"Is she dead?"

"No, but she's got her British citizenship now."

Silence. Then, "So is he sticking around or what?"

"I don't know."

"Does he have a job?" her mother asked suspiciously.

Tabby grinned. Overprotective, but lovable. "I suppose. He certainly seems to have money, but the truth is we spent a lot of time talking about me. It was weird."

Her mom laughed. "If you dated more, that kind of thing wouldn't be so strange. He's been pumping your dad and sister about you for a couple of weeks now."

Tabby smoothed the sheet and blanket over her legs. "Why do you suppose he waited to approach me?"

"Helene said you avoided them whenever he was with her. Maybe he thought you weren't interested."

"I didn't want to intrude."

"I don't think he would have seen it as an intrusion."

"No, I guess not." But how was she supposed to know? This whole thing of being the sole recipient of a man's interest was new to her, and she couldn't help feeling it wasn't fated to last very long.

"My crab salad went over very well last night. I knew it would."

It was all Tabby could do not to blurt out the truth. "It's a wonderful recipe."

"Yes."

They chatted for a few more minutes and then her mother rang off.

Tabby was in the shower when her doorbell rang.

She grabbed a towel, did a quick dry-off, and then wrapped it around herself sarong style to answer the door.

Expecting her sister or someone equally innocuous—like *anyone else*—she reared back in shock when she saw Calder standing on the other side.

"Good morning, love." His dark eyes made a meal of her, and the oversized bath sheet felt like the most revealing piece of lingerie she owned.

"I wasn't expecting you this morning." He'd said he would call, not come calling.

His dark brows rose. "Then who were you expecting?"

"No one in particular."

"But definitely not me?"

"Honestly? No."

He frowned. "Do you frequently answer the door wearing nothing more than a towel when you don't know who is on the other side?"

"Of course not. How often do you think I'm in the shower when someone stops by?"

"I can only hope the occurrence is rare." He sounded annoyed. He certainly looked it.

Which was interesting, if confusing.

"Getting a visitor at my door is pretty rare. People usually stop by the store to see me."

"If you didn't think it was someone you knew, then you thought you were opening the door to a perfect stranger?" he asked as if carefully putting a puzzle together and not liking the way it was turning out.

"Nobody's perfect," she quipped, but his stiff expression said he didn't appreciate the joke. She sighed. "I don't know why it matters so much, but I thought it might be a book delivery made to my home address by accident. It's happened before, though never on Sunday. It could have been someone looking for directions to too."

Suddenly, he was a stranger. No longer the charismatic man of the night before, this guy emanated menace and made James Bond seem like a pussycat.

"If I understand you correctly, you are telling me you opened your door dressed like that"—he pointed to her towel-clad self with a precise movement—"believing a stranger was on the other side?" His tone could have frozen underground lava.

"That bothers you?" Okay, so it was hard to interpret his reaction any other way, but the concept was so foreign to her, she felt like she needed a translation guide to deal with it.

"You have to ask?" He looked pointedly at the swell of her breasts revealed above the towel. "Do you mind stepping back inside to continue this discussion?"

"Uh . . . no problem." She moved back a couple of paces.

He followed, shutting the door behind him, and then reached for her. "In answer to your rather obtuse question, yes, I am more than mildly irritated that you would answer your door wearing nothing but a towel if you were expecting someone besides me . . . or maybe your mother."

"That sounds awfully territorial." And the fingers wrapped around her upper arms certainly felt like it.

"It is."

"Oh." She licked her lips nervously, and then bit them when his expression turned from disapproving to heated. "Um, I don't think we have that kind of relationship yet."

"I beg to differ. I made my intentions clear last night,

Tabby, and I won't share." His voice was like razed steel. His hands moved to cup her face, his touch gentle even if his tone was not. "I don't want anyone else seeing you like this."

"No one else wants to."

He shook his head. "You cannot be that naive. You are a beautiful, desirable woman and even if you were a wrinkle-ridden hag, it wouldn't be safe to answer your door practically naked."

"But Port Diamond—"

"Is on a major highway, and small towns have crazy, nasty people, too, love." He sounded so serious, so concerned.

And she realized he was probably right. It was just that living her whole life in a small town, she sometimes forgot the world was bigger than her own backyard. "I won't do it again," she promised softly, still not sure if this whole territorial attitude of his was good or not.

"Thank you." And then he kissed her—as if he couldn't wait one more second to connect with her lips.

She went under immediately, just as she had the night before, but when she tried to get close, he pulled back.

"Don't, love. I came by to see if you wanted to spend the day with me, not to seduce you in your living room." He looked down at her precariously wrapped towel, his gaze glittering with unmistakable desire. "Though it's a bloody tempting prospect."

"I'm glad."

He closed his eyes, as if the sight of her was too much for his self-control. "If you don't get some clothes on immediately, all of my good intentions are going to disappear."

"Maybe I don't want you to be governed by good intentions." The kiss they'd shared last night had been incredible. She wanted more.

At some point, he was going to realize she was not his type and move on. Was it wrong to want to experience all the passion he had to offer before that happened?

She'd been practical and cautious her whole life, and that had gotten her exactly nowhere in the relationship department. One thing she knew, this man wanted her, not some other woman and not her sister.

That meant their connection had more going for it than any of the others she'd had in her life.

His jaw tightened, as if he was trying to gather inner strength. When he opened his eyes, they were hard with resolve. "We're going to the San Diego Museum of Art."

"This is the last week of their special El Greco exhibit. I've been wanting to see it."

"I know."

Whoosh—the air rushed from her lungs as shock reverberated through her.

It was unbelievable that a man so incredible would go to such lengths to please her. Every bit as overwhelming was the reality that she wanted to stay home and continue their kiss more than she wanted to go to the exhibition. She'd never been this physically stunned by a man's nearness.

"We don't have to go anywhere for me to enjoy being with you," she admitted.

He smiled, that Cary Grant charm on display again. "I am delighted to hear that."

"But you still want to go?" she guessed.

"Yes. I want to see if your expression is the same looking at one of your favorite painter's masterpieces as it is when you look out over the ocean from the front window of your shop. I want to enjoy your company in the car and at the exhibit. I'm hoping you will give your whole day to me."

He'd watched her watching the ocean from her bookshop? Wow. "Um . . . I can't think of anything I would enjoy more."

He smiled, and then looked down at her body encased in the towel and his eyes burned with something besides a desire to go to the museum.

She blushed for no reason she could discern. "I guess I'd better get dressed."

He took a deep breath and turned away as if she, Tabitha Payton, was so irresistible, to look at her one second longer would be to take her. "That would be a good idea, yes."

* * *

Calder breathed a sigh of relief when Tabby left the room to get dressed. He'd bedded women with a lot more sophistication, definitely women with more confidence in their innate sexual appeal, but not one of them had made him feel like a panting, hormone-driven teenager—not even when he'd been one.

He didn't know what was so different about the sexy little bookworm, but he was bloody well going to figure it out.

Chapter Four

The El Greco exhibition was everything Tabby had hoped it would be. Unlike other companions she'd dragged along to art museums, Calder seemed perfectly content to let her sit and contemplate whenever a painting struck her in a special way. He didn't hurry her, didn't talk incessantly, and yet she felt his presence as deeply as she felt the spirit of the artist reaching out to her.

She'd never been so aware of another person while indulging her love of art. Usually, even chatterboxes like her sister could melt into the background like ghosts that made noise, but couldn't impinge on her consciousness.

Not Calder. He remained a solid, tantalizing presence throughout their tour of the museum.

It was only as he led her from the building, though, that she realized he had his arm curved proprietarily around her waist and had done every time they walked anywhere.

"Would you like to stop for an early dinner before we head back?"

"I can't believe you let me stay in the museum so long."

"I enjoyed watching you as much as I thought I would."

She tilted her head sideways to see his face. "You're a strange man, Calder."

"No. Merely an intrigued one."

She shook her head, but didn't demur when he pulled her body closer to his. "Dinner sounds great."

"Good. There's a gallery showing we can attend afterward if you are not tired of looking at paintings."

"I never get tired of it, but I'm surprised you're not climbing the walls at the prospect of more stopping and staring." Which was what her mom had labeled her tendency to become engrossed in a visual image. It didn't only happen at museums; she reacted the same way to a creative window display when she was out shopping.

"The artist has a hint of the master in his style, but his work is definitely no copycat."

"You mean El Greco's?"

"Yes."

She sighed in bliss at the thought. Maybe she would be able to buy one of the paintings. The walls of her home were still bare for the most part because of her pickiness regarding the type of artwork she wanted to hang.

But after a dinner where it was all she could do not to leap across the table and plant her lips in close contact with Calder's—did the man have a clue how irresistible he was?—she discovered the artist Calder thought she would like was already selling way out of her price range.

She sighed over several gorgeous paintings, but one stopped her and held her in its thrall for so long, Calder finally asked if she was all right. Similar to El Greco's *Laocoon*, the painting was not easy to interpret, but it stirred so much latent emotion and pricked at her view of her own sexuality to such an extent that she reached out to touch it.

Only Calder's gentle hold on her wrist stopped her from the major faux pas. She smiled at him with gratitude, even as her heart was caught by the image of him beside the painting. Both were doing serious damage to her ability to control her physical impulses.

"If you don't stop looking at me like that, I'm going to kiss you."

The hushed voices of other visitors to the gallery faded to a whisper against her consciousness. "I wouldn't stop you."

He shook his head. "I'm not sure I could stop at a kiss."

"Oh . . ."

He quickly led her from the gallery. When they reached his car, he put her inside, his face set, his body vibrating a message of sexual hunger even she couldn't mistake. He drove with quick jerky movements until they reached an overlook and then he parked the car.

He turned to her. "Come here, Tabby."

"You couldn't wait until we got home?" she teased, her own voice betraying how much she wanted this.

"If I had, I would end up making love to you and I'm not ready for that step yet."

She stared at him in shock. "You aren't ready? I thought it was the woman who was supposed to want to wait." And her body was clamoring for what she knew his would provide.

Pleasure. Acceptance. A sense of closeness she craved. Even if it was temporary, it would be good.

"Once you take me into your body, Tabby, you'll be mine." He sounded so serious, as if his sexy charm was just a front for the deep and somewhat primitive man under the surface. "You have to be absolutely sure I'm what you want before we take that step."

"You're so serious. You make it sound like making love would be a permanent, irrevocable decision for long-term commitment." Which was how she had always seen it—until now, when she'd decided to take what she could get and live with the consequences later.

He was saying those consequences were different than the ones her heart told her were waiting on the other side of sharing her body with him.

"That is precisely what I mean."

The idea that he shared her solemn, but atypical, view of intimacy made her dizzy. It also confused her. "You're not a virgin."

He frowned, an unreadable expression in his dark eyes. "No. I am not."

"So, you couldn't have always felt that way."

"I have never before felt this way."

"You mean, this isn't a general principle?" That made a lot more sense in some ways and was totally beyond her comprehension in others.

"No . . . it is a Tabitha Payton principle."

What in the world was she supposed to say to that? He couldn't be serious and yet his tone of voice said he was—deadly so.

But he didn't expect her to say anything. Didn't so much as give her the chance.

He kissed her instead, and from the first contact, she knew just how easy it would be to make love with this man.

He tasted like he had the night before, but now she recognized the flavor. He tasted like he belonged to her. She didn't care how ludicrous the thought was, she couldn't dismiss it. They connected on a level not governed by what made sense. It was too elemental for that.

When he dropped her off later that night, her lips were still tingling from his kisses and her body was throbbing from unsatisfied needs. From the pained expression on his face, she guessed he was experiencing the same thing.

She didn't ask him inside, though.

He'd made it clear he wanted to wait and she liked what that said about his feelings for her.

After the first night of torture, Calder was careful not to allow the passion between him and Tabby to flare out of control. He kept the kissing light and their time alone together minimal, which was why he hadn't taken her to his home yet. Even his well-honed self-control wasn't up to the temptation.

The only time they'd come close to making love again was when he'd presented her with the gift of the painting that had so enamored her from the gallery. She'd gotten all teary-eyed and kissed him. They were half naked and panting before he'd been able to rein in his libido.

She'd gotten testy about it, but he could see she liked knowing she had such a strong impact on him.

The unwitting temptress was going to be his soon, or he was going to go stark staring mad.

She seemed to love everything they did together, but when he invited her to the opera, her eyes lit up like stars on a perfectly clear night. When he arrived to pick her up, it was all he could do to take her out to the car and not ravish her right there. She'd donned a silk dress the color of coral flame that accentuated her voluptuous curves. Her green eyes sparkled in contrast and she'd left her hair down in an alluring curtain around her shoulders.

He was painfully hard the entire drive into Los Angeles. By the time intermission came, his erection was past painful. It was a pulsing ache that demanded satisfaction. He'd listened to her sighs, watched her sensual reaction to the performance, and been tormented by her scent, which revealed an arousal he wasn't sure she was even conscious of.

He led her into the pavilion's reception area, the teeming mass of fellow attendees doing nothing to curb the primal need roaring through him.

Without considering whether she wanted to go or not, he led her upstairs and into a small hall that was blessedly quiet. He stopped at the first door to his left. He tried the handle. It was locked. Using techniques he'd learned early in his career, he picked the lock and pushed the door open. It was a meeting room.

He tugged her inside, took a quick look around, but saw no signs it would be, or had been, occupied tonight. He shut the door and locked it again.

Other than the illumination from the streetlights outside, filtering in through the almost closed blinds, it was dark. It was private. And that was all he needed.

"What are you doing? What's the matter?" she demanded, her voice soft in the darkness around them.

He didn't answer, but took her lips with an animalistic growl that should have shocked him. This was not his normal technique, but she brought out things in him no other woman ever had.

She kissed him back, her mouth eager and pliant against his, her breathing erratic.

Cupping her sumptuously curved bottom through the slick fabric of her dress, he lifted her against him until he no longer had to bend his head to kiss her. She liked that, and wrapped her arms around his head as if wanting to hold onto him for dear life. Did she think there was any chance he would pull away?

Not bloody likely.

He nipped at her lower lip. She whimpered and opened her mouth, inviting him inside. He accepted, sweeping her mouth with his tongue and savoring the flavor that was hers alone. Candy sweet and addictive.

Her small feet brushed against him, trying to find purchase. She made a frustrated sound when they couldn't and almost kneed him in the groin, but her lips never stopped devouring his.

When her knee came perilously close to his sex again, he broke his mouth away. "Wrap your legs around me."

She was trying to resume the kiss, oblivious to his demand.

He avoided her seeking lips and spoke directly into her ear, as he was already pulling the skirt of her dress up. "Your legs, love . . . put them around me."

"Oh . . . okay." She obeyed, moaning with sexy abandon when her panty-covered mound rubbed against his abdomen.

He exulted in her unrestrained passion and kneaded the round cheeks filling his hands with fingers that actually trembled. It had been so long since sex had been this important or this uncomplicated . . . perhaps it never had been. But she didn't want anything from him, wasn't trying to manipulate him in any way, and he wasn't using her attraction against her, either.

They were just a man and a woman making love because they wanted each other and that felt incredibly good.

He kissed her again, and to his delight she started moving

her pelvis, pressing the hot apex of her thighs against his torso. He sucked on her tongue and she increased the bucking movements of her lower body. He growled, primal desire coursing through him in a hot rush.

She matched him perfectly.

He could smell her arousal, could taste her passion, and he could no more stop himself from sliding his hands under the silk covering her ass than he could stop kissing the glorious creature in his arms. Her skin was softer than the silk that covered it.

"You're perfect," he bit off against her lips.

She moaned something inarticulate in response.

When his fingertip delved between her cheeks, she went still again. He adjusted his hold on her so that he could reach further and then slid one questing finger down to the heated moisture of her core.

She was slick and swollen—everything a woman should be in her lover's arms—and he shuddered convulsively with the need to be inside her.

She whimpered again, the sound so hot and sexy, his dick bobbed against the tightened muscles of his abdomen. Pushing against his finger, she forced him to penetrate her to the first knuckle . . . and then the second. Wet, silken tissues clamped his finger like a vice, and he ate at her lips, caressing her even more deeply with his finger.

She made a high-pitched, desperate sound and he knew she was close. He wanted her to go over.

Her legs were locked around him so tightly, breathing was a challenge, but he wouldn't ask her to relax her hold for anything. He needed her unbridled passion. He would settle for nothing less than the pure honesty of her response, so different than the world he had left behind.

He moved his hand so his finger slipped out of her silken heat and searched out her swollen clitoris. He swirled and rubbed, then pressed . . . then swirled . . . then pressed again.

And she came, arching her body, convulsing in pleasure.

He muffled her cry of completion with his mouth, swallowing it as appreciatively as the finest wine or most decadent dessert known to man.

Unable to stop, needing as much as she would willingly give, he played her straining body. After only seconds, she convulsed again, throwing her head back, her throat locked on a silent scream and her legs going so tight they threatened to crack his ribs.

Then the tension in her body snapped and her head fell forward onto his shoulder, her torso resting against his. Sighing breaths shuddered in and out of her body as he cradled her close.

He kissed her temple, licking the salty sweat there, the silver path of tears from her eyes. "You are amazing, Tabby."

"You're the amazing one, Calder."

He didn't argue. He was still hard as a rock and it was taking everything he had not to throw her down on the tabletop and thrust inside her silky, swollen heat.

After a few minutes of utter bliss and sheer torture, she unhooked her legs from behind his back. "Let me go."

He did as she asked, gently lowering her to the ground and releasing her. She dropped to her knees. At first, he didn't know if it was because her legs were too weak to hold her, but then she touched the buckle on his belt and he knew what she wanted.

"I don't think that's a good idea, Tabby."

"Oh, yes, it is. I want to taste you." For an introverted bookseller, she could sound bossy when she wanted to.

And he couldn't begin to pretend he didn't want to feel her luscious mouth on him. He moved a few feet backward so he could lean against the wall. "I'm all yours."

She giggled and the sound entranced him.

But all thought fled when she undid his pants and pulled his throbbing member free. He thought he was going to come from that simple touch, but he managed to hold on.

Chapter Five

She explored him with her fingertips and her tongue, making sexy sounds of pleasure when she licked moisture from his tip.

She engulfed his head in the heat of her mouth and curled both hands around him. Her movements weren't practiced, but they were passionate and he bit back the shout of his release in an embarrassingly short time.

She didn't seem to mind. In fact, she acted rather proud of herself.

He couldn't help smiling. "They rang the second bell for taking your seats." He had acute hearing, a benefit in his profession. "If we hurry, we'll be able to watch the second half of the performance."

"I'd like that."

Later, when he dropped her off at home, she snuggled into him for a good-night kiss.

"Did you enjoy the opera?" he asked as he pulled away, wanting nothing more than to stay, but there were things they needed to talk about before they took what would be an irrevocable step for him.

She smiled saucily. "I liked the intermission best."

"I did, too, love. Will you come by my house for lunch tomorrow?"

It was Sunday, the only day her bookshop was closed.

Her smile fell away from her lips, leaving them looking kissed and vulnerable. "Yes, I think it's time."

Tabby showed up for lunch fifteen minutes early. Calder opened the door on her first knock.

She didn't even get a greeting out before he pulled her to him for a passionate kiss.

He swept her inside and then stepped away from her. "This is every bit as difficult as I thought it would be. Lunch and conversation first. All right, love?"

She nodded, unable to make her still yearning lips form words.

They were eating on the deck overlooking his private beach when he broached the subject of his past. "Your friends' speculation about my past wasn't far off."

"You're an earl hiding out in America because you don't want the title?" she quipped.

"Actually, I am MI6."

"Are as in you're still a spy?" Oh, great. She had fallen in love with a man whose life couldn't be more different and less likely to meld with her own.

"At the moment."

She swallowed, wishing she could cling to the implication it was a temporary condition. "I see."

"I doubt it."

She frowned, not liking the amusement lurking in his brown gaze while her heart felt like it was going through the shredder. "Even a small town bookstore owner knows that trying to make a lasting relationship with a spy is asking for trouble."

"So, you finally acknowledge I want more from you than an entrée into your sister's life or a quick coupling we both forget about soon after the fact?"

She rolled her eyes. A lot of good that did. "Yes, but I don't see how that can work. My life is here . . . your life is there." She waved her hand toward the east. "What are the chances? Unless you want me to move to England?"

He shook his head and her bleeding heart plummeted. So much for sacrificing her comfortable existence for love.

"Your life is here. Your bookshop. Your family."

"Yes, I know. I'm the one who lives in my skin," she said with more acerbity than she wanted, but he didn't need to rub it in.

"Tabby, I don't know if I can explain this very well, but I'm not MI6 because I want to be more than anything else in the world."

Hope stirred beneath her battered emotions. "Then why are you? It's not exactly an easy job to come by."

"You'd be surprised, or at least I was. I wanted adventure, wanted a career that used both my brain and my brawn, as it were."

"And . . ."

"And I got hired by the organization right out of university. I made agent very quickly and have enjoyed my job, though I'm not necessarily proud of all I've done to achieve success."

"Like what?" Had he killed people?

"I seduced women with the intention of procuring information. I developed friendships for the same thing." He sighed. "I've never actually killed anyone, but I have shot two agents from opposing governments."

"Does all that bother you?"

"A little, but I have to be honest . . . not much. I did what I had to do to protect my country."

"And now?"

"Now I've met a woman I want more than an adrenaline-pumping career."

"Me?"

"You. Haven't you figured out yet that you generate more excitement in my life than ferreting out dangerous national secrets?"

"Oh." It wasn't the brightest response, but she was reeling inside from an emotional overload.

"I've been considering settling here in Port Diamond, but whether or not I stay depends on you."

She didn't know what he wanted, what he was asking exactly, but she did know one thing. "I love you, Calder. I want you to stay."

There was a blur of movement and then she was being lifted from her chair against a hard masculine chest. The desperate intensity of his kiss stunned her, and at first she was too taken aback to respond.

He pulled away, his gaze probing hers. "Tabby?"

"Calder . . ."

"You said you loved me?"

"Oh, yes, I do . . ."

"You want me. I know you do."

She smiled at his arrogance. "Yes."

"Now?"

"As you English blokes are wont to say, not beforetime."

He grinned at her mock cockney accent and then frowned. "But you hesitated."

She looked coyly up at him, when she'd never looked coy in her life. "I think starting somewhere less than mach speed might help."

Incredibly, his sculpted cheekbones streaked a dusky red. Nevertheless, the smile he gave her was all confident, sensual male. "I think I can handle that."

And then he kissed her again, but it was nothing like that first kiss, so desperate and urgent.

His lips brushed hers as softly as butterfly wings. Barely there and then they were gone, only to come back again and again, and each time she tried to cling. Only he kept the touches light, making her hunger for the deep kisses of the night before.

She moaned with the urgency of her need.

When he'd teased her lips into swollen sensitivity, he moved his mouth onto her cheek and she discovered that her lips were not the only sensitive skin on her face. He blew softly in her ear and then bit down gently on the lobe. She arched toward him and shivered convulsively.

She held onto his shoulders, knowing to let go would mean sinking into a puddle of aching feminine desire.

His lips moved onto the column of her neck, and the sensual shivers wracked her body as each kiss heightened her sensitivity to his touch.

She'd worn a tank top, giving him free access to her bare skin all the way to the upper swell of her breasts. He took advantage, pressing small, nibbling kisses all over and tasting her with the very tip of his tongue until he reached her neckline. He stopped there, with his mouth hovering just above her skin.

She made a small, animal-like sound of need, unable to stand his teasing anymore, and he laughed softly, his breath hot against her.

Then he tugged her top up from the hem until her bra-encased breasts were revealed. "You're beautiful, Tabby."

She couldn't respond; she was too busy experiencing the way he laved her cleavage with his tongue. It felt like she could come right then, without any further preliminaries. Unbelievably, she was more excited than she had been the night before.

He flicked the front clasp of her bra open and peeled it back to reveal her already hard nipples to the air.

Her breathing fractured. "Suck them, Calder, please."

He did, taking one into his mouth and tugging on it with just enough pressure to send her body convulsing in a mini-climax.

She gasped, her body rigid with pleasure. "Oh, man, Calder, you're good at this."

Husky laughter vibrated against her breasts. "I've had a lot of practice." He licked her nipple, swirling his tongue around the aureole, but not taking it into his mouth again, as if he was building her toward another climax.

He probably was.

She sucked in air.

Then he stopped moving and she whimpered.

"I shouldn't have said that." He sounded embarrassed, irritated with himself. "I'm sorry, love."

It was her turn to laugh, but the sound was breathless because she could barely force her lungs to take in air over her skyrocketing excitement. "I don't mind. If your, um . . . en-hanced experience is what makes you such an amazing lover and capable of giving me this kind of pleasure, I'm certainly not going to complain about it."

His mouth moved back to hers with lightning speed and he spoke against her lips. "Tabby, you're so bloody perfect. I love you."

"Are you sure?" she asked, despite a wealth of evidence in favor of his words.

Years of living in her sister's shadow had taken a toll she hadn't fully appreciated until this moment, when the man she loved spoke his own love to her.

He cupped her face and looked her square in the eye. He didn't say anything, but it was all there for her to see in the intensity of his dark gaze: knowledge of who and what she was because he'd taken the time to find out. Not only did he know her on a level she would have thought impossible, he approved of what he knew.

Her shyness did not bother him. He wanted her. Only her.

She had no words to react to such a thing and simply pressed her lips against his, offering her body and her trust.

He accepted with a care that brought tears to her eyes. Knowledgeable fingers brushed down her bare back, drawing small circles against her skin, doing things at the base of her spine that turned the muscles in her legs to water. He caught her around the waist and held her up, pressing her against him for balance.

There was something incredibly erotic about having her naked breasts against his shirt-clad torso.

She wanted to touch him, too, and tunneled her hands under the dark T-shirt. His skin was so warm, but he shivered at the touch of her hands on his back.

As sexy as it felt to be half-naked while he was fully clothed, she wanted his shirt off. She wanted to see and feel him without restrictions. She yanked at the hem and he broke the kiss to help her peel it off him.

"Oh my . . ." she breathed.

He stood there, letting her look her fill, somehow knowing that as simple as it was, this permitted voyeurism was the sexiest kind of foreplay to her. Last night, it had been almost dark. His body had been nothing but a shadow, but now she could see him clearly and what she saw entranced her.

He had a light smattering of dark hair covering his chiseled abs and well-defined chest muscles. She reached out and brushed her fingers down his torso. The silky texture of his hair against her fingertips excited her unbearably and she smoothed her hands all over his hot skin, excitement melting the core of her.

She whispered, "You're incredible," and then blushed. "I mean—"

Once again, he pressed his finger over her lips. "It's okay. I'm glad you find my body as pleasing as I find yours."

It was then she realized that while she'd been enjoying the display of his body, he had been looking at her bare breasts because her shirt was still pushed up under her armpits. She went to cover them in a reflexive action, but he forestalled her with a quick movement that pulled her into his body.

Her nipples pinched tight, rubbing against him, and then pulsed with indescribable pleasure.

He kissed her, his tongue coming out to master her mouth, but he did it with such tenderness that her heart squeezed.

Was it possible to fall in love this quickly . . . to know you needed another person to complete the other half of your soul? She had to believe yes.

She wasn't sure how it happened, but they were completely naked, standing skin to skin, heartbeat to heartbeat, at the end of a bed in a bedroom she had no recollection of moving to.

She'd daydreamed so many times of her perfect lover taking her, sharing his body with her as she shared hers with him. Only daydreams could not begin to compete with this reality. Calder was so in tune to her every response, he seemed to know her body better than she did.

He touched and caressed and tasted, while encouraging her

to do the same. She touched him in ways and places she'd never wanted to touch another man, but with Calder, she wanted to know him completely, intimately, and forever.

Her whole body trembled with the need to be joined to him. "Calder, please . . . I want you inside of me."

"Yes, Tabby, damn it . . . yes!" He swung her up in his arms and then carried her down to the soft bed.

The down comforter was soft and cushiony, but then he was lying down and pulling her over him, and she forgot about her surroundings. "Ride me, sweetheart. Ride me hard."

She'd never seen herself as the passionate type, but with those words, he unleashed the primitive, sensual woman within. She lowered herself over his hardness, realizing only as she did so that he'd managed to get a condom on sometime in the last few minutes. Probably the same time he'd managed to get her clothes off . . . during that kiss that had taken her under in a haze of passion.

She'd been too busy kissing and touching to notice anything else.

She pushed down on his hard penis, but she gained only partial penetration. He was big and she was tight. It had been so long for her, and it had not been all that many times to begin with.

"I know we're supposed to fit, but I can't . . . please, help me, Calder."

He gripped her inner thighs from the front so that his thumbs played across the swollen wet flesh of her clitoris. He caressed her, teasing her into movement in order to increase the friction on her sweet spot. He surged upward, his hold on her thighs keeping her in place. It was a pleasure this side of pain, but so intense she would die if he stopped.

He didn't stop. And though he had told her to ride him, he was the one doing the thrusting. But the wild woman inside her didn't want it to be all him. She matched his rhythm, adding a variation of her own that had him gasping under her.

She leaned down and offered her breast to him. He took

her nipple into his mouth and started to suck, then nipped her with his teeth.

They came together in a paroxysm of surging limbs and hoarse, elemental cries.

Afterward, she collapsed on top of him, her whole body limp with pleasure.

"Marry me, Tabby."

Her heart stopped and then started again at a gallop. It was more than she'd ever hoped for or dreamed of. "I . . ."

"Please, Tabby, say you will. Don't make me spend the rest of my life alone."

Tears washed into her eyes and she hugged him tight, unable to voice the maelstrom of emotions going through her. She understood exactly what he meant. If it wasn't Calder, it wouldn't be anyone. She guessed some people were just so perfectly matched that once they clicked, breaking open the lock would damage them both.

Finally, she choked out, "I want children."

"Yes."

"And a house on the beach."

"What a coincidence, I've got one."

"And a fish."

"A fish?"

"I'm allergic to cats and dogs, but our kids have to have pets."

"I'll buy you a fifty-gallon aquarium for our first anniversary."

"Why do I have to wait?"

"I want to make sure you have staying power. It's an incentive."

She sat up in outrage and started laughing at the expression on his face.

"I was having you on, love. I'll buy you interest in Sea World if it will get you to marry me."

"I only need you. I love you, Calder."

"You'll marry me?"

"Oh, yes."

"Thank you." He kissed her until they were making love again.

When they were once again sated and lying together, this time under the soft, fluffy comforter, he whispered against her lips, "I love you, Tabby, and I always will."

"I love you, Calder."

And a year later, when she told him she was pregnant with their first child and he bought the fifty-gallon aquarium complete with fish and live coral, she knew she would love this man into eternity.

Captivated

Jill Shalvis

Chapter One

She'd really screwed up this time, even more so than usual, and that was saying something. Ella Scott shifted to swipe the hair out of her eyes, but her right wrist caught on the handcuff, rattling the steel, jerking on the tile towel rod that she was cuffed to. With a sigh, she used her left hand, then lifted her head and surveyed the situation.

Having worked the past straight month without a day off, she'd come to her Baja cottage for a desperately needed weekend to herself. But thanks to her surprise goons, she now stood between the shower and the toilet, handcuffed at chest level to the towel rack, wearing only the towel she'd managed to wrap around herself one-handed, with no key to get free, nothing at all within reach that could help her.

Such was the life of the incurably curious. She'd actually managed to parlay that lifelong curiosity into a career, not as a criminal, as her mother had feared, but as an insurance investigator. Except that now, for the umpteenth time, she'd dipped her nosy nose in where it hadn't been welcome, and here she stood in her least favorite position—that being completely helpless.

She'd been cautioned. Threatened, actually. Told time and time again that if she kept at this case, she wouldn't like the consequences. Having been warned too many times to remember by other, more unsavory types before, she hadn't given it a single thought.

Seems maybe she'd been a little premature in that.

But damn, it should have been so easy, a few days off. Some R and R. She'd arrived via plane, then rental car, and had taken a nice swim in the warm Mexican Pacific waves until her muscles quivered before hopping into the shower.

After that she'd planned to lie on the deck and watch the sun set over the ocean and contemplate why, when she'd finally found a job she enjoyed, it didn't satisfy her the way she'd thought it would.

But it'd all been interrupted by two beefy morons who'd hauled her naked and slippery and screaming out of the shower. Luckily for her, they hadn't been interested in her body, hadn't been interested in anything other than handcuffing her to the shower rod, still dripping wet. And even then, they'd only cuffed the one hand, promising her to send someone in a few days to free her.

And that's when she'd known. They weren't rapists or murderers, but *thieves*. They'd been from the yacht company she'd been investigating for suspicious loss of property. Two separate multimillion dollar boats had been sunk in the past sixteen months. Her company had found nothing suspicious with the first downed ship, and the insurance had been forced to pay out. Just two weeks ago, in fact.

Then the second boat had gone down for the count in Santa Barbara, and now Ella was closing in on why. Bad drug deals, and a greedy yacht owner wanting it all. She'd been watching their third yacht, the *Valeska,* all week, but had been unable to get aboard because there'd been activity on it.

Now she was due to present her suspicions to the D.A.'s office, soon as she made one more trip to Santa Barbara, where she was going to get on the *Valeska* come hell or high water.

Clearly the suspects didn't want her to get to the D.A.'s office, at least not before they skipped town with the money from the insurance from the first boat and any physical evidence. Chances were that had already happened, and they were long gone.

Ella shook her head. She should have taken that job at Target out of college like her mother had wanted. Sure, she looked awful in red, but she'd be willing to bet no one would bother to break and enter her place because of *that* job, or handcuff her naked to her own towel rack.

Unless she wanted them to.

A slight breeze blew in the open window, breaking the brutal summer heat as the sun sank. Oh, God, the sun was sinking, and the severity of her situation sank in. It was Saturday evening. Next week was a long time away. God knew she wouldn't starve, not with the five extra pounds she'd been carrying around since puberty—okay, *ten*, damn it. Still, the amount of time looming ahead felt long, and never having been big on self-discipline, she was already hungry.

She could reach the shower and the toilet. The sink was across from her, a leg's length away. Above it was the mirror that assured her she was as frightening looking as she'd imagined, her hair air-dried and a complete frizz bomb, her face not wearing a lick of makeup. *Ack*. She decided not to look at herself again.

Beneath the toilet was a cabinet which, if she stretched, she could just toe open. A box of tampons, two extra rolls of toilet paper, and a tube of toothpaste. Gee, *yum*.

She looked out the window. The cottage was isolated, down a long, sinuous stretch of highway surrounded by bush-lined high desert hills, punctuated by dense groves of date palms and citrus trees and little else.

The sun sank away, the daylight faded, and Ella felt anxiety pit in her stomach. But even stretching her leg out to bionic contortions, she couldn't reach the light switch.

And the dark came.

She'd spent a good amount of her childhood chasing after her three older brothers, and feeling invincible because of them. She'd wear her blankie as a cape and pretend she was a superhero who could fly through wind and sleet and snow, who could do anything.

She didn't feel so invincible now.

Then came a noise. The front door closing. *When had it opened?* Heart in her throat, she froze. Or rather her body froze. Her towel did not. It slipped yet again. She grabbed it with her left hand and hastily tucked the corner back between her breasts, her heart tattooing a crazy beat against her ribs.

No other sound, but she could *feel* someone on the other side of the door.

Listening.

Breathing.

Oh, God. She couldn't scream, couldn't even draw air into her lungs.

The handle on the bathroom door began to turn.

Ella stared at it, her life flashing before her eyes. She hadn't watered her plants. She hadn't tried skydiving. She hadn't reconciled her checking account!

The door creaked open.

She stuffed her uncuffed hand against her mouth to hold back her panicked whimper at what was about to happen to her. What would they tell her family? No one had even known she was coming here, not her parents, her brothers, not even—

"Ella?"

At that low, husky, almost unbearably familiar voice, she squinted into the shadows of the opened door, thinking, *Oh, no*. No, no, no, no, no.

But indeed, the form was tall, wide in the shoulders, narrow in the hip, the body built like the long-distance swimmer he used to be. "*James?*"

The shadow stepped into the bathroom and came to an abrupt halt. Not a shadow at all but the one man she hadn't wanted to see her like this, the one man she hadn't wanted to see, period.

Her mouthwateringly sexy, break-her-heart-and-stomp-on-it husband.

Make that almost ex-husband.

Chapter Two

Ella let out the pent-up breath she'd been holding and tried to look normal. As if being handcuffed in nothing but a slipping towel was anywhere close. But she couldn't pull it off, so she sucked in a breath and went for calm, cool, and collected, or at least the appearance of it.

And reminded herself that as far as the worst-case scenario went, this wasn't it. Close, but not quite. After all, she hadn't been raped, tortured, or killed before the goons had left her, right? She was still breathing, which was a good thing, so she kept that in front of her.

James let out a sound that managed to perfectly convey his surprise and unhappiness at the sight of her.

The fading light fell over him favorably, but *any* light fell over the man favorably. Then he flipped on the switch and the fluorescent bulbs had her blinking like an owl. "Hi," she said.

He just looked at her. His nearly black hair was cut short as always, but no matter the length, it had a mind of its own. His melt-me chocolate eyes could reveal everything in his heart, or nothing at all, depending on his mood. They were pretty stingy at the moment. He had his cop face on, allowing only his tough competence to show as he moved in closer to prop up the wall with a shoulder, his arms crossed casually over his chest. A deceptively relaxed pose. "I'd appreciate it if you wouldn't play sexual games with your boyfriend on my weekend for the house," was all he said.

She registered the urge to knock her head against the wall. He hadn't actually yet signed the divorce papers she'd sent him, which technically made them only separated, but that *he'd* been the one who'd left still rankled. And that it had been her job to drive him away made explaining her current problem a tad bit difficult, because she really hated when he was right. "I don't have a boyfriend."

He lifted a disbelieving brow but relaxed. It was a marginal lessoning of the tension in his shoulders that no one else would have noticed, but she'd known him for a very long time and could read his body like a book.

"If there's no boyfriend, what's this?" He gestured with a jerk of his chin to the way she was cuffed to the rack. "An early Christmas present?"

"Ha, ha," she said, and jangled the cuff. "A little help?"

He took his gaze on a slow roll up her body, starting at her bare feet, past her legs, which she'd thankfully shaved—*No*. Just because he'd been the first, *and the last*, man to drive her to the edge of sanity with a debilitating combination of love and lust and like and more lust, she did *not* care if her legs were shaved for him. Damn, but he could still get to her like no one else, which really topped the cake.

His gaze continued on its tour, landing on her breasts, which were spilling over the edge of the slipping towel, then her throat, and finally her face, his own impassive.

She couldn't blame him there. She'd taken that single, horrified glance in the mirror. She knew her long, curly blond hair had long ago rioted, resembling an explosion in a mattress factory. She knew she looked like a ghost without blush and lip color. She was just surprised he hadn't gone running for the hills.

But then again, nothing scared James. He stood there in black jeans, black athletic shoes, black T-shirt well-fitted to that mouth-watering body, looking like sin personified.

"What the hell are you doing here, Ella?"

Good question, she thought, and since she had no intention of telling him the truth, that she was a complete idiot, she racked her brain for a good excuse. "*Me?* Just . . . hanging." She added a grin, and hoped he bought it.

But he'd never bought the bullshit she'd been able to feed just about anyone else. He stepped closer, a mixed blessing for her. She felt a huge relief, because though he was a lot of things, including a rat bastard, he was incapable of leaving her here trapped and helpless. Or so she hoped.

And then there was her panic, because now she could see him up close and personal: the dark day's growth on his jaw, the way his eyes were like two fathomless pools she could drown in, his tight jaw . . . and then there was his scent, which made her want to press her nose to his throat and inhale. Pathetic.

Once upon a time he'd been everything to her, her greatest fantasy, her most amazing lover, her best friend, and she missed him, mourned him like a missing limb, and if he looked close enough he'd know it. Not wanting that to happen, she dropped her head down, but he only stepped even closer, and her forehead brushed his chest. He was warm and hard with strength, and beneath the shirt his heart beat steady. The waistband of his jeans were loose, low on his washboard abs. She had good reason to know his body looked just as perfect without the clothes, and that he knew exactly what to do with it to drive her insane with wanting.

Why did he have to be so damned perfect?

Why couldn't he have love handles? Or bad breath? Okay, maybe not love handles or bad breath, but it'd be nice if *he* could screw up once in a while instead of it always being her.

"Ella."

Right. He wanted answers. "It's complicated," she said demurely.

"Uh-huh." He tipped up her chin. "Keep going."

Her towel slipped another half inch. Before she could pull it back up, her left hand was in James's, held above her head against the wall in a gentle but inexorable grip. "Look at me, Ella."

She stared at his Adam's apple and hoped the towel was still covering her nipples. His thighs bumped her bare ones and said nipples hardened with hope because they knew exactly how good he could be to them. "Why?"

"Because we both know you can't look me straight in the eyes when you're lying, Super Girl."

A nickname she'd acquired from her various escapades, usually nearly fatal. He kept his other hand on her jaw, holding her head, leaving her stretched and bound like an offering. "M-maybe I really am an early Christmas present."

He stared at her, his eyes no longer the flat, cool cop's eyes. Now they were filled with frustration, temper, and a good amount of the heat and love that had always caught her breath. "It's only June."

"Merry Half Christmas." But he didn't cave, he never caved. "Okay, fine," she said, grumbling. "So I ran into a little problem with a case."

"Surprise, surprise. What was the problem?"

"I found proof that a multimillion-dollar yacht we'd insured and lost this year was purposely destroyed. It didn't click until their second, and more expensive, yacht was destroyed last week."

"Drug runners?"

She nodded. "A few deals in a row went bad. They were hurting for money. Now we think they sank the boats for the insurance money."

"And?"

"And I'm working on getting proof."

His eyes narrowed. "Let me guess. Your suspects are planning to hightail it out of town with the cash from the first boat, and you got in their way."

She bit her lip.

"Jesus Christ, El." Temper dropped, replaced by instant concern as his hands slid down to her arms. "Did they hurt you?"

"No."

His expression was no longer a cool cop's, but fierce and terrified. "Did they—"

"Nothing. They did nothing but cuff me." And okay, maybe they'd made a joke about her being a true blonde. "I'm fine."

He let out a low breath, fighting for control as the muscles bunched in his jaw.

She knew it was more than this particular situation. Her job was the basis of any fight they'd ever had—her putting herself in danger, sometimes stupidly. Him hating it.

He ran a finger over the cuffs on her wrist. "Hell of a mess you've got yourself into."

"Do you have a key or something?"

"Or something," he murmured, and looked her over again, slowly. "You sure do look like my idea of Christmas, all naked and . . ." He ran a callused finger over the edge of her towel, his knuckles brushing over the plumped-up curves of her breasts. "Restrained." His melting eyes met hers and her knees nearly buckled at the memories his words caused.

It'd been their first Christmas together, and she'd bought him two new silk ties, which he'd used not around his neck but for her wrists in his bed. He'd had his merry way with her, and then in return had let her bind him.

The memories made her ache. "Can you just set me free?"

Another slow pass of his finger over the edge of the slipping towel, and though she didn't lower her gaze and look, he was helping the thing fall, damn him. "*James.*"

"Yeah, I could set you free."

Relief rushed through her. Short-lived, as it turned out.

"Soon as you tell me one thing." His slow exhale fanned the hair at her temple, warming her ear, causing a delicious set of goose bumps to raise over her skin.

Her eyes wanted to drift shut. In their marriage, one thing that had never wavered was this . . . this hunger, this un-quenchable need.

Truth was, she missed his arms around her at night; she missed his big, solid presence in their bed. He had a way of making her forget everything but what he could make her feel, and what he made her feel was like a walking orgasm. The man oozed sex appeal, and that hadn't changed. "Um . . . what do you want me to tell you?"

He ran his hand up her free arm, once again lifting hers over her head, entwining their fingers. His thighs bumped hers, and it took every ounce of self-control she had—which wasn't much on a good day—not to rub against him like a cat.

"Tell me that you really don't want to be married anymore," he murmured, and curved his fingers into hers now so that they were holding hands rather than him restraining her. "Tell me you really want me to sign those divorce papers you had sent to my work."

That was so far from what she expected, she blinked. "You were the one who left me."

"Mmm," he said noncommittally, tracing the pads of his rough fingers over her skin. Just that small touch and her world spun. Her free hand automatically went to his arm for stability, even though she couldn't have fallen if she'd wanted to. Her fingers dug his ropey, satiny shoulders. She was close enough to see into his dark, dark eyes, and what she saw there made her go still and quivery at the same time.

"El."

Just that, just her name on his lips, and everything faded away except the excitement that always shimmered between them no matter what they were dealing with. He tipped her face up and their mouths were only a breath apart. With a soft sigh, she leaned into him. A sound escaped him, one of frustration, of need, and then he hauled her close, wrapping his arms tight to her body. "This is crazy," he muttered, and rubbed his jaw to hers. "Stupid crazy."

She nodded. She knew it, knew also if he dipped his head a fraction of an inch and kissed her, it'd be a mistake. It'd taken her this whole time to even begin to get over him, she couldn't do it again, she just couldn't—

"Damn," he whispered, and then his mouth touched the very corner of hers.

She let out a helpless little murmur and strained even closer, wanting more, so much more, but he pulled back. Stared at her as the corner of her towel slipped entirely free from between her breasts.

The only thing holding it in place was James's body, and they both knew it. "Uncuff me," she whispered.

"Tell me that you don't want me anymore," he whispered back.

Damn it. If she said the words, they'd be a lie, and he'd know that, too. He always knew. But here she was, literally trapped, and a complete wreck from just one tiny kiss, ready to toss all pride to the wind and beg him for whatever scrap he had left to give her.

Six months ago, he'd told her all bets were off, that he couldn't love her as wildly and fully as he did and watch her destroy herself with the job. In her stubbornness, all she'd heard was the ultimatum, him or her dangerous job, and she'd reacted. Badly.

He'd left their L.A. condo and she'd hit rock bottom, or so she'd thought.

But she'd been wrong. *Today* was rock bottom. Being forced to admit still wanting him . . . it was too much. "I don't—" But the lie caught on her tongue.

"Tell me," he insisted in a rough whisper, his length bumping hers.

She had to close her eyes in an attempt to deny what he could make her feel with just that barely there touch of his hot, tough bod.

"Tell me."

God, it'd be so easy to do just that, but then they'd be back at square one, with her loving him ridiculously, and him wanting her to be someone she wasn't.

No.

She was stronger than this, and to prove it, she lifted her chin, staring at a spot just over his shoulder. "I don't want to be married anymore."

He studied her for a long beat, his gaze burning a hole in her heart.

Not for the first time either . . .

"That's not what I asked you," he finally said.

"I want you to sign those papers at your office, James."

"And what about me, Ella?" He nudged even closer, slipping a muscled thigh between hers.

She nearly melted into a pool of longing on the floor.

"You don't want me?" he asked softly, silkily.

She closed her eyes, gathered her strength, then opened them again. *I don't want you*, she tried to say, but he shifted again, that thigh moving between hers, rubbing against her, and all that came out was a whimper.

Chapter Three

James waited for Ella's answer with an expectation that he didn't want to feel. He hadn't come to Baja hoping for anything but a few days without expectation, grief, or a page from the beeper he'd left at home. He certainly hadn't expected his estranged wife.

Who stood before him like a tempting, forbidden treat with her long, wild, blond curls playing peek-a-boo with her torso and shoulders, her clear blue eyes full of the wanting she wouldn't admit to, and then there was her mouth. God, that mouth, with the full, pouty lips that could give a grown man a wet dream, damp from her own nervous tongue.

His first response had been a resounding, *Yeah, baby*.

But then they gotten to the part of her story where he realized she hadn't come here for him at all. It'd been her work, *again*, the same work that had split them up. Thanks to the kind of characters she investigated—the scum of the earth, basically—she'd been manhandled into this helpless, compromising position, and that both terrified and infuriated him because one day she was going to get herself killed.

And he'd have to bury her.

His heart clenched good and hard over that. When they'd been together, she'd had him popping Tums like candy, and he couldn't handle it. Now, with a few months of distance beneath his belt, he figured he deserved a little revenge for his heart, which she'd broken.

Make that decimated.

Oh yeah, definitely he had a little payback coming his way, and he was nothing if not a man who made the best of his time. Well aware that the only thing protecting her modesty was his chest against hers, he shifted back an inch.

Her towel hit the floor.

"*James.*"

Probably not his smartest idea, letting the towel fall, because with her standing there wearing exactly nothing, virtually his captive, his every muscle shifted to full alert status.

She tried to turn away, which was not easy restrained as she was. She bumped into his fully clothed body, things shimmying and shaking, mostly her glorious breasts. She had tan lines, which dissolved his bones right then and there. Her breasts gleamed pale and beautiful, and between her legs she'd waxed or shaved, or whatever it was a woman did to drive men right out of their minds.

She let out an infuriated sound and fought with the cuffs. It was sick of him, he knew, but he was getting off on this.

"This is ridiculous," she spat out.

No, what was ridiculous was what the feel of her bare ass to the front of his crotch was doing to him. He spun her back around to face him. "Then you should be able to say the words. And when you do, I'll uncuff you and we'll go on our merry way. Our merry *single* way."

She went very still. "Is that what you want?"

Christ, no. "Just say it."

She lifted her free hand, presumably to cover some part of herself or another, or maybe to smack him, and he caught it, holding it out to her side. "Say it."

"*Fine.* I don't want y—" As before, the words tripped on her tongue and she closed her eyes.

He realized he'd been holding his breath, but something surged through him now. It felt like triumph, but also a bone-quivering relief.

His gut *had* told him the truth. She still wanted him. *Damn, Ella.* He didn't know whether to kiss them both stupid or shake the hell out of her and demand to know why she'd sent those divorce papers. "Finish it."

She licked her lips. "I . . ."

Looking into her huge baby blues, he momentarily couldn't see the body he wanted to drop to his knees and worship but that didn't matter. Her dazzling, lush curves had imprinted themselves on his brain years ago. Had he thought he was merely exacting a little revenge? Like hell. More like sinking his own ship here. But definitely, he liked her tied up. Liked it that she couldn't run, couldn't go off to her dangerous job, couldn't do anything but face him.

Which she hadn't had to do in too damn long.

"Okay, but you'd better listen," she warned him. "Because I'm only going to say this once." She stared at a spot just over his shoulder. "I. Don't. Want. You. Anymore." She shot him a shaky smile. "*There.*"

"Uh-huh." She was gorgeous and smart and funny, and everything he'd once upon a time wanted, but she was a horrible liar. And she *was* lying, he had no doubt, a particularly fascinating fact.

Also fascinating, against him her body was screaming the opposite. Her heart raced, her nipples bore two hard points into his chest, while her skin radiated a heat that had nothing to do with the warm evening. It caused a surge of excitement through his own body that he hadn't felt since . . . since he'd been with her.

"I said it," she whispered into his silence, lifting her head slowly, which had her out-of-control hair tickling his chin and throat in agonizing little butterfly kisses. "So now you have to undo me." Her nose just barely glanced along his throat, and all of it combined, slamming home memories of the times they'd been together, when he'd practically inhaled her every night.

They'd never been able to get enough of each other. "You lied."

"Did not," she said. Her eyes were still wide, dilated nearly black. Her breathing was shallow, and he knew damn well that wasn't fear.

"I have proof," he said, and slid his fingers along her jaw until they sank into her hair. Her eyes drifted shut again, slowly. She'd always loved when he'd played with her hair.

"Don't," she whispered.

"You can't catch your breath." He dipped his mouth to the spot beneath her ear which he knew was incredibly sensitive to his touch.

She shivered.

Now *he* was the one cheating and he didn't care. He danced his other hand down her free arm, then squeezed her hip before skimming up the bare skin along her ribs. He spread his fingers wide, so they rested just beneath her breast as he let his gaze once again fall over her. "God, El." His entire body clenched, hard and throbbing. "How could you have forgotten what it's like between us?"

She drew her bottom lip between her teeth, and he wanted to do the same. He wanted to gobble her up whole. "Your nipples are hard." He glided his thumb along her highest rib, just barely brushing the curve of her breast.

"Maybe I'm cold," she said in that same shuddery voice that told him she was having as much trouble controlling herself as he was.

"It's ninety degrees in here." He was sweating. She had a fine sheen to her skin, as well. He wanted to lap it up. Wanted to lap *her* up. His thumb slid over her nipple, catching on the very tip.

Both of them caught their breath.

Her head fell back and thunked against the wall. He leaned in, mouth open, to nibble at her throat, but that was instinctive, that was affection and heat, and he stopped a breath away because this wasn't supposed to be about any of that. Damn, he'd nearly forgotten. He was trying to prove a point here. "Maybe you are cold," he allowed with some disbelief. "But there's one reaction you always give me that has nothing to do with being chilled." With that, he glided his fingers down her belly, her muscles quivering at his touch.

"Don't even think about it," she whispered.

"Oh, I'm thinking about it, Super Girl."

"James," she choked out as he stroked a finger over her mound, then into her petal-soft folds.

"You're wet." His legs nearly buckled at the feel of her. "Is this for me, Ella?"

Letting out a half whimper, half sob, her free hand fisted in his shirt. Definitely not a sound of distress, he noted, but of arousal, and he groaned as he sank into that creamy heat.

She squeezed her eyes shut. "So I lied. So I want you. It's only because I haven't had sex in too long and I ran out of batteries, so don't flatter yourself."

His gaze met hers as his thumb found her clit and lightly stroked.

Her eyes went opaque. Her fingers dug further into his chest, pulling out more than a few hairs, which made him wince, but he kept up the torment. It was the least of what she deserved.

"I'm going to go off like a rocket," she gasped.

Yeah. And he wanted to see it, feel it. Cause it. Wanted to remind her exactly what she was missing out on. Pride and brainless ego on his part? Maybe. He didn't care. He kept stroking her.

"James." A few more chest hairs were lost. "*Stop.*"

Damn, the magic word. He stopped but left his hands on her.

She dropped her head to his chest and gulped for air. "I told you," she said tightly, head still down on his chest. "I told you what you wanted to hear. Now please, James, get me free."

He didn't want to, but there was something in her voice that stopped him cold, and he was deathly afraid it was tears. "Okay," he said quietly, and stroked a hand over her long, wild hair. She was trembling, and his heart wrenched. Christ, he

was an ass. "Okay," he murmured again softly. "I'll free you."
He just wished she meant only the handcuffs, and not their
marriage.

Or that he'd been the one bound, because one thing was
damn sure, he didn't want to be free.

Chapter Four

Ella turned from James and set her hot face to the wall. She felt him move away, even out of the room, and she told herself she didn't care.

Then, though he didn't make a sound, she knew he was back. She didn't look at him.

Couldn't.

She still wanted him. She'd never stopped wanting him.

Neither was a crime, but thanks to his torturing of her for his own amusement, she had so many emotions battering her, she didn't know which one to start with. Furious, aroused, and embarrassingly close to tears for reasons she didn't understand, she shifted to hug herself.

Only to discover she could use both arms.

James had released her.

Still facing the wall, she rubbed her wrist, gave herself a bolstering pep talk along the lines of, *You can do this, you can face him and not let him see how much he's destroyed you,* and slowly turned back.

She was alone.

Bending, she grabbed the towel and wrapped it around her torso. With her armor back in place, she stared at herself in the mirror. Yikes. She needed an entire tube of no-frizz and an hour with her makeup bag.

But first things first. She stepped out of the bathroom. The cottage was cozy but small. Single bedroom, living room, and kitchen open to each other. It'd come casually painted in beachy, muted colors of light blue and earth tones, and the little bit of furniture they'd put in matched. They'd bought the place as a fantasy escape, but their harsh reality had been that they'd rarely had the time to come.

Or Ella hadn't. In the past two years her job had cut into her personal time considerably, something else James had hated.

But for the first time she'd had a career, not just a job, and Ella had loved feeling needed.

With perfect twenty-twenty hindsight, she could admit she'd given her job more than she'd given her marriage, and that shamed her to the core.

But James had never needed her. He'd loved her, passionately, of that she had no doubt, but he'd never needed her. Not like she'd needed him.

Still, their relationship had deserved more. James had deserved more.

In one sweeping glance she could tell she was entirely alone. The west-facing wall was all windows, open to the ocean. The sun had gone down, leaving the sky flaming in purples and blues, and there, at the water's edge, stood the shadow of a man.

James.

As she watched, he stripped out of his shirt and pants in economical movements, his tanned, sleek, hard flesh nothing but a blur in the night as he lifted his arms and dove into an oncoming wave. She lost sight of him after that.

It wasn't the first time. She'd lost sight of him when he'd walked his damn fine ass out of their house six months ago, which had nearly killed her.

But thoughts like that one only made her sad, and she didn't have time for sad. She needed to get home. Needed to get back home to Los Angeles, and then up to Santa Barbara to get onto the *Valeska*.

And yet she stood staring out at the ocean, at the occasional flash of James, swimming as if the devil himself was on his heels. It used to be she'd go to him . . .

But his problems were no longer hers. *He* was no longer hers, and to prove it she turned away to grab her duffel, still on the couch. She'd grab some clothes, get dressed, and go.

Any minute now.

With a sigh, she dropped her towel and grabbed the bikini off the floor, the one she'd stripped out of a couple of hours ago, before hopping into her fated shower. She slipped back into the wet scrap of material thinking the modesty was silly, considering James had just seen her stretched out and captive for his perusal, but she figured it might put them on more even ground.

Even ground was good, and she was a master of finding it. After living with well-meaning but hard-to-please parents all her life, then a string of boyfriends who'd lasted for less time than her string of meaningless jobs, she'd learned what she wanted.

And that was to be appreciated for being who she was. Whoever *that* woman turned out to be. She'd thought James had been the man to do it, but she'd learned things didn't always turn out how she wanted. That was life.

She stepped outside into the warm night. There were no city lights, no highway noises, nothing marring the still, humid air but the sound of the waves pounding the shore and the small sliver of the moon lighting her way. She walked the sand until the water lapped at her toes. Every few seconds or so, as the waves shifted and moved, she could still see James bodysurfing, working his long, lean muscles for all he was worth, swimming out some nameless demon that she had a feeling might have a name after all.

Hers.

He took a four-foot swell, diving into the arc of water with skill and precision. He'd always swum like a fish, and standing there watching him, Ella was hit with a wave of her own, filled not with water but yearning and memories that made her want to sink to her knees and pound the sand in frustration.

She'd missed him, so damn much.

They'd met three years ago when she'd still been just a clerk at the insurance company. Big surprise, she'd butted into a case that had gone bad, and had been mugged coming out of her parking garage late one night.

James had been the responding officer.

And the rest was a sweet, sexy, shivery, heavenly blur as he'd insinuated himself into her life until she couldn't remember what she'd done without him.

She'd been forced to remember that very thing these past six months.

The water was nearly the same temperature as the air, and as she waded out, the black swirling depths and the dark night sky above her blended into one, like a comforting blanket. When she could no longer touch the bottom, she began to swim.

As if sensing her coming, James turned. She couldn't see his features but felt his eyes search hers as he waited for her. "Still here?" he asked.

"I wanted to talk to you before I left."

"Why?"

Why? She blinked at that, but he took the next swell, giving her time to think about her answer. When he came close again, tossing back his wet hair, his face and shoulders gleaming in the moon's reflection, she tried a smile. "Maybe to thank you?"

Treading water, Ella remembered in vivid Technicolor how they used to thank each other for things. *With sexual favors.* She'd always wanted the same one, his talented mouth on her body. He, however, had been forever inventive with his own owed favors, and she'd never known what to expect—maybe to find herself bent over the arm of the couch for him to take her from behind, or on her knees before him . . . and then there'd been the time he'd requested a raunchy striptease on their brand-new kitchen table, culminating in dinner, which, in fact, had turned out to be her.

"You'd have been fine if I hadn't shown up," he said now, his eyes dark and glimmering with the same memories. If that was so, she marveled at his ability to keep his cool, because even in the water, she was beginning to sweat.

"Yeah, maybe." She managed to smile at him. "But I'm glad I didn't have to find out."

He treaded water effortlessly beside her, saying nothing. His manner bespoke quiet, rock-solid confidence. It always had.

She, however, had to work at feeling confident on the best of days. "I know I was unwise today," she admitted, getting a little breathless from keeping herself afloat. "Letting my guard down like I did."

"Wasn't the first time," he said, not at all breathless.

"No, it wasn't. But at least I didn't get myself mugged in the parking lot, and then splashed across the human interest section of the paper."

One black eyebrow shot up. "Or locked in the meat freezer of a packing plant, and then on the *front* page."

That had been last year, and after his fury had worn off, he'd had the nerve to laugh at her. "Or locked in a trunk," she said softly.

Another episode, from eight months back, and he let out a sound that might have been frustration or dark humor as he shook his head. "Good thing you had your Nextel on you that time."

"It's a good thing I had *you* on the other end of my Nextel," she corrected. "Come on, admit it, some of my more colorful cases might have brought me trouble and grief, but you eventually always found the humor in the situation. You think I'm cute."

He shot her a baleful look and caught another wave.

She watched him vanish beneath the black, swirling water, then caught sight of his strong, lean body riding the crest. When he came back, she reached out for him, setting her hand on his rock-solid shoulder to hold herself up.

"Tired?" he asked.

"Nah. Just wanted to make sure you weren't too cold."

He snorted and slid his hands to her hips, still treading

without effort, now supporting both of them. "Still stubborn, I see."

"And you still have to be right all the time."

"Yeah." He toyed with the bathing suit string low on her hips. He'd always loved this particular suit, and as he tangled his fingers in the ties on either side, her brain tangled with memories of what exactly those fingers could and had done to her. "I'm thinking of switching departments," she heard herself say. "Back to investigating worker's comp cases instead of fraud."

Once again she felt his assessing stare, though he said nothing as he kept running his fingers in and around and under the string on her hips in a way that seriously hampered her thinking ability.

"Did you hear me?" Her breath was soughing in and out of her lungs now, and since he was holding her, it wasn't from the effort of remaining above water.

"I heard you." He towed her closer to shore so she could stand. "Before you drown. So did your own personal insurance company beg you to change jobs, or what?"

That sounded like amusement in his voice now, and she set her jaw in annoyance. "I just thought you'd like to know."

"What you do for a living is no longer my concern, as proven by the papers you sent to me."

She'd sent the divorce papers out of hurt, not that she'd tell him so. "I figured you might be in a hurry to get rid of me."

"Why would you figure that?"

"Because your brother told me you were dating again." Just the thought left her cold. Terrified. "He said you needed a date for some charity event."

He sighed. "Cooper has a big mouth."

"No, he doesn't. He's protecting you. And anyway, what you do is your own concern now, right?" she asked, tossing his words back at him.

"Ella—"

"It's okay, James." She shrugged in the water, the motion bringing her breasts in direct contact with his broad, wet chest.

Because that hit her with a jolt like an electric shock, she began to turn away, wanting to hide the madness that overtook her whenever she thought about him touching someone else, kissing someone else, loving someone else.

It haunted her. He was a sexual man, demanding, earthy, rawly sensual, and she couldn't imagine he'd really gone six months without—

"Oh no, you don't." Grabbing her arms in his big hands, he whipped her around in the water, frustration written all over his face. "I hate this," he ground out. "Hate the doubts, the anger, the fear—"

"James—"

"You're standing there picturing me with someone else. I know it because I'm doing the same thing and it's killing me. Killing me, Ella."

"I haven't—"

"I haven't, either, damn it. God, I hate this, hate all of it, especially the missing you." He gave her a little shake, then hauled her up against him. "So you know what? The hell with that part, at least."

And he covered her mouth with his.

She had exactly one coherent thought: *Yum.* Then her every brain cell checked out, replaced by pleasure cells, of which he hit them all.

It amazed her. One second they were standing there in the ocean, the water pummeling them, staring at each other with all the pent-up emotion and exhilaration that was never far from the surface with them, and the next his mouth opened on hers, making her whimper with a carnal need so powerful it shook her to the core, taking away all rhyme and reason.

Then he pulled back and stared at her, water dripping into his face, eyes dark and hot.

Her own heart was drumming so hard and heavy she could hear nothing but the blood roaring through her ears.

"I can't do this again, El," he said. "But I can't not, either." And he came at her again.

Chapter Five

He tasted the same, Ella thought dazedly, like heaven on earth, and in the water as they were, their bodies being gently battered by the rise and fall of the swelling waves, she pressed closer.

At her movement, James groaned, low and throaty, and then he was inside, his tongue tangling with hers, his taste hot and sweet and so right she felt her eyes sting as she opened to him with a low murmur of acquiescence.

He shifted in the water so that she was flush to him, her breasts mashed to his chest, her soft, giving belly pressed to his hard, ridged one, her legs entangled with his. She'd always loved the way she felt so small and protected in his embrace, and that hadn't changed. Neither had the fact that he could still thoroughly ravish her mouth with a skill that rendered her completely witless.

And only when he'd accomplished that did he rip his mouth from hers. "God, El. You feel so good." This was punctuated by hot little biting kisses along her jaw to her ear, which he nibbled while breathing with thrilling unevenness, all of which combined to make her eyes cross with stabbing lust.

"I can't stand anymore," she gasped.

"Here." He lifted her up. "Wrap your legs around me. There. Oh yeah, like that. I can't get enough of you," he muttered as a wave washed around them, lifting them up and then down on the endless tide. "Just can't." Holding her head still with one hand fisted in her hair, his other slid down her spine and into her bikini bottoms, squeezing, molding, pressing her against his shorts, thin and wet now, hiding nothing, especially not the hot, pulsing erection nudging between her thighs.

"More," he growled, palming one butt cheek and then the other before dipping his fingers between and exploring there.

"James—"

He cut her off with his lips and teeth and tongue, coming at her hard and fierce, still holding her head in place as if afraid she'd pull away.

Fat chance. She couldn't get enough either. Slippery strands of her hair caught in the stubble on his jaw, stabbed into her eyes, clung to their shoulders, releasing the scent of her shampoo in the air along with the tangy salt from the ocean spray.

Inhaling her as if he wanted to gobble her up whole, James sank his teeth into her earlobe and pulled lightly as he exhaled slowly, raising a delicious set of goose bumps along her flesh. Lifting his head, still holding hers, he stared down into her eyes, then at her lips. When she licked them to get the last taste of him, he groaned.

All while his fingers gripped her bottom hard, grinding her against him, his hips moving, moving, moving, in a slow, snug, rocking motion that had her whimpering in helpless delight, gasping, sobbing for breath as she squirmed to get even closer. Her skin felt too tight, her heart too full as he drove her toward climax with nothing more than those maddening, increasing oscillations of his hips.

When he pulled back for air, breathing fast and shallow, Ella nearly died. No stopping! She moaned low, a protest deep in her throat, and slid her fingers into his hair, trying to bring his mouth back to hers. Her hips were still rocking, her heart still pumping, her nipples had shrunk to painful, tight little ball bearings that ached, *ached* for his attention. Between her legs she felt hot and desperate, and with him holding her open, spread to his rocking hips, his erection within easy access of every critical nerve ending she owned, she couldn't stop, just couldn't stop.

"James." The word was a mere whimper, dark and disturbingly needy, and in another time and place she might have spared the time to be horrified to hear herself begging, but not now. Now she needed him, hard and pulsing, needed him to tear away her bikini bottoms and his shorts, needed him thrusting into her, taking her over the edge, now, now, now. "*Please . . .*"

"Yeah, I'll please." He rasped a thumb back and forth over her nipple, then drew his hand down her belly to do the same over her bikini-covered sex, outlining her in slow precision.

"Ohmigod."

"Here, Ella? Now?"

"Here," she panted. "*Now.*"

He dragged her out of the ocean. She thought maybe he intended to take her inside the cottage, but apparently it was too far away because the moment their calves were free of the water, he sank to his knees and brought her down with him.

Their hands fumbled for purchase, hers skimming over his glorious body, touching his shoulders, his flat belly, his thighs . . . between them.

His were no less desperate, his fingers spread wide as if to touch all that he could with every sweep of his hands.

She tugged down his wet, clinging shorts.

He bit her shoulder.

She licked his Adam's apple.

He growled and tumbled her all the way down to the sand, spreading her legs and making himself at home between them, cupping her bottom and pulling her forward in a quick, hard movement that settled her more completely against his straining erection before he covered her body with his and kissed her, hard and wet and deep. She tried to get her hands between them, to draw him inside her, but he manacled her hands in one of his and drew them up over her head. Towering over her, he stared down at her. "You're not going to rush me. Not after six months of this, getting hard at the mere thought of you beneath me like this."

Then he sank his fingers into her hair, drawing her head back, forcing her to arch beneath him so that he could drag his mouth down her throat towards the curve of a breast. His handling of her was presumptuous and aggressive and she didn't care. She knew what he could offer her, knew how far he could take her, which was further than anyone had ever taken her before. And she wanted to go there, *now*.

Water and sand swirled around them in the dark, dark night as he tugged her bikini top off and tossed it aside before dipping his head and capturing her nipple in his mouth, lashing the tender tip with his tongue.

Stars burst in her vision, but she had no idea if they were the real ones hanging in the sky above them or only manufactured in her head from what he was doing to her as she cupped his head in her hands and held him to her.

Water lapped at their feet with each wave. She loved the weight of him, thrilled to the way he thrust a thigh between hers, spreading her, holding her open as he lifted his head and blew hot breath over her wet nipple. "I missed the taste of you here," he said.

"Keep tasting, then."

Curling the fingers of one hand around the bikini tie on her hip, he tugged until the wet, stretchy material popped free. Then he was scraping the bikini bottoms off her. "I missed the taste of you everywhere." His knuckles brushed her trimmed pubic hair, the very tips of his fingers just barely skimming over her folds as he kissed his way past her belly button. "But I especially missed the taste of you right"—he nipped at her inner thigh, brushed his nose over the center of her and then kissed her—"*here*."

Ella gasped and tightened her grip on his hair.

"Mmm." He kissed her again, using his tongue this time to circle her clit, and her entire body bowed, tightened. She was going to come, thank God, but then he pulled back a fraction of an inch, and she dug her fingers into his shoulders. "*James.*"

"Still here. God, El." He nipped at her other inner thigh

again, then a little higher, moving tantalizingly close to where she throbbed for him, for release—

Yes.

But the man only danced his tongue over her, moving half an inch to the right. Frustrated beyond speech, she gripped his hair tight and tried to direct his head.

"Easy," he murmured as a wave teased just past their knees.

Easy? She'd give him easy! Again she gripped his hair and shifted his head and felt a puff of air in the right spot.

He was chuckling. Bastard. *Rat bastard*. "Goddammit, James, do me!"

"I intend to. My way." He took her with his mouth then, by turns soft and gentle, demanding and aggressive, and yet when she was a quivering, desperate mass—which took all of two minutes—he pulled back again. "Anyone else ever make you feel this way?" he murmured, nudging her legs even wider with his shoulders, cupping her bottom in his big hands, making himself at home while she let out urgently needy, panting sobs. "Ella?"

"No one," she admitted in a strangled voice, crying out when he finally sucked her into his mouth, his own uneven pants against her captive flesh sending her even further onto the edge. "No one," she managed to say. "But you."

He rewarded her by moving to the preciously correct spot, unerringly laving at her with his tongue in the rhythm he knew she needed. Each heartbeat, each breath, shoved her closer to the unrelenting, building heat threatening to consume her, and she went willingly. Her fingers slid out of his hair and went to his shoulders, roped with lean muscle as he bent to his task. Her skin tightened, her muscles began to shake.

"Mmmm," he murmured, lapping her up like cream, sliding two fingers deep inside her, stroking her both inside and out now, in a way she couldn't have resisted if she'd tried.

"Don't stop, don't stop," she panted as water lapped at their lower bodies.

"I won't," he promised, and then she was coming, bursting

apart at the seams really, with the water hitting her at mid-leg now, the dark night sky drifting over them, and James doing as he promised, not stopping, licking her more softly now as he held her frantic hips, slowly bringing her back to earth.

Her hands fell to the wet sand at her sides as she fought to catch her breath. "My God. What was that, a hurricane?"

His hair brushed over her as he turned his head and kissed her inner thigh. "Hurricane James."

She laughed breathlessly. "F-5 strength. I think I have sand in all my parts," she said, but then the laughter caught in her throat because James surged up to his knees, gripped her hips in his hands, and stared down at her with burning eyes.

"I have something else to fill you with," he said, and in one smooth, controlled thrust, buried himself to the hilt.

Her pleasure-filled cry comingled with his. Wrapping both her arms and legs around him, she tipped her mouth up for his crushing kiss as he began to move. Water continued to lap at their feet and calves, the sand warm and giving beneath them. The light hair on James's chest teased her nipples as he stroked her smooth and sure, then harder, grazing her already sensitized, wet flesh with each flex of his hips.

Then he tore his mouth from hers and lifted her hips higher for the thrusts she couldn't get enough of. The breath plowing in and out of her lungs, she felt her body tighten again, but she struggled to hold back, to wait for him.

"No, you don't," he growled, and spread the fingers of the hand on her hip so that he could glide his thumb over her clit.

She exploded again, from an even deeper, darker place than she had before, and even as she let go and cried out his name, she knew. God, she knew.

She was still hopelessly, helplessly in love with him.

When she came back to herself she realized he was still hard as iron inside her, holding himself rigid. He hadn't come. She ran her hands down the taut, damp, quivering muscles of his back.

"Don't," he choked out. "Don't move, don't touch."

"But—"

"Don't talk either." He buried his face in her hair and took several long, gulping, deep breaths before speaking in a tight, guttural voice. "I don't have a condom."

He was barely clinging to control, and a burst of warmth and affection for him nearly overcame her, so much so she could hardly breathe. "But I do."

He lifted his head, his eyes black and glittering.

"In my purse," she said.

They both craned their necks and stared at the little beach cottage, a good hundred yards away.

"Fuck," he said tightly.

"We can do that," she said coyly.

He met her gaze, his unwavering and no-holds-barred dark and hungry. And *not* playful, not at the moment. "One condom isn't going to cut it," he growled. "Not tonight."

Good thing she was flat on her back because her knees went rubbery at his thrillingly rough tone. "Then we'll have to get creative, won't we?"

With a groan, he rolled off her to his back and tossed his arm over his eyes. "You're going to kill me. Give me a second." His chest rose and fell rapidly as she watched him fight for control. A fascinating sport.

And arousing. His chest, defined and delineated with lean, hard muscles, heaved with each breath, his flat, ridged belly quivering. She straddled him, murmured "Shh" at his low, tortured groan, and slid down that delicious body. "Let me get started on that creativity," she murmured, and ran her tongue up the length of his rock-hard penis, swirling it over the tip.

James groaned raggedly, struggling with that control she always admired but wanted no part of at the moment. She *wanted* him to lose it. *Wanted* to watch. Just as he'd watched her. And she had the advantage of knowing that *this* act was one of his favorites, guaranteed to take him over the edge. She licked him again, then raised her head and surveyed him, sprawled out before her, back bowed, body drawn tight as an arrow, his face a mask of both pleasure and pain. "Want me to stop?" she asked softly.

"No." His head thunked back on the sand as his fingers tunneled into her hair, clutching her head. "God, no."

Chapter Six

Afterwards, they staggered through the dark, balmy night toward the small cottage like a pair of drunks. *Drunk on lust,* James thought, grabbing Ella's hand before she could fall over as she tripped over her own feet yet again.

She collapsed against his chest with a muffled snort of laughter, and just like that, with her hair up his nose and her naked, warm, damp body sliding against his, his heart melted.

Maybe not just lust.

She curled into him and somehow he found the strength to hoist her up.

"Mmm," she murmured, burying her face in his throat and inhaling deeply as if she loved the smell of him. "I love it when you do the he-man thing."

"No, you don't." He looked down at her in his arms and laughed. "You hate it when I try to protect you."

Her eyes were clear of amusement now, gleaming in the night and full of things that made him reel. "Maybe I've changed."

He wasn't sure how to take that as he nudged open the front door with his shoulder and dropped her down on the couch, lit only by the slant of moonbeams coming through the blinds. Nor was he sure what she wanted when she reached up and tugged him down over the top of her.

Her kisses, as she rained them over whatever part of him

she could reach, were greedy, her hands demanding, and she urged him close, touching everything she could.

Not understanding how it was that they could ravish each other like they just had and still want more, he gave into it, into her, gathering her close with a confusing mix of heat and tenderness. He'd only been half kidding earlier when he'd said she was going to kill him—she was. Death by broken heart.

"Love me," she murmured, holding his head to her breast.

He kissed her there, curling his tongue around her nipple until it beaded hard for him. "I am. I do."

She bucked, and together they toppled to the floor, mouths and fingers frantic as they rolled, jockeying for position. She crawled to her bag, dug through it, and came up with a condom.

He grabbed it, and her, tucking her beneath him, kissing her, smiling when she rolled them again. They bumped into a lamp, nearly upending it over the top of them, then bashed into the coffee table. Beneath him, Ella laughed breathlessly and dug her fingers into his butt. "What's taking you so long to get inside me?"

"I have no idea."

"Make it up to me."

"Done." He tore open the condom and protected them both with fingers that actually trembled, then grabbed her bare thighs, opening her to him. They were bathed only in the meager moonlight from the window, but it was enough to have him moaning at the sight of her spread for him, vulnerable and fragile, pink and glistening. "Mine," he said in primal instinct. "All mine." He sank into her, a movement that had them both going still, flummoxed by pleasure.

Slow down, he told himself but he was tense and quivering, his every muscle straining with the need to posses and take.

Then Ella surged up and sank her teeth into his shoulder, and any good intentions flew out the window. "Take me, James." She soothed the bite with a lick of her tongue. "Hard. Fast. Now."

He opened his mouth to quip "Yes, ma'am," but he couldn't

speak. He slid his hands beneath her thighs and rocked his hips, going even deeper now.

Tossing back her head, she gasped his name, and just like that he was a goner in the control department. He drove himself into her again and again. She was wet and mewling for him, hips pistoning to meet him thrust for thrust. Hot and wild. Hard and rough.

Out of control.

Outside, the ocean crashed into the shore with the same uncivilized force of them pounding into each other, damp flesh slapping against damp flesh, hearts thundering, wordless murmurs and cries, breath ragged as lungs fought for air . . .

James forced his eyes open as he felt the inevitable tightening between his legs.

Ella opened hers, too, and hit him with a one-two punch of those two baby blues, drenched and brilliant and glazed over. In them was everything he'd ever wanted, and his heart tightened with the rest of him as he barreled toward a freight train of an orgasm he couldn't stop to save his life. "I'm too close—"

"You're perfect," she panted, and wrapped her legs around his waist. "God. Right *there*—"

"El, I can't hold on—"

"I know, me either—oh God, James . . ." Her body constricted, then was wracked with a shudder as she let go, milking him with each contraction, throwing him right off the edge with her.

For those few moments being held by James, being touched and kissed, hearing his low, husky voice murmur things in her ear that made shivers rise on her spine, Ella felt like her old self.

Not lonely.

Not worried that her heart might never feel full again.

Not struggling just to make it through her next breath.

But happy. Full of hope.

It'd scare her if she could muster the energy for it, but at the moment she lay facedown and sprawled across the bed, sated and exhausted in a way that completely excluded thinking. That was good because she didn't want to think, didn't want anything to pierce this lovely protective layer he'd given her, or she might have to remember that being with him was a sheer accident of fate.

And temporary.

A warm, callused hand smoothed up the back of her thigh and her exhaustion vanished. "Careful," she murmured into the pillow. "My husband is home."

The hand came down on her butt in a light smack that made her laugh. She tried to roll over but James held her still, nipping lightly at the back of a thigh, then higher, and a rush of excitement surged through her. "Again?" she whispered, fisting her hands in the sheet at her sides.

He yanked her hips up so that she was on her knees. "Yeah, again. I can't get enough. Christ, I still can't get enough of you." One hand smoothed up her belly to cup her breast, his other slid between her legs, testing the way, which was already wet enough to make him groan. Leaning over her, he put his open mouth on her neck and drove into her, and just like that they moved from the eye of the storm back into the frenzy. With his fingers stroking on the outside, his erection filling her to bursting on the inside, he began to move within her, until with a sobbing cry, she came. From a long way away, she heard her name ripped from his throat and realized he'd had to pull out of her to come, and that he trembled around her.

Her entire heart caved, just opened up and let him in. Stupid, she knew, but she couldn't help it, or hold back, not with him.

"James—"

"Shh." He gathered her close as he took them both back down to the mattress. Stroking the hair from her face, he pressed his lips to her temple and breathed her name. Breathed it again as she drifted off in his arms.

James woke as Ella carefully slid out of the bed. With dawn nothing more than a purple tinge in the far eastern sky, he propped up his head with his hand, watching as she tried to pull the corner of the sheet from beneath him. She had the rest wrapped around her already. "Where are you going?"

She went still, and he knew. Damn it, he knew because his heart gave one bruising kick to his ribs. "You're running," he said flatly.

"Actually, no. I'm walking." She tugged on the sheet.

He just looked at her.

She tugged again. "Let go."

He could have let go of the sheet, if he wanted. But he found he couldn't let go of her. He'd been wrong to think he ever could.

"Damn it, James."

He fisted his hand on the sheet and gave a yank, and the thing came off her entirely. "There," he said, deliberately mis-understanding her. "You're free."

Nude, she let out a sound of pure exasperation and shot him a look that said, Grow up. Her sweet little ass sashayed across the room, where she bent for her clothing. He could see the bite mark he'd left in the crease where her thigh met her buttocks, and smiled grimly. He could leave all the marks on her he wanted, she still wouldn't be bound to him. Not by hook or heart.

His own heart suddenly aching like a son of a bitch, he plopped to his back and stared at the ceiling. "Hell if I'll watch you walk away."

"I watched *you* walk away."

At that, he swore again, more creatively. Then he got off the bed and moved to her.

She stood before him in a pair of panties, holding a camisole tank top in front of her breasts. He took it out of her hands and tossed it over his head. "I didn't *want* to walk away."

"I was driving you crazy, I know." She went back for the top, then stepped into it and yanked it up, fussing with her straps. "I tend to do that to a person."

He lifted her chin with a finger. "It wasn't you, Super Girl, it was your job."

"Really?" Her huge eyes searched his. "I think it was more than that."

His heart caught at the look of pain on her face. "What do you mean?"

"I loved you. *You*, James. I loved every single part; your loud rock music, your silly big oaf of a dog, the way you sneak sips out of the milk container when you think I'm not looking, how you snore when you're tired—"

"I do not."

"I loved every part," she said again in that terrifyingly soft and final voice. "But what kills me is that you can't say the same about me."

And on that shocking statement, she walked out of the bedroom.

He followed her to the living room, where she was digging through her duffel bag. She pulled out a khaki cargo skirt and shimmied into it. She was putting on her sandals when he found his voice.

"It's your job," he said quietly. "It scared me. You scared me. Still do, damn it. I want you as my wife, Ella. I want that more than I want my next breath, but I want you alive and well and *safe*."

She gave him a long considering look as she zipped up her bag and prepared to walk out of his life the way he'd once walked out of hers. "That's funny coming from you."

"What? *Why*?"

"You're a cop. *Your* job terrifies me but I don't tell you to change."

"I'm not the one who's been shot at, kidnapped, stuffed in a trunk *and* a freezer, and nearly killed at every turn!"

Slowly she shook her head. "I'm not going to do this, James, not again. I . . . can't."

His heart began to thud hard and fast. "You said you were thinking about making a change. Was that just what you thought I wanted to hear?"

"No, I meant it. But I'm not a quitter. I'm going to finish

this case first. They made it personal now, and that pisses me off."

"See that's exactly what makes this so dangerous," he said, feeling desperate. "You've got to get it through your head, El. With these guys, it's not personal. It's drugs. It's drug money. It's you getting in their way—"

"They handcuffed me in my own home."

"Because you wouldn't stay out of their way! Christ, El, just stay out of their way."

"And let the police handle it?"

"Yes!"

"And I just bet I know which cop wants to handle this for me."

"You've got that right."

They stared at each other, and right then, he knew. He'd blown it. She was going to go, and he couldn't stop her.

Sure enough, she grabbed her keys and stalked to the door.

He snagged her wrist, pulled until she looked at him. "Don't go," he said quietly. *Begging*.

But she tore free. "I have to. I have to do this for me." She shut the door quietly, with a finality that frightened him more than anything else had.

Chapter Seven

Ella knew what she had to do, but just in case, she made a list on the long, bumpy flight back to Los Angeles. She committed it to memory on the two-hour drive from Los Angeles to Santa Barbara:

1. Get onto the *Valeska* and find *something* to nail my suspects.
2. Switch departments to a safer investigative job that doesn't involve being stuffed into any dumpsters or getting handcuffed to towel racks, and as a result, live happily ever after.
3. Without James.

That last made her throat tight as she navigated the windy Highway 1, the summer-browned California hills on her right, the sparkling, whitecapped, azure Pacific Ocean on her left. She'd had months to get used to the idea of being without him, and in that time she'd learned to spend whole minutes without dwelling on it, but her heart just couldn't wrap itself around the idea of this being permanent.

Angrily, she swiped at a tear and told herself it'd been caused by the sun in her eyes. No more of this. She was her own woman, and didn't need nor want a man who didn't love her for all her little pieces and neuroses. It was all or nothing, damn it.

And in any case, she didn't have any tissues with her, so she sucked it up, parked in the marina, and slipped her binoculars out of her purse. She checked out the long rows of boats harbored. There were many, certainly more than a hundred, and they ran the gamut from small dinghies that hardly seemed seaworthy to party-sized catamarans and sailboats, to the multi-million-dollar yachts such as the ones she'd been investigating.

She sought out the *Valeska*. She sat in her car and watched the boat carefully for ten minutes, and saw nothing. No maintenance, no guests, no movement at all. Hoping her luck had finally turned, Ella twisted into the backseat and grabbed her disguise: a white cap with a bobbling plastic pizza on it, and the pizza delivery box, which didn't hold pizza but her Mace, tape recorder, and ID, just in case. Once, she'd been arrested snooping around in a shipping yard because she hadn't stowed her ID and couldn't prove who she was. James hadn't enjoyed bailing her out, or the crap he'd taken for it from his station, but he'd enjoyed teasing her about it later.

Not this time.

Taking a deep breath, she shoved him out of her mind, exited the car, and made her way down the wooden planks of the docks with purpose. As a pizza delivery girl, she'd want a tip. As Ella, she just wanted a damn break. She was due for one. This sort of thing used to excite the hell out of her but she felt no rush of adrenaline now, nothing but a confusing mix of duty and dread. She had no idea what was the matter with her. Catching bad guys had always been so thrilling.

But actually, in truth, she did know what was wrong. It wasn't the job that amped her life up and gave her a buzz.

It'd been having love. Having James.

Hell of a time to realize that, since she'd left him a thousand miles away, with a finality she didn't want to think about right now.

Couldn't think about.

She came upon the *Valeska*. Sleek, shiny, posh, and so expensive she couldn't imagine planning to destroy it, insurance money or not. She shielded her eyes from the sun and called out from the deck. "Hello? Anyone home?"

No response.

It wasn't too difficult to get on board; she simply hopped the waiting plank and walked on. She figured if she could just get belowdecks, she could check out the place, look around, and . . .

And she had no idea. She just hoped to God some sort of evidence leapt out at her. She ducked beneath the bowline and walked along the bulkhead, heading astern, marveling at all the glass and flashy gold trim, at the lushness and sophistication.

At the back, on a vast white deck, she came across two wet suits and a pile of diving gear.

Still wet.

Roped to the back just below the deck was a small motor boat that hadn't been there last week. She stared at the diving equipment at her feet and understood. The drugs had been held on the second yacht, the one that had been purposely sunk, and they'd just gone back to retrieve the drugs, thinking they were safe because she, with her questions and interest, was locked up in Mexico.

Now that they had their insurance money from the first boat, and the drugs from the second boat, they thought they had it all.

She was about to change that perception.

The brass door heading belowdecks wasn't locked. A strange oversight with a boat as expensive as this one.

Or, and much more likely, the divers were still on board. As she stepped over the threshold, she heard the telltale muted voices. Heart kicking into high gear, she flattened herself against the inside bulkhead, between two large gold framed paintings that she recognized as museum quality, but because she'd skipped more art history classes than she'd actually attended at UCLA, she had no idea what they were other than pretentious renderings of some fancy gardens.

The voices came from below. Ella kept moving and found herself in the galley, surrounded by a luxurious crystal and china lunch spread that had been ravished. Leftover lobster, shrimp, and fancy pasta salads lay around with three empty bottles of champagne.

Seemed someone—several someones—had been celebrating.

Ella reached into the pizza delivery box and flipped on the small tape recorder. No one in their right mind was going to believe she really was delivering a pizza to this ship, but it was too late to change her disguise now. And she wanted to hear what was going on.

What would they do to her if they found her snooping?

Didn't bear thinking about, she decided. Tiptoeing through the galley, she came out into a stateroom with plush seating, state-of-the-art entertainment center, and—

Her husband coming in the opposite door, dressed in black jeans, black running shoes, and a black T-shirt draped over the bulge of his gun, looking fiercely intense as he met her gaze.

"What are you doing here?" she hissed across the thirty-foot room.

He took in the pizza delivery hat and shook his head. "You're kidding me, right?"

"This is *my* case. Get out."

"Can't do that, sweetheart. You need backup. Jesus, tell me you're at least armed with something more than pepperoni."

"I'm fine solo."

"Sure you are, but wouldn't it be nice to know someone had your back?"

She let out a soft breath and felt her stomach twist. "More than anything in the world," she admitted. "But it's more than that, James. You want to change me. Dominate me. Run my life."

"*What?*" He looked around them and then hissed back, "I don't want to change you, damn it. I don't want to dominate you, or tell you how to run your life."

"So you're saying you love all my parts?"

"Every goddamn one," he said fervently. "And trust me, I need all those parts, El. So let's get out of here—"

"Even this one?" she asked, gesturing around her. "The part where this is my job? You love that?"

"Look, all I want is for you to live long enough to love me back—" His head came up at some sound that she didn't hear, or maybe it was just his sharp instincts.

"What?" she whispered.

"We're going to have to discuss this somewhere else, say far away from the three guys downstairs divvying up their drugs, armed to the teeth."

"There's drugs?" *Her proof!* "Where—" But she broke off because someone was coming into the galley behind them.

She froze.

James drew his gun and jerked his head toward the door from which he came. He wanted her to get out, and she knew he'd stand there in the open, covering her, until she did.

But no way was he going to risk himself for her. She shook her head and dropped down behind one of the couches.

James didn't make a sound as he shot her a look filled with sick dread and fear, *for her*, then backed out the door from which he'd come just as someone opened the door from the galley.

She ducked low, her heart going high. James loved her. He'd never stopped loving her. And he needed her. *Her*. The woman she was. God, she'd been so stupid, chasing after all this adrenaline within her job when everything she'd ever wanted had been right there in front of her.

From her perch behind the couch she couldn't see him, couldn't do anything but wait and hope and pray she hadn't just given them both a death sentence.

A man entered the room, and another behind him, both in nothing but swim trunks, their hair still wet. Ella recognized the voices as the men who'd been speaking belowdecks.

The divers.

"We should get a move on," the first one said. He was in his thirties, built like a heavyweight boxer, with tattoos covering most of his upper body. "Our flight's in a few hours."

"No rush now that our resident insurance investigator slash pain in the ass is detained." This guy was thin and lanky, with no tattoos, just plenty of scars, and a chuckle that gave Ella a shiver. "Lou and Raul said they handcuffed her nosy naked ass to her towel rack. I can't believe they didn't take pictures of her, man. She's still there, you know. Maybe we should go see her for ourselves."

Ella fisted her hands. James had in all likelihood saved her life.

"Raul said she squirmed a lot." Tattoo Guy let out a lecherous grin of his own. "He kept getting handfuls. Damn, we should have been the ones to catch her."

Fully creeped out, Ella huddled behind the couch, her finger on the Mace trigger.

"Got the shit?" Tattoo Guy asked.

"Oh, yeah, and it's pure, baby."

Ella felt the couch shift as both men sat on it. It was a low back, thick cushioned leather number, and though she flattened herself to the floor, if either one so much as craned his head an inch to either side, he'd see her.

Her eyes searched frantically for a way out. There was an end table to her right, a glass and chrome deal that had some fancy steel sculpture displayed. The sculpture was about a foot high and looked like a wire cage, though she knew better and figured it was another ridiculously priced piece of art.

The thin thug opened a baggie, and Tattoo Guy stuck his pinkie finger into it, then brought it to his mouth to taste. He nodded and smiled. "Nice."

"Our cut's going to set us up for life."

"Then let's go get started on that life."

No. No one was leaving. But just as Ella went to make her move, a big, hot, sweaty hand settled on the back of her neck and hauled her up.

Bad guy number three. Heck of a time to remember the *three* bottles of champagne.

Tattoo Guy and his partner whipped around, jaws dropped. "What the—"

Ella hung from the third man's grip, feet swinging a few inches off the ground. Bringing her hand up, she nailed her attacker in the face with her Mace.

He screamed like a baby and let go of her. She hit the ground hard, scrambling to crawl away, but he fell on her, all three hundred pounds of him, a full dead weight.

Tattoo Guy let out a howl and dove over the back of the couch, landing on top of both of them.

Ella took the weight, her mouth opening and closing like a fish, her poor lungs uselessly attempting to drag in some air. Her one last thought was that she'd screwed up again.

Then there was rapid gunfire and suddenly she was free of the weight pinning her down. Sitting up, she saw Tattoo Guy rolling in agony, hands to the bullet hole in his thigh. Scrawny guy and James stood face to face, each holding a gun on the other.

"Drop it," James demanded, but the scrawny guy just shook his head.

Ella glanced to her right just as the third guy sat up and glowered at her.

She'd dropped her Mace. Bad.

Without thinking, she grabbed the steel sculpture, which was heavier than she thought. She chucked it at his big, meaty head. By some miracle, it actually beaned him between the eyes, and with a sigh he toppled back over.

"Drop the gun," James said to the skinny thug.

He just leered and pivoted, abruptly changing from pointing his gun at James to pointing it at Ella.

Uh-oh.

She dove to the floor as gunshots pinged and ricocheted around her, crawling beneath the coffee table. Before she could even attempt to peek out to see James—*God, please don't let him be hit*—she was hauled up against a warm, hard chest.

"Are you hit?" a rough voice asked as gentle hands ran over her body. "Ella, Christ, *say something*."

She could hear Tattoo Guy squalling about his leg. There were sirens in the distance, and she realized James must have called it in on his cell before he burst back into the room and saved the day. Her hero, she thought dreamily, and grinned. "You still smell good."

He stared at her for one beat and then yanked her closer, burying his face in his hair. His arms were banded so tightly around her she couldn't breathe, but that was okay because breathing was entirely overrated. She could feel his heart thundering steadily beneath her ear, could hear his not quite steady breathing as he nuzzled close. The feel of him warm and hard with strength surrounding her had always worked like an aphrodisiac, and now was no exception, except it was deeper than mere physical wanting. "You were scared for me," she murmured.

"I think I had a coronary."

"You didn't."

"Then I definitely got gray hair."

Throat tight, she ruffled his jet black hair, completely free of gray, and burrowed in closer.

"You know I love you, right?" he demanded. "I need you, too. So much, Ella."

And because she did know it now, she smiled through her tears. "Don't let go, okay?"

His arms tightened. "I won't."

"No, I mean don't ever let go."

"Never." He lifted his head and cupped her jaw. "Let's go home, Ella."

"Yeah, leave." Tattoo Guy pulled himself to a sitting position, sweating and gritting his teeth in pain, but lifted his hands in surrender when James pointed the gun his way. "Look, I'm not stupid. I'm staying right here."

James looked at Ella again, and everything within her quivered with hope. She'd wanted this, had ached for so long. "Really? You want to go home with me?"

"Yes. I want both of our shoes in the closet and both cars in the garage."

"Just one bed, right?"

"One bed, and you in it," he murmured, dipping his head to rub her jaw with his. "Beneath me. Wrapped around me." He lifted his face again and held her gaze with his dark one. "And I don't mean just for tonight."

"Good, because I'm free tomorrow night, too," she quipped, her stomach jangling with hope and what she was deathly afraid was nerves. She'd faced three crazed drug runners without blinking and now she was going to fall apart. It didn't make sense, and yet it did.

Because this, with James, was the most important thing she had going on in her life. She had to get it right. *They* had to get it right. "And the night after?" she whispered.

"All of them," he said gently, and kissed her. "It's okay, El. We're going to be okay. We're going to have the forever after we promised to give each other."

She meant to laugh confidently but ended up letting out a gulping sob instead. "I want that, too. I want that so much. In fact, maybe you could take me home right now and we could get working on that forever part, with your pager in the freezer and my cell phone turned off. And without any clothes on."

Tattoo Guy rolled his eyes. "Hey, felon in the room."

James smiled and kissed her, and everything was in that kiss—his promise, his hope, his love. All she ever needed.

SISTER SWITCH

Susanna Carr

To Mary-Jo Wormell and Sue Curran

Chapter One

With every set of twins, there is a leader and a follower.

"You're bailing out of your wedding rehearsal? Are you crazy?" Jessica asked with a squawk. She gripped the armrests of her chair. It was unclear if the move was for support or for restraint. "They kind of need the bride to be there!"

Tracy Parks shrugged her shoulders. When her sister put it like that, it did sound bad. Almost cowardly. Spineless. Which was *so* not her!

It took someone with nerves of steel to even come up with the plan, she reminded herself as she strolled along Jessica's cluttered bedroom. It was a bold move. It meant taking a big risk that promised a bigger payoff. And the plan required her twin sister's help. Who just happened to be a scaredy-cat, unfortunately.

But did Jessica see it that way? Of course not. The self-appointed conscience for the duo thought she was being the smart and sensible one. She also saw this as an opportunity to give the lecture of all lectures.

The warnings and sermons wouldn't do any good. Never had and never would. Tracy didn't bother with the codes of conduct that her sister held dear.

As far as Tracy was concerned, those rules didn't make sense and only served to get in the way. By disregarding the rules, she had been able to zigzag her way to success in the Seattle software industry while her peers were eating her dust, clinging to the vague promise that good behavior would ultimately be rewarded.

Jessica certainly believed that. Once again, Tracy was amazed that they were related. They were so different, right down to what they wore. Even now, Tracy's power red business suit and tight chignon were at odds with Jessica's baggy jeans and messy ponytail.

She would have thought that her sister was adopted, but the fact that they were identical twins totally ruined that theory.

"The rehearsal is tomorrow," Jessica reminded her in a fierce whisper.

"Yeah, I'm aware of that." Tracy paused and fiddled with her pearl earring. Okay, she'd really flubbed up the presentation of her plan. She might as well get to her point. "I'm hoping that you can take my place."

Jessica's mouth sagged open. "Take. Your. Place."

Well, duh. What did her sister think she was leading up to? "I can't let anyone know that I'm going to be out of town, and I can't postpone the wedding rehearsal."

If her plan worked, then the rehearsal would have been a waste of time. Everyone knew that her marriage with Devlin Hunter was a merger between two software dynasties. Devlin would usurp her role as the heir apparent, and she would get to be married to power.

Big whoop. Why marry power when she could *steal* it out from under her intended husband's nose? Even better, she didn't have to get all dressed up and promise to love, honor, and obey a guy who she could care less about.

Of course, the best time to snatch the power was during its most vulnerable moment. Namely when the power was being transferred to Devlin. However, it just so happened that the only time she could get the needed shares was on the day before her wedding. And she had to travel across country to New York in order to get them. That was where Jessica came in.

Tracy knew being identical would come in handy one of these days. Usually it sucked. She was rarely treated as an individual. There were also the constant comparisons. Not to mention the unending annoyance of being called the wrong name. All. The. Time.

But implementing this plan would make up for the twenty-some-odd-year suckfest. That is, if her sister would agree to it.

"Can you pretend to be me?" Tracy requested softly, folding her hands into prayer. "Just for a few hours?"

"A few hours!" Jessica parroted, her eyes widening at the understatement.

Okay, so those few hours just happened to be when Tracy would be the main attraction. She was kind of hoping to finesse that weak spot of her plan. From the look on her sister's pale face, Jessica was fixated on the one itsy-bitsy drawback.

"It won't work," Jessica declared.

"How do you know? We haven't tried it before." Tracy had always wanted to, but her sister would never let them do it. Now was probably not a good time to point out that they sure could have used the practice.

Tracy leaned back against Jessica's untidy bed, prepared to use every persuasive technique she possessed. And she still didn't know if it would work. She found it amazing that everyone thought she bossed and bullied Jessica. Ha! If only!

Jessica vetoed every brilliant idea Tracy ever had and wouldn't change her mind once she made a decision. She might have fooled the world into thinking she was soft and sweet, but Jessica Parks was the epitome of stubbornness. Trying to get the woman to agree on anything—from what would be the theme for their sixth birthday party to where they should go for dinner tonight— was an unbreakable check and balance system.

One of these days Tracy would figure out a way to shatter the system and get whatever she wanted. She could practice by taking over the world. But one coup at a time. First she had to assume control of the family's company and boot out all of the relatives who refused to let a woman run the show.

"We've never traded places before because it won't work!" Jessica said with a touch of exasperation.

"It'll work. And I'll explain to Mom what's going on," Tracy continued, knowing Jessica would need backup. "I have to, since she would tell us apart instantly."

Jessica cast her a disbelieving look. "What makes you think Mom would go along with this plan?"

"If I can convince her, would you do it?" Tracy asked, keeping her face expressionless. No need to mention that Mom already knew the plan and was gung ho about it.

"Oh, sure," Jessica said with deep sarcasm. "If you can get Mom to back you up, I'm in."

Tracy smiled. "I'll hold you to that."

Damn and double damn! The words swirled around Tracy's head like background music. Her sweaty hands shook as she swiped the card key to the honeymoon suite, but the red light glared back at her. Nothing was cooperating with her today.

To top it all off, she'd messed up. Crashed and burned. Big-time. Tracy leaned her head against the door and closed her eyes. It was bad enough that her brilliant plan backfired, but she couldn't believe she missed her freaking *wedding*!

Thank God, Jessica was secretly—and oh so reluctantly—filling in for her. Tracy knew she was going to hear about this for the rest of her life. When she was ninety years old and in the old folks' home, Jessica was going to be in the next bed complaining about it.

She just might deserve that special kind of purgatory, unless she came up with a quick save. That and a lifetime of really, *really* good birthday presents for her twin.

How did it all go wrong? Tracy wondered as she swiped the card key again and again. Yesterday she was getting down and dirty with a high-risk deal, experiencing a buzz from the cut-throat atmosphere.

Then suddenly everything went sour. Her head was still spinning from it, but the results remained the same: she hadn't gotten the shares.

Plan B had bombed and she had to hurry back to Seattle and follow through with Plan A, whether she liked it or not. Only she hadn't gotten home in time. Damn airline computer glitch.

And now she was trying to break into her own honeymoon suite undetected while the wedding reception was going on several floors down. How could her life make a 180 degree turn in such a short space of time?

Tracy almost didn't notice when the card key finally worked. Tears of relief pricked in the back of her eyes when the green light went on. She slipped inside and looked around the empty suite.

Devlin Hunter didn't spare any expense, Tracy realized as she walked through the sitting room, gliding her hand along the raw silk of the sofa. The suite was enormous. Luxurious. Spacious. Too bad it didn't offer a lot of hiding places.

She crossed the threshold into the bedroom and stumbled to a halt when she saw the big bed. It was really big. Like you could do a whole tumbling routine for Olympic judges and never step out of bounds.

Okay, maybe not, but she didn't want to look at the bed. Or think about sharing it with her new husband. That didn't help in the least.

She needed to concentrate on trading places with her sister. Tracy glanced at her watch, wondering how much time she had to come up with a plan. She didn't like the idea of switching back in such close proximity to her groom, but there was nothing she could do about it.

She heard someone at the door. Tracy whirled around and stared at the doorknob. *Shit*. Devlin and Jessica were back earlier than she expected.

And they managed to unlock the door with one swipe of the card key.

Shitshitshit! She frantically looked around and bolted for the bathroom.

She heard the door swing open and close with a thud.

Shitshitshitshit—Tracy's feet skidded along the tiled bathroom floor. She restrained herself from closing and locking the door. Just barely.

Her heart pounded against her ribs as she felt her way through the dark. Her hands batted the shower curtain. Wishing there was a better hiding place, she stepped inside the bathtub.

Pressing her back against the slick tile wall, Tracy hid in the shadows of the curtain, wondering if the day could get much worse. *Don't ask that! You'll jinx yourself!*

She needed to think positively. Wish with all her might that Jessica stepped into the bathroom first. And hope that her sister was in the right frame of mind not to scream.

Now, if it was her intended groom who found her first, then she would be well and truly screwed. She could see it all now, the obvious question: "What are you doing here?" Tracy reviewed her three possible responses:

(a) "This isn't the sauna?" Tracy played it back in her mind and winced. No, too lame.

There was always the generic (b), "Surprise!" Uncommitted but required a follow-up.

She could go for broke and do (c), "Funny thing happened to me on the way to the church . . ."

Yeah, that wouldn't go over well. She'd go for (b). Hold on. . . . Tracy stood absolutely still. Why was it so quiet out there?

She listened intently, but didn't hear any mushy gushy sounds. Good thing, too. She and Devlin hadn't even held hands, which was something that was so obvious she forgot to mention it to Jessica. She hoped her sister wasn't giving any mixed messages. That wasn't something she wanted to follow up on if she could help it.

There was nothing except for hushed, determined steps. Definitely singular and absolutely masculine. *Son of a bitch.* Tracy stomped her foot in frustration and almost slipped against the porcelain.

Was Devlin by himself? Tracy wondered as she flattened her hands against the tile wall and regained her balance. That didn't make sense. Even if it was the worst-case scenario, like Jessica making some great escape, her groom wouldn't stay in the honeymoon suite.

It must be someone from the hotel staff, Tracy decided. No, that couldn't be right. They would have announced their presence.

That left only one explanation. A strange sense of resignation filled her chest. It had to be an intruder.

Tracy tossed her hands in the air. Figures. She should have hidden under the bed. Hopefully the thief was more interested in the minibar than a random search.

But this was her life, Tracy reminded herself as she placed her hands on her hips. Therefore, the guy was heading straight for the bathroom. Trust her luck to be stuck with a thief with a weak bladder.

Tracy flinched when the intruder slapped on the bathroom lights. Her knees crumpled. *Fuck*. How did she get herself into these situations?

The footsteps echoed against the tiled floor. A shadow appeared on the shower curtain. Grew bigger. And bigger.

Fuck, fuck, fuck. She forgot to breathe as his hand reach around the vinyl curtain. The guy was tanned and had long fingers. His hand was big and strong . . .

Fuckety-fuck-fuck. She pressed her back firmly against the wall and clenched her eyes shut. She didn't move. Until icy cold water hit her full blast.

Tracy yelped. She felt the shower curtain being ripped away. She wiped the water from her eyes and blinked when she saw the man standing in front of her.

"Nick?" Nicholas Taggart. Devlin's assistant and best man. The only guy who could make her lose control with just one touch.

Nick turned off the water and stared back at her. He cocked back his head to one side. "Jessica?"

Jessica?! Tracy's mouth dropped open. Okay, that was it. Tracy had been able to coldheartedly dump Nick when she found out he betrayed her. And since then, she had no problem going for his jugular every day in the boardroom. But when the love of her life can't tell her apart from her sister, he was going to pay big-time for that mistake.

Chapter Two

Unless you've seen one of them naked, you won't be able to tell identical twins apart.

Tracy's eyes narrowed as her jaw locked in anger. The nerve of that man. The absolute nerve. They once had shared a life-altering, mind-bending fling. Okay, so it only lasted a week, but Nicholas Taggart should have the decency to recognize an ex-flame.

Ex-flame. Tracy didn't like that label. Nick was supposedly her soul mate. The guy almost made her believe in love at first sight. Almost. Until she discovered it was all a Machiavellian maneuver in the name of business.

Normally Tracy would admire such technique. Actually, she would be kicking herself for not thinking of it first. But this time it was different. This time she fell in love and couldn't seem to shake it off.

"What are you doing here?" Nick folded his arms across his chest. The movement pulled his exquisitely tailored tuxedo jacket against his sculpted arms.

"Uh . . ." *This isn't the sauna?* No, she scratched that idea. What was the plan?

His brown eyes darkened. "Don't you have the flu?"

"Yes!" she said hoarsely. It didn't sound familiar, but she'd go with it. "Yes, I do." She dragged her gaze away from the sleek lines of his shoulders. Now was not the time to remember how strong they felt under her arms . . . or her legs . . .

It took a superhuman effort to yank her gaze up. The ribbons of tension swirled and tightened around her. She reluctantly met Nicholas Taggart's gaze head-on.

She wanted to look away. Needed to look away. But Nick's brown eyes held her fast.

She didn't understand how this guy had so much power over her. It certainly wasn't his good looks. His dark brown hair was too short and his cheekbones were too high and square. The bridge of his nose looked like it had seen a fist or two in the past. Lines bracketed his straight mouth and his lips sported a small white scar.

And for some reason, Tracy could stare at his face for hours. It didn't help that Nick was the most fascinating and most annoying man she'd ever met. The guy always seemed to be one step ahead of her whether she was swooping in for the kill or faking a fever.

Fever! Right. She was supposed to be suffering from the flu. Tracy gave a dry, hacking cough. She quickly clasped her hands against her throat as the pain ricocheted. *Wow, that hurt.* But it worked. Nick got out of her way fast.

"You should be in bed," he said with a frown.

No shit, Sherlock. This day definitely rated as one in which she shouldn't have gotten out of bed. But it was too late for that. She'd settle for getting out of the bathtub without falling and cracking her skull.

"You shouldn't be here," Nick continued.

Tracy faked a whiplash sneeze in his direction. "I . . . I didn't want to miss my sister's special day." That sounded very Jessica-like. Tracy was quite proud of the response.

Nick arched an eyebrow. "So you're waiting for her in the bathroom?"

Hmm . . . That did sound illogical. "Yeah."

Nick's forehead wrinkled. "Are you taking medication?"

"Why?" Was he thinking of upping her dosage or withdrawing treatment altogether?

"You look like hell."

That bugged her, even though it was the point she was trying to get across. "So kind of you to notice," she said with a closed-mouth smile.

Tracy glanced at herself in the mirror above the sink. Tendrils of her long blond hair had escaped the simple ponytail and were now plastered against her bare, shiny face. The wrinkled T-shirt and jeans she'd grabbed from Jessica's closet did nothing to improve her mood. They were tight and uncomfortable. Tracy still couldn't get over the fact that her twin sister wore a smaller size. There was obviously no justice in the world.

But just because she was wearing sloppy, damp clothes didn't mean she looked sickly! She glared at Nick's reflection. *You try taking a cross-country flight*, Tracy thought bitterly. *Try missing your own wedding and breaking into your own honeymoon suite, lying in wait to pounce on the proxy bride. Then we'll see how chipper you're feeling.*

"Okay, Jessica." Nick reached for her arm. "You better leave before Devlin and your sister get here."

She dodged his hand. "No way." Her self-control was already weak. If he touched her, she'd be lost.

"No way?"

Right. Tracy gritted her teeth. Jessica would get her point across much more politely. If she wanted to be successful in this masquerade, she needed to act all ladylike and proper.

That meant no swearing, no talking back, no public displays of anger, sitting with her legs crossed . . . Aw, hell. Tracy's shoulders drooped. She might as well give up right here and now.

Tracy tried again. "I mean, I would prefer to stay. I went through all this effort, and I'm quite determined to see my sister."

"That's not a good idea."

"Who—" She bit her tongue. Hard. This ladylike image was going to be the death of her. "I'll let my sister decide that," she said sweetly. Tracy strode out of the bathroom with regal grace before she punctuated her reply with her favorite cuss word.

She walked into the bedroom, purposely looking away from the bed as her mind whirled at top speed. How was she going to get Nick to leave when he was dead set on throwing her out? And how much time did she have left before the bride and groom got here?

It might help if she knew what Nick was after. If it was something as simple as looking for a cell phone, she'd help him find it and send him on his way. "What are you doing here, Nick?" she asked over her shoulder.

"Checking to see if the honeymoon suite was ready," he said right behind her.

His answer stopped her in the middle of the bedroom. Was he for real? "You really take your best man duties seriously, don't you?"

"And I'm serious about you leaving." He wrapped his fingers around her upper arm.

Tracy softly gasped as the jolt of awareness startled her. Her skin tingled and flushed as the sensations forked through her body, heating her blood. *Well, isn't that freaking fantastic.* His touch was just as potent as ever. Probably more so.

Focus! She had to get away from him but stay in the honeymoon suite. The man had the strength and the strategic mind to throw her out. And once he slammed the door behind her, the chances weren't good of regaining entrance. Unless . . .

She placed her hand on her forehead and weaved a bit on her feet. "Oh . . ." Clockwise and then the opposite direction for effect.

He instantly released her. "You okay?"

She placed her other hand on her stomach. She couldn't decide if she was going to be light-headed or nauseous. She'd go for both. "I need to sit down."

"There's a bench next to the elevator."

You're all heart, Nick. "I need to sit down *now*." Tracy allowed her knees to buckle. She rolled her shoulders as if the dry heaves were imminent. "You go on ahead. Just give me a couple of minutes."

Nick shoved his hands in his trouser pockets and rocked back on his heels. "I can wait."

"No, no." She waved him off, wondering if she could break out into a cold sweat on command. "That's not necessary."

"Yes, it is."

Tracy glanced at him from the corner of her eyes. She didn't like the hard edge in his voice. It was like he wasn't buying her performance.

She couldn't have that. Okay. Time for Plan C: faint dead away.

Tracy rolled her eyes and went limp. She fell backwards and belatedly realized Nick was making no move to catch her before she went splat on the floor.

She should have known not to expect Nicholas Taggart to save her. The rat bastard never did have any manners.

Chapter Three

If you cause pain to one twin, the other twin will feel it.

Nicholas Taggart winced as he watched her collapse onto the floor with a sickening thud. *That had to hurt.* He thought she would have made a duck-and-roll at the last minute. Anything to soften the impact, but no, she went for the full effect.

He should have expected that. If there was one thing he'd realized long ago about Tracy—and it was most definitely Tracy Parks lying at his feet—when she went into action, she was one hundred percent committed to see it through.

He studied her face with a mix of yearning and grudging admiration. Tracy never flinched or groaned when she hit the floor. Her expression was as peaceful and serene as an angel.

Yeah, she was definitely up to something. Tracy never looked that innocent, even when she was sound asleep. He'd better get out of the way before she rose from the dead like something from a horror movie.

Nick stepped over her and walked to the bed. He sat on the edge and loosened his black tie. He might as well get comfortable, or at least try to. For the first time in months, he felt alive. Tracy always had that effect on him. Life was never boring around her.

Even now, while she was pretending to be comatose, her vibrant energy made him ache with need. Nick knew he couldn't afford to get distracted. He needed to remember that this latest scheme had her signature all over it.

Trust Tracy Parks to cause trouble, Nick thought as he released the top button of his shirt. He dealt with her enough in the boardroom to have expected something like an ambush or guerrilla warfare. She was ambitious, double-crossing, and determined to rule.

In other words, his equal. It was no wonder she captured his imagination from the moment they first met. They would make the perfect team. That is, if they didn't kill each other first. Or if she didn't marry his boss.

Nick's gut twisted over the last reminder, just like it had spiraled tight when the engagement had been announced. He knew it had been a business deal, and that the marriage merger was essential to Devlin's plans, but he didn't have to like it.

Tracy Parks was his woman, and he wasn't ready to give her up. He wanted her to return to his bed and his side. He wanted Tracy watching his back instead of stabbing it.

Nick's lips slanted into a wry smile. Yeah, he always did like those impossible challenges. Tracy Parks, most of all. And this time he was playing for keeps.

"Jessica," Nick murmured in a low, husky tone. "Jessica?"

Why didn't she ever notice how annoyingly persistent Nick could be? She might as well wake up before he called an ambulance. She blinked her eyes open. "Where am I?" she asked dazedly.

"Devlin and Tracy's honeymoon suite," Nick answered as he pulled his black tie from his collar. "How are you feeling?"

"Like I broke every bone in my body. No, no." She waved her hand. "Don't knock yourself out helping me up. You've done more than enough breaking my fall and bringing me back to consciousness."

"Jessica, you're sounding more like your sister every day. She's a bad influence on you."

"I'll be sure to tell Tracy." She gingerly rose from the floor, every bone creaking in protest. "She should be showing up any minute."

Nick shook his head. "I just came up from the reception. Your sister will be there all night."

All night? Impossible. Jessica was not a party animal. And Devlin? No way could she imagine him waltzing until the wee hours of the morning. Nick had to be overestimating.

"It's time I took you home." He tossed the tie aside.

Okay, she had to come up with another strategy than falling on the floor every ten minutes. She'd be black and blue before the night was over. And she wouldn't put it past Nick to grab her by the ankles and drag her outside the door.

"You know," she said as she weakly climbed up on the bed. "I don't think I can handle a car ride right now. Unless you don't mind me getting sick all over your dashboard." *When all else fails, threaten the state of the man's car.* "Let me lie down here."

"Isn't it bad luck to sleep in someone else's honeymoon bed?" Nick shrugged off his tuxedo jacket and tossed it down next to the tie.

"I don't care." She crawled to the headboard and plopped down. "And you're thinking of the wedding rings," she corrected him, the soft pillow muffling her voice. "It's bad luck if you try on someone's engagement or wedding ring."

Uh-oh. Her gaze darted to her bare fingers. Her sister was wearing her ring. Oh, puhleeze! What was she so worried about? She didn't believe in those superstitions.

"Same concept," he decided as he removed his cuff links. "Probably carries the same bad luck."

"Why would you care?" she murmured, trying not to get too comfortable. She had to come up with a Plan D. Or was she on E? "You made it clear that you think Devlin and Tracy shouldn't marry."

"Yeah, and I still feel that way," Nick said as he folded up his sleeves. "But business is business—even if it's unsound business."

Business. His answer sent her reeling. Business! She should have thought of that. Applauded it. But instead it left her gasping for breath.

He wasn't motivated by jealousy or envy. It had nothing to do with the possibility that he couldn't live without her. No, he was against the union because he thought it was bad business.

"Now, you and me," he continued. "We're very alike."

She didn't think Nick could have said anything more shocking to her. "*We* are?"

"Yep."

Her eyes widened with alarm as he lay down on the pillow next to her. "How do you figure that?"

"We would never marry for the sake of business."

She scooted back and eyed him cautiously, but his scent still beckoned her. *Stay strong. Under no condition are you to curl up against him.* "I wouldn't," she answered as if she were Jessica. "But I'm not too sure about you."

"I wouldn't."

What a liar! She would have loved to shoot his statement down, but she couldn't risk getting into an argument. It would reveal her true identity. "You would if the stock options were right."

"Think again." He laced his hands behind his head. "When I marry, it'll be for love."

"Love?" Her eyebrows shot up. "You?"

"Why is that so hard to believe?"

Hmm . . . This sister switch was proving more useful than she anticipated. "Have you ever been in love before?" she said as casually as she could.

He looked directly into her eyes. "Yes." His answer was so certain, so simple, it pierced her.

She swallowed, the movement painful against her tight throat. "What happened?"

"She dumped me." The glimmer in eyes dark eyes vanished. "She thought I was seducing her to get insider information."

Her heart skipped a beat. *Oh, my God.* He was talking about her! Why did he mention this after the fact, when she couldn't do anything about it? "And . . . and . . . and were you?"

"No. It was love at first sight. At least, it was for me." He sighed and looked up at the ceiling. "Not that she'll believe that."

"Well, why should she? You don't strike me as someone who would fall head over heels."

Nick appeared surprised by her opinion. "Why not?"

"It's not"—she sought the least inflammatory description— "devious enough for you."

"True," he said with a nod. "Maybe that's why it turned my world inside out."

It did? Why hadn't she seen that? Or had she been too busy protecting herself that she didn't see that he felt the same way?

"But the next time I fall in love . . ."

Jealousy ripped through her like a jagged bolt of lightning. She didn't want to hear it. Tracy didn't want to imagine him with someone else. "Isn't that a song?" she asked with a brightness that she found exhausting.

He flashed a warning look in her direction. "The next time I fall—"

"Yep, I'm sure it is." She was tempted to stick her fingers in her ear and sing, but that might give her away.

"It will be with someone who is *completely* different," Nick finished.

Tracy flinched at his decision. "Different?" There went any possibility of a second chance. "What was wrong with the woman you fell in love with?"

Nick propped his head up with his hand. "Well, for one thing . . ."

He had a *list*? Tracy clenched her back teeth. It better not be long.

"I need someone who would trust me unconditionally."

"Is this a requirement, or is it more like, 'To qualify for the position, she must love and honor me. Unconditional trust preferred'?"

Nick acted as if he hadn't heard her. "Someone who is gentle and kind. Sweet."

Sweet? "Are you kidding me?" Spicy with a surprising kick, absolutely. But sweet?

"Someone who is concerned with the environment and is good with animals."

"You forgot to serve mankind and to live by the Girl Scout laws," Tracy muttered.

He pinned her with a look. "Someone who would obey."

Tracy stopped her snort too late and it sounded like a kersnuffle. "Good luck on that."

His eyes brightened. "Someone like you, Jessica."

Tracy stared at him. Her mouth opened and closed. Fury bloomed inside her chest, threatening to consume the fragments of her hard-earned control.

She couldn't believe it. It shocked her to the core. Nicholas Taggart was hitting on her sister!

And there was nothing she could do about it.

Chapter Four

Twins share everything.

Tracy looked away sharply as chaos erupted inside her. She would not react. She would play it cool, even if a dark fury swept through her.

It was essential that she didn't show how his words hit a weak spot. *Never show what was important to you, or someone would try to take it away.* She'd learned that lesson early in life, and it had served her well.

She didn't even know why she was so upset. Who cares if Nick had moved on? Tracy asked herself as she tightly bunched the quilt in her fists. She and Nick were no longer together. He could go after whomever he wished. It had nothing to do with her. Even if that meant he pursued her sister.

She felt Nick's gaze sweep across her. The atmosphere crackled with intent. She wanted to ignore him, but it proved impossible. Tracy cast a quick glance in his direction. Her skin flushed under his intense scrutiny and she turned her head away.

The whole thing was academic anyway. Her twin would not be interested in Nicholas Taggart. Jessica had some hang-ups about following rules. Laws. Basic principles. She would never give Nick the time of day. Unless it was one of those opposites-attract kind of deal.

Tracy gnawed on her bottom lip as she considered the possibility. Even if Jessica was remotely interested in Nick, although hell would freeze over first, so be it. That was fine with her. Jessica was more than welcome to her hand-me-downs.

Tracy could almost feel Nick commanding her to turn and face him. The fine hairs on her nape prickled. She battled against his silent insistence while fighting against her wish to comply.

Okay, she was lying. Tracy closed her eyes and burrowed deep into the pillow. Lying to herself, of all people. That had to be a new low.

She might be able to ignore Nick's searching gaze on her, but she couldn't hide from one undeniable fact. There was no way she wanted Nick to pursue someone else—especially her sister!

But what did that mean? *Well, hello.* Tracy wanted to roll her eyes. She wasn't over Nick. She might have cut him out of her personal life with a staggering ruthlessness, but her success could be measured in degrees.

That could be a drawback, since he was moving on. And there was the small detail that she was three-fourths of the way married to his boss. Not insurmountable problems, Tracy admitted, but they could prove pesky.

Okay, Plan . . . what plan was she on? Tracy couldn't remember. Never mind, she'd start fresh. Plan AA: no follow-through with the wedding.

Tracy braced herself for the wave of failure to crash upon her, but it didn't form. Undoubtedly it would hit her when she least expected it. At the moment she felt relieved. Rejuvenated. She was sure the effects were temporary.

After all, she was going to have a mess on her hands. Deal with the fallout with the business merger. Spin the scandal of a society wedding that was quickly annulled. Come up with a strategy to pursue Nick on her own terms and time frame.

But first she had to warn her sister about the change of plans. *Come on, Jessica!* Tracy opened her eyes and stared at the ceiling. *What is taking you so long?*

She impatiently splayed her hands out on the crumpled quilt. The one time Jessica didn't have her phone with her! Stupid etiquette rule. Considering it was one of the most important days in their lives, brides should be allowed to carry cell phones.

She'd have to wait until Jessica arrived. She could explain it while they made the switch. Now if only Nick would leave! Or, better yet, how about if he would stop staring at her!

She twisted her head to the side and glared at Nick. "What are you looking at?" she asked, not caring if she sounded like a grouch.

Nick moved his head closer to hers. Tracy fought against the heavy sensations flooding through her. It would be so simple to shift slightly and nestle against his body.

"I wonder," he said in a seductive drawl, "if you taste as sweet as you look."

Tracy's lips parted and snapped shut. *Oh, right.* He thought he was talking to *Jessica.*

"Looks can be deceiving," she said in a warning growl. "I'm not that sweet."

"I love your modesty," Nick said. The mattress dipped and his leg bumped hers. "It's hot."

"What?" She skittered her head away from him, wincing as her long hair got tangled and pulled at her scalp. "What is hot?"

"I don't know how to explain it," Nick said. "There's an angelic quality."

He couldn't be serious. But then, she never heard him utter a pickup line before. When she first saw him at the software convention, Nick had sliced through the crowd with a slow, purposeful swagger.

She remembered how the panic had welled up inside her. Tracy had instinctively known that this man wanted to take her in the most elemental way. And that she was ready to be claimed by him. From the feral gleam in his eyes, it was obvious that he wanted to grab her above the hips so they would meet eye to eye, mouth to mouth.

He hadn't used any line to express himself. He didn't need to say anything about the fact that he wanted to span his hands around her waist, press her against the wall that had been holding her up, and sink into her.

He stopped himself just short of doing that, but followed through on the silent promise later that night. And from their first meeting, Tracy knew Nick wasn't confined by basic courtesy. That, unfortunately, put her at a distinct disadvantage. Her disregard for rules had been her secret weapon. It shocked and disarmed her prey. But it turned out Nick was much, much better at it.

"There's nothing angelic about me," Tracy told him gruffly. And if that was what he wanted from a woman, it was too damn bad. She wasn't going to change.

"You're wrong," Nick said. "There's something about you that makes me want to shout hallelujah!"

Ugh. Tracy hunched her shoulders and curled her chin into her neck. What kind of pickup line was that? And was it wrong for her to be pleased that he sucked at it? "Shout it from your side of the bed," she suggested.

"Virtuous, too." His eyes shone with admiration. "Sexy-y-y."

Her pulse tripped at the burr in his voice. "Nick, please." She blocked him with an outstretched hand. "I'm already nauseous."

"That's right. I forgot. I'm sorry."

Tracy did a double take. "O . . . kay." Nick was being solicitous and he was apologizing. Tracy wondered if she should be scared.

"Do you need anything?"

"Yeah." She settled more comfortably on the bed. "I need to be left alone."

Nick shook his head. "Not a good idea. Because you already passed out, someone should watch over you. Since I'm already here, I'll do it."

Damn! Tracy wanted to stomp her foot. She was trapped in her web of lies. She should have seen that one coming. Obviously she was slipping at being a master tactician.

Was she ever going to get Nick out of the suite? Acting sick wasn't doing the job. Neither was the sweet and innocent routine, although she had a feeling she'd flubbed that up.

Her expertise wasn't about being sweet. It was about irritating people to no end. *Hmm . . . That might work.* She was going to have to irritate him. Gross him out. Work every one of his pet peeves. And, even better, he'd think Jessica was the disgusting one. Tracy couldn't wait.

She jerked back when he placed his hand on her forehead. "You're not feverish."

"Good to know." Did he have to be this attentive?

"Let me try again." Nick leaned down and brushed his lips against her forehead.

Tracy stiffened in surprise. Her heart clenched as his mouth pressed softly against her heated skin. Her eyes drifted shut. She knew she should turn away, but she couldn't. Not yet.

Nick trailed his mouth down her temple and along her cheek. By the time his mouth hovered over hers, she tilted her chin up, desperate for his kiss.

He didn't make her wait long. Instinctively parting her lips, Tracy drew him in. She wanted to taste him, inhale his scent, and feel Nick's body against hers. Wrap his strength around her just one more time before she came to her senses.

She resisted the urge to rush the kiss. Nick's touch wasn't anything she expected. It wasn't hard or fast, but leisurely. He savored her mouth.

Correction: he was savoring *Jessica's* mouth!

Tracy opened her eyes at the thought. She had to stop kissing him. She couldn't ruin the charade now.

Okay, she had to act like Jessica. But how would her twin react? Tracy couldn't think properly as Nick's tongue surged inside her mouth.

Would Jessica faint? Knee him? Lay still and not move a muscle? Whatever it was, Tracy knew she was doing something wrong. She was positive her sister would not be kissing back.

To hell how Jessica would act! Tracy knew what she felt like doing and bit his lip.

Nick jerked back. Color slashed his cheeks as his eyes glittered with frank need.

"Like I said, Nick." Tracy strove for a prim response, but it was ruined by the breathless quality of her voice. "I want to be left alone."

He gave a slow, knowing smile. "That's strange."

Tracy rolled her eyes and took a deep breath. She might as well ask. "What is?"

Nick darted his tongue along the sore spot on his bottom lip. "You kiss better than your sister."

Chapter Five

Twins are highly competitive with each other.

Come on, Tracy, Nick silently urged her. *I really zinged you good. Let me have it.*

But she had refused to give him the satisfaction. Instead she went all Jessica on him and acted like he hadn't said a thing. It was beginning to drive him crazy.

Nick slid an uneasy look at Tracy as she opened another package of chips from the minibar. He obviously had gone too far with the last comment.

He had wanted to provoke her. The plan was to make her slip up and expose her masquerade. Instead, he was the one who had been edgy for the past half hour and ready to abandon his strategy.

Tracy hadn't argued with him, like he had expected. She didn't even defend her kissing technique or throw a pillow at his face. Nope, she decided he was to pay for that comment. Tenfold.

A jarring belch ripped past Tracy's lips.

"Sorry," she said, sounding anything but repentant. "That one got right by me."

Nick didn't know if his patience was going to last much longer. She had pushed him to the brink and was ready to give him a big shove.

From the corner of his eye, he watched Tracy open her mouth. He looked away when she started to pick the food from her teeth with her fingernail.

Wasn't it bad enough that she'd already covered every one of his pet peeves? And created a few new ones. The worst part was that she took over the remote control.

"Yes, Nurse?" the jovial male voice boomed from the television speakers, vibrating against the walls of the hotel room. *"What seems to be the problem?"*

"I feel so hot, Doctor."

Nick rubbed his face with his hands as the breathy female voice grated on his nerves. He couldn't take much more of this. He should go into the other room, but he wouldn't give up an inch of his hard-won territory.

"I'll need to check your reflexes."

He was in hell. It could be worse, Nick decided, shifting his back against the headboard. Tracy could have found one of those boring Jane Austen movies where the characters either stared at each other or fell down. He couldn't understand why she liked those films so much.

"Oh, Doctor!" the nurse said in a groan.

Nick glanced at the TV screen. Big mistake.

He quickly looked over at Tracy, his body tightening at the sight of her. With the pillows propped up behind her, she lounged on the bed, noisily eating her way through the minibar. She absently nibbled on a cheese puff, her attention riveted on the television.

Oh, yeah. She was up to something. There was no way she could watch this as if it was a medical drama.

"Nurse, you'll need to disrobe."

Nick winced at the bad dialogue and tried to concentrate on something else.

"Lie down, Nurse."

Anything else! He would not look at the TV. *Do not look at the TV . . .*

"Doctor, please take my temperature."

Nick knew Tracy was doing her best to make him leave.

"Stick your thermometer in me, Doctor!"

Obviously she wanted him to race out the door, screaming for mercy. A cheesy porn movie just might do the trick.

"Open wide and say ah."

Okay! That was it. He had had enough. "Change the channel," he said in a growl.

Tracy's attention remained on the movie. "Is it bothering you?" She licked the orange dust off her fingertips.

Nick was mesmerized by her darting tongue. He swallowed roughly. "Yeah." Orgasmic moans from the movie punctuated his answer.

"It'll be over soon." Her lips curved into a sly smile. "I have a feeling I know what the nurse is suffering from, but I want to see if I'm right."

Nick dragged his gaze away from her mouth. He shouldn't have kissed her. It stirred up memories he wasn't strong enough to resist.

And that smile was just like the one she gave him when they first met at the computer convention, which seemed so long ago. Tracy's cool beauty had captured his attention, but it was her attitude that made his head spin. The fierce attraction and equally competitive nature made a potent combination.

When she eventually dumped him without ceremony, for the first time in his life, Nick retreated. He couldn't charge forward and grab what he wanted. He couldn't risk another rejection.

As he licked his wounds, he had replayed every minute of their time together. Should he have let Tracy know how much he loved her? Or was it for the best that she didn't know how much he had been willing to give, and give up, for her?

Now he knew he had played it wrong. He had been too intent on protecting his heart when he should have left himself wide open. But that went against every instinct and everything he knew about life.

While he knew he should have surrendered unconditionally, his gut twisted at the thought. It was a risk he had to take if he wanted Tracy—the one person who had the power to hurt him.

But when he had her cornered in the honeymoon suite, had a once-in-a-lifetime opportunity to change the course of their relationship, what did he do? Messed with her mind like he always did.

No wonder she didn't trust him an inch. Could he blame her? How could he expect absolute trust from Tracy when he couldn't take the same risk?

It didn't matter now, Nick thought with a sigh. She still considered him the enemy. Tracy would probably think worse of him after today.

He'd blown any chance of reconciliation, but he was still hanging in there. If all else failed, at least he'd prevented Tracy switching back with Jessica.

"Tell me if this hurts . . ."

But even his tenacity had limits. "Give me the remote."

Tracy didn't look in his direction. "No."

"Now." He reached for it.

She lunged for the remote control and rolled over a bag of chips. Crumbs spilled onto the wrinkled quilt. "The show isn't over."

"You might feel a slight discomfort . . ."

"I mean it." He couldn't stand this torment any longer. He couldn't hear, see, or even think about sex when he was alone in a room with Tracy with nothing to stop him. Not unless he planned on losing this battle.

"Is it better like this? Or like this?"

Tracy jumped off the bed. She slapped the remote control against her palm, echoing the sound of a spank from the TV. "You want it?" she asked, wiggling her eyebrows. "Do you *really* want it?"

"Turn your head and cough."

Nick stretched out his hand. "Give it to me."

"Are you *suuuure?*"

"Oh, yes!" The TV nurse groaned. *"The doctor is in!"*

He clenched his teeth and felt the muscle pop in his jaw. "I've had enough of your games, Tracy. It's my turn now, and I'm changing the rules."

Tracy froze. "W-what?" she asked.

"Yes, I know it's you, Tracy," he revealed impatiently. "I saw you when you snuck into the hotel and followed you. How else would I know you were in the shower?"

She stared at him as if he had lost his mind. "Why are you calling me Tracy?"

He was not going to humor her anymore. "Because that is who you are," he said through clenched teeth.

"You know, I get this a lot. Let me explain." She pointed to herself. "I'm Jessica."

"Drop the act."

"I don't know what you're talking about," Tracy said, as she aimed the remote control at the TV and turned the power off.

"Let *me* explain," Nick mimicked Tracy. "Your sister switch isn't going to work."

"Sister switch?" Her voice went up with each syllable as she stepped away from the bed. "Are you crazy? Why would I do such a thing?"

"Because, as usual, you're up to no good."

"Trading places is the one thing I have always refused to do with Tracy," she said, oh-so-casually backing away from him. "And do you know why? I'll tell you why. It's because they never work."

He flashed Tracy a warning look. For once, it served its purpose as she immediately changed tactics.

"I can't believe this." Tracy tossed her hands in the air. "All my life people have confused me with my sister, but this is ridiculous."

He knew she was going to argue it to death. Tracy won many of her arguments based on endurance alone. Nick could admire that trait if it wasn't always used against him. "Tracy—"

"*Jessica*." She corrected him with a touch of exasperation. "The name is Jessica. Jessica"—she paused as if searching her memory bank—"Ann Parks."

Nick folded his arms across his chest. "Wanna bet?" he asked. It was time to call her bluff.

"Yeah, actually I do." She propped her fists against her hips. "Let's see what you got."

"Call Devlin."

She raised her eyebrows and clucked her tongue in disgust. "Devlin had his cell phone on during his wedding day? That is *so* tacky."

"And," Nick continued, as if she hadn't spoken, "I can have him ask his bride a few questions about Parks Software Systems that only Tracy would know."

"You'd interrupt his reception for that?" Tracy shook her head. "I wouldn't do that if I were you."

"I would." He strode to where his jacket lay on the floor and picked it up. He dipped his hand into the pocket to retrieve his phone.

Tracy pursed her lips as she mulled over her predicament. "Okay, fine. You got me." She held her hands up in surrender. "I'm Tracy."

Nick left his phone untouched and dropped the jacket back on the floor, saying nothing.

"You won," Tracy said, and shrugged her shoulders. "You figured it out. Why don't you go tell everyone how smart you are?" She gestured at the door.

He wasn't going anywhere without her. She'd realize that soon enough. "I would rather hear why you and your sister traded places."

Tracy tilted her chin up with defiance. "I would rather not discuss it."

He took a step towards her. "Would it be because you got cold feet?"

"Are you kidding?" She folded her arms across her chest. "There's not a cowardly bone in my body."

"But you are having second thoughts." He said that with

much more confidence than he felt. He was guessing, playing a hunch. Acting on a wish.

"Am not."

"Are too."

"Am—" She pressed her lips into a straight line and visibly reined in her temper. "I don't know why you would think that."

"It's obvious," he said as he stood in front of Tracy, resisting the urge to reach out and grab her. "You thought it would be easier to marry a guy you feel nothing for but indifference."

Tracy made a face at his assumption. "I wouldn't necessarily say *easier*."

"Safer," he corrected softly.

Her startled gaze collided with his for a second before it darted away.

But she didn't contradict him. Hope swelled inside him. His blood pounded through his veins.

"It amazes me that you can negotiate million-dollar deals and not break a sweat," Nick said, his chest rising and falling. It was like he couldn't catch his breath. "You never hesitate to take risks that would make your coworkers cringe in fear."

She studied her tennis shoes, the tension shimmering off of her. "What's your point?"

He almost couldn't say his deepest desire out loud. "You wouldn't take a risk on me." Nick was relieved his voice didn't crack.

Tracy's forehead crinkled with a frown. "That's different."

Yeah, and he was hoping it was because he meant more to her than anything else. His heart was pounding so hard that it hurt. If he was wrong, he didn't think he would recover.

"The minute you thought I had an ulterior motive to get close to you, what did you do? Run," Nick said bluntly. "And you didn't look back."

She swiveled her head and glared at him. "That's your interpretation. And you're wrong. But, once again, what's your point?"

He had to ask for it. He had to make the first move, whether he was ready or not. *No pressure, though.* "I have an offer to make you."

Tracy seemed surprised. She hesitated before curiosity got the better of her. "What is it?"

His instincts told him to pull back. Divert and confuse her until she couldn't stand straight, and then go in for the kill. But that wouldn't get him what he wanted more than anything.

Nick looked deep into her eyes and didn't pull back. "Take a chance on me."

Chapter Six

The link between twins is so sacred that they always put their siblings first.

"That's it?" She couldn't believe the audacity of the man. His sheer ego! "That's your offer?"

"Yep," he replied without a smile.

He was serious! "Why would I do that?" She splayed her hands out, trying to make sense of his request. "I learn from my mistakes."

"Your only mistake was distrusting me."

"Right." Of course he would think that. It wouldn't have anything to do with the fact that few trusted him. "So, tell me, Nick. Do I get any kind of guarantee this time around?"

"No return. No guarantee."

"Wow. What a deal." She shook her head, trying to make sense of it all. "You really expect me to jump at the offer?"

"No." A muscle bunched from his jaw. "But I hope you will."

"You're asking me to give up marrying a guy who would give me all the power, money, and control I need. And for what?"

Nick nervously darted his tongue across his mouth. "For us."

Us. The simple word packed a punch. She missed being

with Nick. She yearned for it as much as she missed the make-my-toes-curl-backward moments.

Tracy had no idea how much she had once craved that kind of connection until she found it with Nick Taggart. It had exceeded anything she had known before. Surpassed any sense of belonging she felt from being a twin.

When Tracy had first gone to bed with Nick, she had nothing to lose and everything to gain. It had been a heady, scary, roller coaster that had her begging for more. The world was suddenly one big circus—bigger, better, more colorful—and she was the ringmaster.

But when their fling came to a screeching halt, she wished she had never taken the chance. After living off of her wits and shielding her heart for years, Nick inadvertently had exposed the harsh truth to her. She had been living a masquerade and didn't even know it. She wasn't the brazen and bold woman she thought she was.

The world was now a dull shade of gray. Her sense of vulnerability was a constant companion, something she had worked so hard to prevent. Tracy had always danced along the tightrope of success and failure, keeping her eye on the target and never looking down. It was easy when nothing had mattered.

She managed to fool everyone into thinking she was invincible: her colleagues, her sister, her family. Even herself. But somehow she hadn't fooled Nick. What had he seen in her that no one else did?

He reached out and brushed the line of her clenched jaw with the sweep of his knuckles.

A shower of sparks trailed behind his gentle touch. She was tempted to lean in and rest against his hand. So tempted.

"You think you know me," Tracy said, her throat tight as she held her emotions in check. "That you know what I want, but you don't."

He cradled her face in his hands and looked into her eyes. She wanted to pull away, but he wouldn't let her. She felt too raw, too exposed to handle his direct gaze.

"I do. I know what makes you tick and what drives you wild," Nick declared with a certainty that made her spine tingle. "I know your dreams, your fears, and your past. I know everything about you."

God, she hoped not. Panic fluttered in her stomach. "So why aren't you running in the other direction?"

"Because I like what I see," Nick replied and kissed her. His touch was hot and fierce. It made her head spin. Left her breathless. Rocked her world. Scared her.

She remained still as sensations stampeded over her. Nick's callused thumbs rubbed against her cheekbones and her skin stretched tight against her bones. His mouth took over hers. Her lips grew full and heavy. Voluptuous.

What was she doing? Tracy wondered as his tongue pushed insistently against her mouth. She had to stay strong and deny herself this.

But she couldn't after tasting him again. Tracy parted her lips and he invaded her mouth. She suckled the tip of his tongue, drawing him in deeper. Each thrust of his tongue echoed the increasing pressure between her legs. Her nipples tightened and stung.

Desire rippled through Tracy. She wanted to chase after the feeling. Catch it, grab it, and hold tight. She needed to feed on it and let it push away the emptiness that had been taking over.

Only Nick could give her that power. It was never like that with any other guy. When she was with Nick, Tracy felt she could take on the world. That she was invincible.

She needed to be invincible again.

Tracy tore her mouth from his and yanked at his tuxedo shirt with desperate, fumbling fingers. The snaps broke free, exposing his hard, muscular chest. She pulled the white linen off his shoulders and sculpted arms, feeling the heat billowing from his smooth, bronzed skin.

Nick licked and nibbled her ear, his hot breath curling around her like steam. She gasped as he darted his tongue in her ear. The wet caress drove her close to the edge.

Tracy pressed an open-mouth kiss against his collarbone.

His moan rumbled deep in his chest. She ventured further down his chest, indulging in the salty, masculine taste.

Nick plowed his fingers through her long hair, pulling the rubber band free. Tracy followed the path of his sternum with her mouth as she sought for his belt with her hands.

What was she thinking? Tracy twirled her tongue around Nick's hard, flat nipple. She winced as his hands flexed and tightened in her tangle of hair.

Why was she doing this? She and Nick were over. Through. Kaput. Tracy closed her eyes, trying to remember that as Nick made her feel hot and restless. This night didn't guarantee a future. The colorful lights would eventually fade, leaving nothing but gray.

Tracy wrestled with the decision to make. It wasn't easy as Nick's hands were on the move again, this time at the hem of her shirt.

The answer hit her hard and fast. She wanted Nick. Even if it didn't last. Even if she went through hell again. She wanted him more than anything else.

Tracy refused to second-guess her decision. She grabbed for Nick's belt buckle. So she was weak. So she was greedy. Especially when it came to Nicholas Taggart.

She wanted Nick and she wanted him the way it was supposed to be. No ulterior motives, no manipulation. No watching her back.

Nick's hands moved under her shirt. The fabric pulled against her sensitive skin as he sought her breasts. Pushing the bra up and out of his way, he claimed her breasts with a boldness that left her reeling.

God, she forgot how much she missed this. Tracy bit the inside of her lip as his thumbs rubbed her tight, crinkled nipples. She had made herself forget or else she would have gone crazy.

When she gave up Nick the first time, it was like ripping her heart out. But she always thought that if she became powerful enough, if she was in total control, she could get Nick back. On her own terms.

She had played it safe and missed out. She wasn't going to

make that mistake again. Tracy hurriedly pulled his zipper down and shoved his clothes past his lean hips. The sight of his cock made her wet with anticipation. She grasped his length at the base and stroked him to the weeping tip.

She wanted to take him now before the brilliantly colored world passed her by. She needed to feel every inch of him. Wrap her legs around his waist and take everything he had to offer.

"Lie down on the floor," she commanded in a husky voice. She pushed against his shoulders when he didn't respond.

"No." Nick dragged her jeans and panties off of her legs. He cupped her sex and she felt her knees buckle.

Tracy grabbed hold of his shoulders as his fingers dipped into her wetness. Each stroke tightened a powerful coil inside her, ready to spring uncontrollably.

"Lie down." She swallowed roughly, the desire thick inside her. "Please."

This time he gave in. Nick lay down and pulled her forward. She quickly straddled him before he changed his mind. Tracy grabbed the hem of her shirt, pulled it over her head and tossed it onto the heap of clothes. The bra followed and Nick covered her naked breasts with his hands.

Tracy clasped her hands onto his, reveling in the strong, possessive touch. She lowered herself onto him inch by inch. Her breath hitched during the slow, teasing descent.

Nick's hands clenched as she made her journey with pauses and retreats. She saw the muscles in his jaw trembling as he struggled for control. She saw the haze of desire in his eyes.

She let out a shuddering groan when she took all of him. Tracy instinctively rocked her hips. A blanket of sensations swept her skin. *Oh, God. Did that feel good!* Tracy smiled as she swiveled and rocked again. Her body tingled. She felt the sparks just underneath her skin.

She bucked again and again. Faster. Harder. She laughed with pure pleasure as she chased the sensations rolling inside her. Her knees rubbed against the carpet. The friction wasn't anything compared to the sliding, sleek cock inside her.

Nick guided her hips, accepting her pace. He reached for where they joined and found her clitoris. And then it hit. The climax burst free. Tracy arched her neck, tilted her head back as the wild, chaotic sensations took flight, letting her soar.

She was vaguely aware of Nick rolling her underneath him. His sweat-slick body shrouded her. He surged into her and Tracy felt her flesh grip tight. Each powerful thrust, each retreat, was wild and untamed. Almost savage.

Tracy stared into his face, tight with need. She saw it in his dark eyes. Felt how he was savoring each move. Nick was willing to take the wildest, craziest ride of his life. If she was by his side.

He wasn't promising her forever. He wasn't even promising her marriage.

She closed her eyes and she felt the kick in her bloodstream. The fierce sensations gathering inside her. Tracy held tightly onto Nick as he strained against the impending release.

He was worth the risk.

No, Tracy thought as joy tickled deep inside her. *They* were.

Chapter Seven

With every set of twins, there is a "good" and a "bad" sibling.

An hour later reality hit her upside the head. Tracy gasped as she bolted upright from the bed, the sheets slithering down her naked body. "Oh, my God."

Nick sat up, his muscles tight, his senses on full alert. "What? What is it?"

She covered her face with her hands. "I just had sex with the best man in my wedding!"

Ow. That hurt. "It was more than that," he said in a low, harsh tone. *I'm more than that*, he wanted to say. "And you know it."

"In my honeymoon suite!" she wailed.

The woman was getting hysterical. He'd never seen her like this. Was this another ruse? "Tracy . . ."

She shoved her hands in her mussed up hair. "Can I *get* any more trailer trash?"

No trick. Her eyes glimmered with unshed tears. The taut, pale skin clearly indicated her distress. Nick reached for her. "Tracy—"

"I'm one step away from those TV talk shows. I can see the name of the episode right now: 'Women Who Cheat on Their

Wedding Night in the Honeymoon Suite With the Best Man.'"
She winced and shook her head. "But I'll be the only guest for
the hour because no one else would be so *stupid* to do such a
thing."

"Tracy!" His sharp tone got her attention.

"You have to get out of here." She pushed at his shoulder,
but he refused to budge. "Go! Before Devlin finds us. I can't
call off the wedding while you're lying naked next to me."

She had been planning to call off the wedding. Satisfaction
flooded through his veins. That's all he needed to hear. It was
time to come clean. "Devlin's not going to notice anything."

"Your naïveté shocks me." She shifted on the bed and
started pushing his leg with her feet. "And it's very inconve-
nient at the moment."

Nick grasped her wrists and pulled her against him. He
swallowed a groan as her soft curves pressed against his chest.
"Devlin is not going to notice because he's not showing up."

Tracy stilled. "Say what?"

"He's not coming by the honeymoon suite," Nick explained,
wondering what he could say to make her wiggle against him
again. "He's on his way to Las Vegas. With Jessica."

Her expression darkened like storm clouds. "Run that by
me again," she said with dangerous calm.

"Since his bride bailed," Nick said as he lowered Tracy down
on her pillow, "Devlin's going to try and convince Jessica to
marry him."

Tracy snorted at the thought. "Good luck with that. I hope
Jessica gives him hell."

Nick held her arms on either side of her head. He didn't
want to think about his boss's mission. He had a quest of his
own to complete.

"How long have you known?" Tracy asked, arching her
back as he settled between her legs.

"We've known since the wedding rehearsal that you traded
places with your sister." He paused, wondering if it was too
soon to test her newfound trust in him. "We weren't sure why."

Her arms jerked under his grasp. Tracy's gaze nervously
darted away. "That doesn't really matter . . ."

She didn't fully trust him. He pushed back the wave of disappointment, knowing he was going to have to be patient. Sooner or later she'd trust him enough to mention her trip to New York. And one of these days she'd trust him enough to marry him.

"We also weren't sure if you were coming back," he added as he stroked his thumb along her wrists.

"Of course I was." Tracy looked offended by the suggestion that she would take the cowardly route.

"I knew you would," Nick admitted, lowering himself onto her. "Which gave me the opportunity to stall you."

She bit down on her bottom lip. "Why did you want to do that?" she asked softly.

The beat of his heart pounded loudly in his ears. "Maybe I didn't want to watch the love of my life getting married to my best friend."

She gasped softly. "Oh."

Nick got braver when she met his gaze. The love in her eyes mirrored his own. "Maybe I wanted a second chance," he said as he threaded his fingers through hers.

He watched her throat work as she swallowed roughly. "You have it," Tracy whispered.

"Or," he said as he brushed his mouth against her lips, "maybe I liked the challenge of stealing the bride."

He felt her smile. "Took you long enough," she said, and captured his mouth with hers.

Three months later Tracy leaned against the balustrade of her sister's elegant veranda. She sipped the white wine from her glass and stared up at the moonlit sky. The stars seemed to wink back at her, as if they knew all of her wishes had been fulfilled.

"I am never trading places with you again," Jessica declared.

"Stop being so dramatic." Tracy rolled her eyes as the night breeze wafted over her. She pulled the tangled blond strands from her face and hooked them behind her ear, wondering why Nick liked it when she wore her hair down. Or why she indulged him, for that matter.

"I'm serious." Jessica thrust her chin out. "Nothing will ever provoke me to do that again."

Tracy glanced over to where Nick and Devlin were talking. Her pulse leapt at the sight of Nick, and a secret smile played briefly on her mouth before she returned her attention to her sister. "What are you griping about? Everything turned out perfectly."

"In spite of your plan," Jessica pointed out. "Not because of it."

Tracy decided not to argue. One had to humor pregnant sisters. "Let's hope there will never be a cause for another sister switch."

Jessica shuddered delicately. "There will *never* be a good enough reason. Got that?"

"Got it." Nine months of agreeing with her sister was going to be agony.

Jessica took a sip of juice from her wineglass. "So you and Nick are getting married?"

"Yep."

"Let me give you some advice about weddings."

"Here we go," Tracy muttered to herself. Jessica was the first to get married and the first to get pregnant. She was going to revel in her expert status for as long as she could. Tracy wondered if all of her "because I'm the oldest" moments were going to come back and haunt her.

"Take it from someone who had the ritzy ceremony and the Vegas quickie in one night," Jessica said. "Go for the quickie."

"As you wish, Obi-Wan Kenobi."

"I'm not kidding." Jessica leaned forward and lowered her voice. "When I wasn't on the verge of vomiting because I was so afraid of being found out, I was in physical pain. Not to mention going insane."

"Really?" Mental and physical anguish. Sounded like a regular Parks family get-together.

"During the wedding reception, I could barely move my back." Jessica motioned at her spine. "It was like someone knocked the breath right out of me."

"You don't say?" Tracy nibbled her bottom lip. "What do you think caused it?"

"It might have something to do with all the boning in your wedding gown," Jessica suggested and glared at her.

"Don't blame me." Tracy held her hand up in self-defense. "Mom picked it out."

"That figures. Anyway, once I managed to breathe normally again, I was having some bizarre conversation with you, but it was all one-sided." She motioned at her ears. "Like we were on walkie-talkies, but mine wasn't working."

Uh-oh. "Did I say anything profound?"

"Had you done so, I would have checked myself in the psych ward."

"Ha, ha. Funny." Tracy wrinkled her nose. "That's coming out of your next birthday present. What did I say?" *Please don't let it be something like, "Yes, Nick! Yessssssss!"*

"Weird stuff like 'brides should carry cell phones.' And 'what's taking you so long?'"

"Huh." She took a gulp of her wine but didn't taste a thing. There was no way Jessica could have heard her that night. She must have suggested it to her sister when she had been begging for forgiveness for missing the wedding. That had to be it.

"But I'm not warning you off getting married," Jessica assured her. "I wasn't too sure about marrying Devlin. But what do I do? I go through two wedding ceremonies with him in one night."

"You didn't have to."

"I know, but somewhere along the way I fell in love, and it turned out he preferred me all along." Jessica grimaced. "No offense."

"Believe me, none taken."

Jessica's eyes lit up. "And the sexual attraction between Devlin and me is a bonus."

Tracy closed her eyes in protest. "I don't want to hear it."

"I always thought Devlin was gorgeous, but I wouldn't call it sexual attraction. Then after our wedding reception—pow!"

"Pow?" Tracy repeated. "What do you mean, pow?"

"It was like I was having a life-altering orgasm without any warning."

Tracy choked on her drink. The wine splurted out of her mouth before she could clamp her hand against her lips.

"Now look who's being dramatic." Jessica let out a long-suffering sigh. "Are you shocked that I said the word orgasm? Or that I've experienced them?"

"No to all of the above," Tracy said in between coughs. "Now about this random orgasm thing . . . Has that happened to you before"—she cringed, not sure if she wanted to know—"or since?"

Jessica pursed her lips as she thought about it. "Well, there was that one week. But it happened way before Devlin showed up in Seattle."

"Oh?"

"I figured I was coming down with something." Jessica brushed the concern aside with the wave of her hand. "Like a form of heat stroke. Or mono."

"Yeah . . . I can see where you could make that kind of mistake." She raised her glass for another sip but realized it was empty. "Why didn't you tell me about it?"

Jessica shrugged. "You were off at the COMDEX convention."

Where I first met Nick! Tracy gripped her wineglass, vaguely surprised it didn't snap under her whitened knuckles. *Son of a bitch, there might be something to those urban legends about twins!*

"It passed after a couple of days and I never thought about it until my wedding night. Now I feel it all the time. Every. Single. Night."

"I bet you do," Tracy muttered under her breath.

Jessica glanced over at the men and lowered her voice another level. "It can happen more than once a night. I could be fast asleep and then hootchie-wawa!" she exclaimed, raising her hands up to the sky. "I tell you, I'm exhausted."

"Uh-*huh*." Okay, life was so unfair. Her sister got double the pleasure, double the fun. But was she getting any frequency from Jessica's side? Hell, no.

"Last night was really wild," Jessica confided.

"Yeah." Tracy froze in midnod. "I mean, yeah?"

"You wouldn't believe what happened. I almost—"

"Fainted?"

Jessica drew back and studied her sister. "How do you know that?"

Tracy touched her forehead with her fingertips. "I felt a little dizzy myself last night."

"Really?"

"Maybe it's one of those twin things," Tracy suggested as she stared at her empty wineglass. "Like I'm having sympathy morning sickness."

"Aw, come on." Jessica gave Tracy a playful push. "You don't believe that."

Tracy shrugged. "Anything is possible."

Jessica's mouth quirked. "Then you're in for it for the next nine months."

Tracy frowned. Her sister didn't need to look so pleased at the prospect. Knowing her luck, she'd get the hootchie-wawa moment when Jessica gave birth. Her pelvic muscles flinched at the thought.

"Um, Jessica." Tracy's knees knocked together and she struggled to remain upright. "Speaking as this child's one and only aunt, I think you should go for full anesthesia when giving labor."

Jessica chuckled at the thought. "No, I'm going to have it as naturally as I can. I'm quite determined about it. Here, let me get you a refill."

Maybe there was a need for one more sister switch, Tracy thought as she watched her sister walk away. This definitely went under the heading of a good enough reason. First she needed to find the phone number of her sister's obstetrician . . .

SPENCER
FOR....EVER

Morgan Leigh

Chapter One

Kip Spencer was halfway to the back of Charley's Hardware Store when the chimes over the door sounded, and she followed him in. He slowed his stride, but didn't stop until he'd reached the back table at the rear of the store and the old-timers milling around it. He figured there was safety in numbers.

Conversation came to a halt; a female in their midst was cause for shock, and by the look on the men's faces, this one in particular had the attention of every male in the shop.

Arden Prescott was back in town. Kip got the feeling that he was the only one not pleased by the fact.

He forced himself not to look. *Lot's wife turned to a pillar of salt when she looked back on Sodom and Gomorrah,* he thought. What might happen to him if he faced Arden head-on? Having had glimpses of her at various intervals today, he'd kept a good distance between them. He'd experienced her closeness once before—the heat, the need that he'd always banked. It was long ago, but he was afraid he'd go up in flames if he turned and took a good, long look at her.

Pouring himself a cup of coffee from the pot that Charley kept for his regular patrons, he took two gulps of the now tepid brew. It was the consistency of mud after hours of sitting out, and he grimaced at the bitter taste, but it hit the spot. It gave him the fortitude he needed to steel himself against the woman he once thought was so right for him—the same one who convinced him just how wrong he was.

With a deep breath, he turned around, the muscle in his jaw jumping as he faced Arden. At one time, he'd have given every penny he owned to see her again. Now he'd pay a privateer's booty if she'd go back to wherever it was she'd been.

Standing only ten feet from where he was rooted to the spot, she tried to appear fascinated in the displays of scented car air fresheners that hung from the peg on the shelf. She was as bad at being contemplative as she was at being inconspicuous.

Why the hell did she have to look so incredibly sexy?

He hadn't seen her since he was nineteen. None of the Prescotts had been on the Vineyard in a decade, and though they still owned the huge manor on the bluff, it had been closed up after that last summer they were here.

The years had been damn good to her, though; she was as beautiful as he remembered—more so, even. She was a woman now.

Her tall, sleek body was covered by a crisp white tank top. It was tucked into a pair of denim shorts that stopped mid-thigh. His eyes traveled down her sinfully long legs; even the work boots she wore were adorable on her. It was the height of summer, and she looked like she was working construction. All she needed was a tool belt and a hard hat to complete the outfit, he mused, his mouth curving in a reluctant grin. He tipped his head, deciding against the hat; her golden and honey blond tresses would be covered, and Kip had enjoyed many a fantasy in his youth dreaming about that hair. It hung straight and silky down to the middle of her back, just right for tangling his fingers into.

He swallowed the lump forming in his throat. Christ, but she still had the ability to kick-start his heart. It beat like a drum in his chest as he shamelessly stared at her.

He thought he saw her yesterday, up on the widow's walk at Prescott Manor. He was on the back deck of his much smaller house, and something made him glance up at the mansion. Nothing was amiss, and he'd shrugged it off.

Then this morning, when he was in line at the post office, Kip could've sworn that he was being watched. He couldn't shake the restless feeling. He'd searched the room, but his gaze was drawn to the window, and what lay beyond it.

Across the street, at a table outside the little café, sat the source of his uneasiness. His vision locked on her, and Arden's eyes went wide when she realized she'd been spotted, and she'd quickly averted her eyes.

It was no wonder he felt like a wall of seawater had crashed down on him.

He hadn't even been within shouting distance, and yet his body reacted as it always had; his heart rate picked up, his skin heated, and he wished he'd worn a roomier pair of pants; his cock had swelled to a painful thickness in his jeans. That pissed him off as much as the idea of her stalking him. He didn't want to want that woman. But he did. God help him.

Up until the last summer she was on the island, the division of the classes had kept him and Arden from socializing in the same groups. She was rich, and only here three months a year. He was local, a fisherman's kid, and poor by comparison. He was full of pride and arrogance, and she was shy, timid. They shouldn't have been a match.

But ten years ago, they'd shocked everyone by forging a friendship, though it was tentative at first. There had been bad blood between their families for years. But he liked Arden, not her money, and she seemed to like him, too. Neither wanted old rivalries to come between them.

When they'd begun to get more involved, Kip would've died if he frightened her by moving too fast. He'd taken it slow, holding hands, talking, and they became closer as each day went by. He'd never even kissed her, but in his dreams, Kip knew her intimately. To him, Arden was worth the wait.

Then on that Labor Day weekend, things went terribly wrong between them. She left the next day, and she never came back. It took him longer to recover than he cared to admit.

He'd be damned if he ever let himself go through that hell again.

The last few days, a feeling of déjà vu had plagued him, but Kip attributed it to a storm that was fast approaching the island. He was the captain of his own charter boat business now, and he taught sports fishing to his clients. The summer months were his biggest revenue, and he'd be the first to admit that he'd done some crazy stunts when they were after a huge catch, but even he wouldn't risk lives to haul in a prize-winner when forecasts came with warnings of dangerous swells and alerts of high winds. He'd been forced to cancel bookings for the weekend.

With two days free, he used the time off to do chores he'd neglected since the season started. Now that he realized who was messing with his peace of mind, he almost wished he'd taken the chance and sailed the boat up the coast like he'd planned. The tight twisting in his gut told him Arden Prescott could do more damage than even Mother Nature was capable of. Not to his business, but to his heart.

He didn't know why she was back on the Vineyard, or why she was following him all over town, but he wasn't sure he could remain unaffected long enough to find out. Even if he gave her a wide berth, she was his very close neighbor. The land her house sat on used to belong to his family nearly a century before. He didn't like the odds of avoiding her. His brain might fight against speaking to her again, but every other part of him was amenable to it. Damn it all.

His eyes swept over her again, wondering how the hell he was going to hold out and keep away from her until September, when the summer people wrapped up their vacations and went back to their real lives. Labor Day was almost two full months away!

Then she tipped her head, and a growl threatened to escape as his mouth went dry, imagining his tongue licking along the smooth, warm column of her exposed throat.

Her teeth sank into the soft flesh of her bottom lip, as if undecided between two items on the shelf.

Would she bite her lip like that to hold in a scream when pleasure commanded her? he wondered. Or would she give her passion free rein? How would her teeth feel sinking into his—

"Okay, that's about all I can take for one day," he grumbled, swallowing the sudden flood of saliva in his mouth. His hand trembled as he set the coffee mug on the table.

As if he had tunnel vision, he afforded her only a curt shake of his head and a look of dire warning before clamping a hand around her arm and escorting her out of the shop. She was going whether she wanted to or not.

"Kip, what the hell—"

He didn't slow down, but one brow rose in mild surprise. "You've learned to swear since you left. And you remembered my name. How nice."

She began to struggle. "I'll say a lot more than that if you don't take your paws off me."

She tried to twist her arm free from his grasp; he merely tightened his grip on her small, curiously firm bicep. He wished he didn't notice the little details. It was only going to make it that much harder to tell her to get lost.

"Ow, you're hurting me—"

When they'd exited the store, he stopped to stare down at her. "Stop being a baby, Arden. I'm not hurting anything but your pride." His head dipped until he was almost eye to eye with her. "And you brought this on yourself, princess."

The muscle beneath his palm bunched as she stiffened, her eyes narrowing to slits.

He looked around for a place that would lend them a little more privacy. He almost snarled at her as his gut clenched; it irked him that even her anger stirred his blood. He needed to put a stop to this before he abandoned his own pride, and let the wrong head do the thinking for him.

Deciding that anywhere was better than where they were, he started off again with Arden in tow. Lowering his voice as they passed people on the sidewalk, he tipped his head toward her. "You may not care about making a scene, but this is my home, and I'd rather not give the gossips any more fat t'chew."

She gasped, and Kip took wicked delight as his words sank

in. Her eyes darted across the street, up the block, then back to him as it dawned on her just where they were—Main Street, downtown Menemsha, Martha's Vineyard Island.

He chuckled humorlessly at her mortified expression. "That's right, kiddo. You seem to have forgotten how small this community is. You can sneeze on one side of the island, and someone from the opposite side will shout out a 'God bless you.'"

The wind picked up, and her hair whipped unheeded around her face. He tore his gaze from her before the thoughts in his head turned to actions. He ached to tuck the wayward strands behind her ear so he could see her face, press his lips to her soft cheek, follow a path to her jaw, her neck, her—Damn it! She was getting to him, and it was pissing him off.

He sneered at her. "You're supposed to be the refined, well-mannered one here. This isn't the big city where no one pays you any mind." He shrugged. "When you go home, look around; you'll see the difference."

Kip could just imagine what people were thinking right about now. Things moved at a sedate, more leisurely pace up here. Odd behavior was remarkable, and her conduct today would surely keep lips flapping for weeks.

Until the next time, he silently amended, rolling his eyes. There was still plenty of summer left. He had no doubt if she kept this up, she'd be guilty of some other newsworthy event before the end of the season. He shuddered to think what that might be.

This was different from the last time they'd locked horns, though. She was only seventeen then, and when she'd run home crying, he'd been left feeling like a bully. He wished he hadn't had to yell at her, but she'd put herself in danger, and she'd scared the hell out of him. His temper was warranted.

Somewhere in those ten years, she'd found a fighting spirit that was turning him on like crazy. He wished being in private wasn't just as dangerous as being in public, or they'd be having this conversation back at his cottage.

She grumbled. Kip grinned, reasonably certain they were actual words, but she knew when she was being chastised.

It didn't take her long to rally, however. "There's something you should know, but it'll keep."

He just grunted, not really caring what she had to say at the moment. She kept pace with him, walking at a fast clip past shops and tourists; she didn't even seem to mind anymore that he had hold of her. In fact, he'd bet his boat that she liked it.

When he'd first spotted her this morning, he was amused enough by her less than skillful reconnaissance that he decided not to confront her; it didn't matter that he hadn't a clue why she was tailing him. If she wanted to make a fool out of herself, let everyone in town observe her odd behavior, then who was he to object?

It wasn't until he got a really good look at his would-be stalker at Charley's did he realize that not only had she not gone unnoticed by at least the locals, but that he could be in serious trouble with this woman. She was too enticing for her own damn good.

She had a life somewhere else, and he'd built one here, he reminded himself. It couldn't work.

Why was he mulling it over? It wasn't going to happen. *They* weren't going to happen. Period. Whatever her intentions were, he couldn't worry about them. It was his own behavior he was beginning to have serious doubts about.

It rankled that nothing he told himself could stop the sensual heat racing through him and settling in his groin simply from touching her bare arm. His control was chipping away with each thought, every glance. He didn't bother to hide his annoyance as he ordered, "Just keep your pretty mouth shut until I find somewhere less visible to watchful eyes. Then you can explain this outrageous behavior of yours."

Her mouth opened and closed again like so many fish he'd caught on a hook or in his nets. When he shot her a murderous glance, she thought better of speaking, but she let him lead the way.

At the corner, he hustled her into the alley, allowing them at least a modicum of privacy he'd been looking for. He wanted answers, and this had to be the place he was going to get them.

Spinning her to face him, her startled eyes looked at him as if she questioned his sanity. He wasn't so sure of it himself.

He backed her against the brick wall; even her hands were flat to the side of the building. Only then did he trust himself to release her.

His own palms pressed to the wall on either side of her head as he dipped his toward her. His nostrils flared as her perfume surrounded him, and Kip forced himself to concentrate. He had to forget the memory that the arousing scent invoked, and remember the anger and bitterness that resulted from it. There was no other way. He was wise enough to know that if he let his guard down even a little, he was a goner.

His eyes pinned to her sea green ones, his jaw so tight it ached, he said, "Okay, Prescott. You've got my attention." His voice sounded rough, strained. He hoped he looked more menacing than he felt.

"Huh?" Arden looked up at him, totally at a loss for words. She'd been hoping for a confrontation. She just didn't think it would be here, on the street. And she certainly hadn't anticipated this. She knew he wouldn't welcome her with open arms, but she at least thought he'd be civil. This wasn't going at all like she'd planned.

Of course, following him around today might have something to do with his ire, she thought.

"Why are you stalking me?"

She was surprised he'd use that word. "Stalking you?"

He frowned, and advanced closer. "What would you call it?"

She had nowhere to go. And he acted as if he was perfectly justified in crowding her.

She tipped her face up, showing bravado that was as fake as a three-dollar bill. "I'd call it giving you the opportunity to greet me like a gentleman should. I've been gone a long time. You could've come up to the house when you saw that I was back."

His eyes darkened from a bright blue to a deep navy color, belying his outward calm. "I didn't know you were back for sure until just this morning when I realized you were trailing me all over town. And if you ask me, you weren't gone nearly long enough." He dipped his head closer, his lips brushing along her cheek. His breath fanned her ear, and his voice lowered to nearly a whisper as he informed her, "And I stopped being a gentleman a long, long time ago."

Arden's eyes drifted shut. She had to remember to breathe. With him so close, her thoughts became muddled, confused. Her knees almost buckled when his lips touched her cheek; the rough stubble on his jaw sent shivers down her spine. She ached to slide her fingers through his hair, to turn her head and pull his mouth to hers. She wanted it as much as she wanted anything. But revealing weakness to this man would be a critical error.

She had to show some grit, or he'd use this bullying routine to keep her at a distance. She'd had enough intimidation in her life. Kip may not want her here *now*, but he was a good man, and she wanted more than acrimony between them. She knew in her heart that she belonged here. And she belonged with him.

Pulling herself together, her hands left the wall to rest flat on his chest. Then she pushed. "Keep it up, and you'll find out the hard way that occasionally I'm no lady."

His face went blank. Taking her at her word, he stepped out of her personal space.

Parts of him were still vulnerable to a well-placed knee, but he recognized a challenge. She'd fight back if she had to.

Not that she wanted to, Arden thought. She'd like nothing better than to slide her arms around his ribs, sink into his warmth.

His brow rose. "I'm impressed," he said.

"With what?"

He grinned. "You swear now, you stand up for yourself . . ."

Arden looked away, knowing the hell she'd gone through in

order to *get* that backbone. Her ex-husband had never laid a hand on her in anger, but there were other ways to abuse a soul.

"Arden?"

Where annoyance had made his chest rumble moments ago, now concern laced his voice. She slammed shut the door to her past, except the part with this man in it, and met his gaze. "I'm an adult now, Kip. And I've learned to go after what I want."

Her hands slid over his T-shirt, his pecs rippling beneath it. A rush of power surged through her, seeing that cocky grin of his falter. His eyes darkened with desire and suspicion, and she bit the inside of her cheek. She couldn't reveal her triumph just yet. He wasn't ready.

"And what exactly is it that you want?" He asked.

Now's your chance, she thought.

With deliberate slowness, her hands snaked up around his neck, into his coal black hair. She tipped her face up, staring at his eyes, but his were focused on her mouth.

She said one word, "You," and pulled his head down for her kiss.

He groaned into her mouth, and his body seemed to sag in relief. His hands slid off the brick and wrapped around her waist, bringing her in contact with his hard angles, insinuating her smooth legs between the springy hair of his.

His tongue darted into her mouth, searching its mate, and Arden was terrified she'd broken the spell when she whimpered, overwhelmed to be tasting him for the first time.

She needn't have worried. He was as caught up in the moment as she was. His arms seized around her, lifting her off her feet as he rolled his hips, his sex grinding against her cleft.

Her gasp of painful pleasure was answered by a growl of need, and he lifted his mouth, only to change angles and devour her lips again. He was all male, and he was ravenous, as if he were starving for her.

She wanted to see him, look into his eyes, but when hers opened to slits, his were squeezed shut, as if he couldn't stand to know who he was kissing. It wasn't relief he felt to be kissing her; it was defeat. Anguish that he couldn't resist. From the strong band of his arms around her, his erection so hard between them, he wanted her. That much was obvious. But it was tearing him up inside.

The truth hit her hard. Plunging into Nantucket Sound would've felt less icy. Her fingers clutched at his hair and pulled.

"Ahh! What—?" Kip's eyes opened, glaring down at her as if she'd lost her mind.

She furiously struggled to be free of his embrace. When he finally let her loose, he stepped back from her, putting his hands up in surrender. She wiped the back of her hand over her mouth. "The next time you wanna get off, Spencer, find someone else. I don't want to be your biggest mistake."

That got his back up. He retaliated, his eyes still dark with passion. Temper replaced lust. "You started this, baby. You kissed me."

"Yeah, I did. Because I want you."

"Well . . ."

Her throat closed on the lump forming there, and tears threatened. "I saw your face, Kip. You had your eyes closed tight. Like kissing me was a nightmare." She nearly choked on a sob. She'd come back for him, and he considered his body's response to her a betrayal.

His eyes closed again, but he didn't deny it.

"Uh-huh. So I was right," she said. Stepping around him, she retreated down the alley, back the way they'd come. She turned, walking backwards. "I'm sorry I made you sacrifice your principles."

Then she spun on her heel and ran the rest of the way, rounding the corner, getting as far away from him as she possibly could. An argument had ruined them years ago, but it was nothing compared to the humiliation she just experienced. She didn't know if she'd recover from this one.

Chapter Two

The storm, strong as any nor'easter raged outside; lightning brightened the sky and thunder clapped so loud the walls shuddered. Arden felt akin to the tempest as she stood at the bay window, looking into the night. The fury and destruction were parallel to what her life was like right now. She'd taken a chance on coming back here, hoping to recapture the sense of well-being she'd always felt when she'd summered here. She'd made so many mistakes in her adult life that when she was finally free of obligations and expectations, the Vineyard was clearly the only place she could go. It all came back around to this island.

She'd lived through the deaths of both her parents, her mother to cancer when she was nineteen, and her father dying of the same disease six years later. She'd endured four years of a loveless marriage of convenience, trusting more than she knew she should've. Then along with the realization that her husband was verbally abusive, she also learned too late that he was a compulsive gambler and really, really bad at his habit. She got out before he lost everything she had, including Prescott Manor. She'd be damned if he would get this.

She saw nothing through the darkness, but it made her ponder how strange it all was. She'd done everything her father wanted her to do. Then Gregory took over that role. But when the prospect of losing this place became a very real possibility, she'd found a backbone, gumption she didn't even know she had.

Her ace in the hole was that Gregory cared more about his social standing in the community than he did about the house on the island. She'd been careful never to bring him here. She didn't want him to see it in dollar value, nor just how much it meant to her.

When she asked for the divorce, she'd stood toe to toe with him and informed him that if she so much as heard a whisper of him protesting it or demanding even one more penny, she'd expose him for the fraud he was. He wouldn't be welcomed in any of the circles in which he'd become accustomed to traveling. The threat had worked. Last week, before she handed over her keys to the brownstone in the city, she'd accepted her final divorce papers by way of private messenger. It was done.

She'd figured out how she'd make a living, and be able to live on the Vineyard at the same time. In the months leading up to her freedom, she'd secured a loan with the bank for renovations to the manor, thanks to some of her father's connections. With her credit report in shambles thanks to her husband, whom she liked to refer to as the albatross around her neck, she wouldn't have been able to get one on her own. She'd earned a degree in interior design before she got married, and she'd wheeled and dealed with contacts of her own for material, fabric, and furniture. Prescott Manor had officially been renamed Prescott House, and she went from owning a large estate home to owning a bed and breakfast. This place was her link to peace, contentment. But without Kip, she didn't think she'd find happiness here now.

Another flash lit the black night, and Arden saw the railing of the widow's walk. The only entrance to the narrow walkway was through this room in the attic, which she planned to make her quarters when she started accepting guests. This was her favorite space in the whole house. The built-in bookshelves that lined the walls were filled with dusty romance novels that she'd read over and over again as a young girl, too shy to find out for herself what it was all about.

She smiled, remembering that Kip was her girlhood fantasy. She'd be on the widow's walk every day, looking down onto the harbor when he and his dad came into port after work. He was like her very own sea captain, or more appropriately, her pirate, with the gold earring he wore, and his shoulder-length black hair pulled back with a strip of leather. His skin was darkly tanned from the sun, muscular from hours working the nets on the trawler, and so handsome that she couldn't help but dream of him, want him for her own.

Love that could conquer all was in those books, and men who were honorable, kind, protective. Kip fit the description of every hero she'd ever read. He possessed pride, compassion, and fairness.

They'd only ever fought once, but it was a whopper. She'd done something he'd considered dangerous, dumb. Thinking about what could have happened to her had scared him, and he'd lashed out. Then he and her mother argued. She'd looked for him that night, but he'd made sure they didn't meet. She left with her parents the next day. It was the last time she'd been on the island until last week.

That's when she'd learned something new about Kip. That man held a grudge. She saw it in his eyes today. If he only knew what he meant to her, he'd know she wasn't a threat.

She stepped out onto the widow's walk, her bare feet slick on the wet planks. She skimmed her hand over the worn, splintered wood of the railing. The wind rushed around her, sending her hair and her nightshirt billowing out. The cold rain felt like needles stippling her skin, but she barely gave it notice. She had something else on her mind.

Crouching down, she carefully swept her fingers over a rough section of the timber on the rail. It was there! She closed her eyes, knowing it was the omen she'd been looking for. She couldn't give up. No matter how Kip treated her now, she had to break through that wall of resistance he'd erected and get her man. She sighed in relief, leaning against the wood with words carved into it that still rang true after ten years.

* * *

Kip pulled open cabinets and dragged boxes from the closets, sure that he'd put the candles all in one place the last time they'd lost power. The lights had been flickering on and off for almost half an hour. With the force of the storm bearing down on the island, it wouldn't be long before the whole Vineyard was plunged into darkness.

He found the kerosene, and topped off the hurricane lamp that had been collecting dust on the sideboard. Next, he filled gallon jugs with water, cursing himself that he wasn't better prepared for the storm. He knew it was coming. It was the reason he was home this weekend. When he'd run errands today, it was on his list to buy a new bulb for his flashlight. But then he saw Arden, and his schedule had been shot all to hell.

The muscle in his jaw twitched as he bit down hard, her parting words still making his gut pitch as bad as any sailor who was dumb enough to be out on the water in this weather.

"I'm sorry I made you sacrifice your principles."

She hadn't made him do a damn thing, but she was right about his principles. When her lips touched his, all he wanted to do was cast his pride aside and love her, long and slow, just once.

He'd always made sure the women he'd taken to his bed knew he'd never marry, never commit to more than casual dating. Every encounter he'd walked away from, both he and his partner were sexually satisfied, free of guilt or promises. No harm done on either side.

But Arden. Christ! She looked at him today as if he were the love of her life. Not even the sight of her gorgeous body, or the feel of her hands sliding over him had the effect that one look did. It was why he'd closed his eyes so tight. He'd swear he was looking into her soul, and he saw the real Arden, not the one he'd conjured in his mind—the one that made it possible for him to forget her.

He actually considered using her desire against her to take what she offered. Maybe then he'd finally get her out of his system, and bid her farewell at the end of the season.

If they'd been anywhere else, he might've, Kip thought. If they'd been here in his house, he'd have kept on kissing her. He'd hate himself for it afterward, and he'd be a bastard for doing it, but he would've stripped her of her clothes and dispensed of his own to slide into her, to finally have what they'd both been building toward so long ago.

God, even now he wanted that! Wanted to be so deep inside her, plunging into her warmth, dragging cries of pleasure from her throat. It was all he'd thought of since this afternoon, but his shame lay in the fact that she recognized it, and was hurt by his reaction to the image.

"Damn it all to hell, anyway," he growled. "She should've just stayed gone. We'd both be better off," he said out loud.

Now he was going to have to apologize for his own outrageous behavior. He owed her that, he supposed. She said she wanted him, but she didn't deserve to be used because of it.

He sighed just as the lights flickered again, and gave up the fight. He stood where he was, anticipating the electricity to come back on in a few seconds, but it didn't, and he made his way to the sideboard where he'd left the lamp. Lightning flashed outside, and through the sliding glass doors, something caught his eye up at Prescott Manor. He paused, staring up the hill, waiting for light to replace the blackness again so he could see it.

"You little idiot!" he shouted as he saw Arden up on the widow's walk, just like he'd sworn he'd seen yesterday. Only this time, it was dark, wet, and the gales ten times more powerful than the soft summer breezes that usually blew in from the harbor. That fool woman was up there, standing against the onslaught of a dangerous storm, her white shirt plastered to her body, so drenched he could see her curves with every strike of lightning, the rain pummeling her face and hair. If he weren't so angry, the sight would be purely erotic.

He shook his head, grabbed his slicker from the back of his dining room chair, and threw open the door. The lightning lit the sky again, and at first he thought she'd gone back inside.

But as his eyes adjusted to the darkness, he could see her crouching down against the rail, her white shirt standing out through the inky nothingness.

Raincoat on, he shifted to close the door firmly against the elements, determined to go up to the manor and give her a piece of his mind. Wood could be heard breaking away and becoming debris that flew like projectiles in the swirling wind. She'd been away from the island too long; she obviously didn't remember just how dangerous these summer storms could be.

He turned again toward the mansion, and a bolt of lightning brightened the night as he looked up. His heart stopped dead, flat-lined. His stomach rolled at the sight, and for a split second fear paralyzed him.

And then he ran, adrenaline pushing him harder and faster than he'd ever moved in his life. He couldn't even take a breath until he reached Arden. *God, please,* he thought, his eyes never leaving that spot on the widow's walk as he sprinted up his lawn onto the Prescott grounds. He slipped and fell more than once, but he didn't stop. He couldn't. She needed him.

The next flash brought a choking howl of relief. She was still there; hanging onto the deck where the railing had given way, her legs kicking at air as she struggled to lift herself back onto the walk, but—

"Ah, God," he rasped as one of Arden's hands slipped on the wet wood, and she almost plummeted back to the earth. One hand still gripped a rail, but he doubted that post was any more stable than the ones that had torn off. He wanted to shout for her to hang on, help was coming, but she wouldn't hear him above the roar of the rain and wind. He couldn't pull enough air into his lungs to yell anyway. She was dangling three stories up, and unless he could get in the house, there wasn't a damn thing he could do to save her.

He found the back entrance to the manor and tried the handle. Locked. "Damn it!"

With as much force as he could muster, his elbow punched through the thick window above the knob, sending shards of glass shattering onto the tile inside the house. He reached in, unlocked the door, and burst through it, running and tripping through the maze of furniture, papers, and boxes until he felt a banister along the wall. He'd never been in the manor, but he knew "up" would lead him to Arden. He took the stairs two at a time; the chill that gripped him wasn't cold, but stark, desperate fear.

When he hit the landing on the second floor, he had to feel along the hallway, opening doors, searching for the flight of steps that would take him to the attic. It was at the opposite end, and when he found it, he heard a most unmanly sob, and realized it was his own.

He bolted up the narrow passageway, urgency and darkness making his normally agile frame clumsy as he reached the open attic floor; he stumbled over a chair, then the bed. The room lit again from outside, and he spotted the bay window straight ahead, and to the right of it the door that opened to the widow's walk. He lunged for it, terrified that he might already be too late.

Edging out onto the deck, he cast his raincoat aside, cautiously making his way along the wall. Keeping his shoulder to the building, he didn't trust the soundness of the weather-beaten, untreated wood. He prayed with every heartbeat, and as he rounded the corner, he let go of the breath he was holding. She was still there, one arm wrapped around the post at the elbow, the other hand trying to find something solid to latch onto.

He reached out, careful not to frighten her or to put himself too close to the edge and pitch himself over, too. Deciding against using the rails as leverage, he lay flat on the deck and seized her free hand in both of his, holding as tight as he could.

He gave her a second to rest her other arm, and sob that there was hope of survival. But they weren't out of danger yet. He hollered above the storm, "You'll have to pull yourself up, Arden. There's nothing sturdy enough for me to brace against."

"Don't let me go, Kip," came her thin voice, but even as

terror filled her, her arm unwound from the post and gripped their clasped ones. Damn, he was proud of her courage.

"You fall, I fall," he vowed, his own voice raw with emotion. She was a fighter, and he'd see her through this. His muscles bunched, and he pulled hard. Her head emerged from below the deck, her face a mask of fear. She looked like hell, but it was the most beautiful sight he'd ever seen. Their eyes met, and he grinned assuredly. "That's it, sweetheart, hang on tight," he told her.

She nodded, her nails digging into his skin. She kept her gaze on him, focusing, willing him to pull her up.

"Ahh," she cried out as he dragged her, his hold on her never faltering, but the years-old wood abraded her chest, her nightshirt catching on the splintered slats, the swell of her breasts taking some of the rough treatment, but he didn't let up. Not until she was safe.

Inch by inch, for what seemed like hours when only moments had passed, Arden managed to get first one, then both legs firmly back on the deck. Kip sighed and let her hands go, crawling backwards along the walkway, but she didn't move.

On her hands and knees, she stared at him, her face stricken with horror. She'd just cheated death, and the knowledge rendered her immobile.

He cocked his head, his tone incredulous as he said, "You almost plunged into the sea, and *now* you freeze?" He actually chuckled at the absurdity of it, but he figured she was entitled to a moment of grim reality.

"Come to me, Arden," he coaxed, his command gentle, soothing. He wouldn't feel better until they were back in the house, safe, dry, and warm. Then he could unleash his wrath all he wanted.

His hand reached out carefully, sliding along her arm, and he lifted her hand from the deck, holding it and urging her toward him. "That's it, Arden," he pressed, crawling back as she began to move forward. "Come to me, honey, I'll get you inside," he promised.

When both of them were clear of the tempest outside, Kip

let go of her hand and fought the rush of elation that was so strong, he thought he might vomit. He completely ignored the fact that he'd seen Arden in all her glory every time lightning struck. Her nightshirt gaped open and it was soaked to her skin. He'd been too anxious to enjoy the sight. Now all he could hear was her teeth chattering. The rain that had pelted her skin was only a part of it. She was in shock, and he knew well what it could do to a body if he didn't attend to her.

He shut out the wind, and on shaky legs, hauled himself up off the floor, feeling around in the dark for the bed. He grumbled about how easy it had been to find when he was tripping over it.

His knees bumped the mattress. He stripped the covers from it, and turned back to where he'd left Arden by the door.

Crossing to her, his survival instincts were still engaged, and he dropped the blanket, reaching down for the hem of her drenched shirt. She didn't utter a peep of protest when he dragged it up her body, over her head. He tossed it aside, and it landed in a sopping heap on the floor across the room. She was left naked except for her scant, drenched panties.

Next, he knelt in front of her and wrapped the dry bedspread over her chilled form. He rubbed her arms hard for a few seconds, trying to work some circulation back into her limbs, then lifted her into his arms. He refused to acknowledge how right it felt to hold her like this, instead concentrating on what he needed to do. He laid her back on the bed with her feet elevated on the pillows.

The lost, blank look in her eyes squeezed his heart. He smoothed her hair off her face and leaned down to press a chaste kiss on her forehead. "Stay here," he murmured. "I'm going to get some towels and candles," and under his breath he added, "And peroxide." The abrasions on her chest didn't look bad, but he hoped she'd had a tetanus shot in the last few years. There were rusty nails out there, and he wasn't positive she hadn't scraped her skin on them somewhere. He'd check more thoroughly when he had something other than lightning to see by.

When he returned, the room was illuminated by the oil lamp he carried from one of the bedrooms on the lower level. He found Arden sitting on the edge of the mattress, facing the bay window, watching the storm rage on outside. She'd pulled the blanket tightly around her body; her hair hung in tangles and snarls down her back. It was already beginning to dry. He grabbed a brush as he passed the dresser.

He moved around the bed, dragged a wooden stool close to it, and set the lamp on its surface. Placing the first aid kit beside Arden, he knelt in front of her. He looked up at her face. "Still with me?"

Arden's mouth curved into a wobbly smile, and she nodded. Her brow rose in question. "Yell at me later?"

It was the first time he'd felt like laughing since he saw her again. "Oh, honey, you can count on it," he assured her, chuckling.

She was thinking of it, and Kip hurt just watching her. It was a close thing.

Her eyes welled with unshed tears.

Oh, God, he prayed. *Please don't let her cry.* He knew he couldn't take that.

But she didn't shed a tear. What she did instead almost made *him* cry.

She stared down at him and unfolded the blanket, letting it pool around her on the bed, laying bare her body to him. She'd even shed her panties while he was gone.

And whoa, was it a good thing he was already on his knees. They surely would've buckled. He had an unobstructed view of her incredible curves, and neither life nor limb was at stake. *Not her life anyway,* he thought. The crisis was over, but he wasn't anywhere near safe.

His clothes were still wet from the soaking he'd taken outside, but they were drying rapidly, becoming stiff and uncomfortable. Some places more than others. And no wonder, he mused. His body was like an oven. Hell, he wouldn't be surprised if steam was coming off him. He was on his knees in front of Arden. What man wouldn't get overheated?

The scrapes that marred her flesh weren't as bad as he'd first thought, but in examining the abrasions, he was gazing at both her breasts, the nipples hard and puckered.

Oh yeah, he thought. He was in trouble, all right.

Then the walls he'd made sure were solid and unshakable crumbled when she lowered her head and kissed him. Not just any kiss, either. He tasted elation, desperation. He felt it, too. Knowing how close she'd come to falling to her death, he kissed her back, hard, shutting out the too-vivid image. This was affirmation of life, raw passion. Whatever remorse would surface in the aftermath of the storm, he gave himself up to the pleasure and joy of her tonight.

"Ah, yes," she murmured when she dragged her lips from his, trailing her tongue along his jaw and throat, her nose nuzzling the collar of his shirt out of her way.

He cupped her face, pulling back and looking into the depths of her bright green eyes. "I almost lost you," he rasped, feeling his throat tighten.

Burying his face in her throat, he breathed in her scent, and dragged her to the edge of the bed, wrapping his arms around her tight, her legs on either side of his torso.

I'll regret this, Kip thought. He felt it in his bones, but he couldn't stop the rush of arousal, the need that drove him. He craved Arden, just as she was starving for him. Tonight, nothing mattered but sating their hunger for one another.

Chapter Three

A rden knew that Kip being here was a miracle in itself. When she was hanging from that ledge, she'd been so close to giving up. Then out of nowhere, his hand touched hers, gripped it, and wouldn't let go. He was her lifeline in so many ways.

She owed him her life. He'd risked his own to venture out on the widow's walk to save her, and she wanted so badly to tell him what was in her heart, that she loved him, but she kept the words locked inside. He wouldn't want to hear them; he'd think it was because of his heroic act, when in reality she'd always felt that way. She'd expect nothing less from a man like him. She was just so glad he'd spotted her up there.

More than that, he was *still* here, returning her kiss, and his resistance was gone. Her lips skimmed along his collarbone, but she pulled back, needing to see his face. She'd meant it that she didn't want him giving up anything to be with her. She knew in her soul that this was where she was supposed to be, not just on the island, but with Kip. There wasn't a doubt in her mind, but she wasn't so sure he felt the same.

That daring grin of his had the same effect it always had; her insides tightened with need and a shiver raced up her spine. His fathomless blue eyes darkened as she tugged hard at his shirt, sending buttons popping and scattering all over the wood floor.

His eyes burned into hers, and she knew he wanted her just

as much. She wouldn't question it, she resolved. She didn't want to cause him more trouble than she already had, but he was everything to her. For just this once, she was going to be selfish, and take whatever he was willing to give. She'd figure out the rest tomorrow.

She held the sides of his oxford shirt tight in her fists, and pulled him, covering his mouth again, needing the physical contact, to be as close as she could. Her tongue searched for his, and she answered his groan when it joined hers in erotic play.

I'll never tire of this. The thought swirled through her mind. The taste of him, the feel of his late-day beard against her smooth skin, she loved it. She loved him. He made her dizzy with desire and she thrilled at letting go of her own inhibitions.

Her fingers sank into the soft hairs on his chest. She kissed him deep, her tongue tangling with his. He shuddered and dragged his mouth from hers, trying to catch his breath. She raked her nails over his dark male nipples, and along his ribs. He growled in response, his brow furrowing as she played with him, teasing his body. Arden kept her gaze on him. He was coming to realize that she wasn't the shy, timid girl who'd left the island ten years ago. Now she was a woman whose needs were as fierce as his own, and she was going to satisfy every one of them. She trailed her fingers around the band of his jeans.

"Arden." His voice had a warning edge to it. "Be very careful."

His eyes were almost as black as his hair in the lamplight, but there was no mistaking the passion that blazed. He started to get up, to push her back on the bed, but she would have none of it. This was her fantasy, and in it, she was in control. The first time, anyway.

"Let me. Please?"

She could've laughed at his agonized, forlorn expression, but reluctantly, he nodded and dropped his hands back to his sides.

Her palms flattened on his hard, defined abs. He did manual labor, none of that sissy gym stuff, she mused. She had the real McCoy at her mercy, and she nearly cooed when her touch made those muscles tighten and a growl escaped his lips.

She'd waited forever to be in this exact place. She wanted to indulge herself. "Stand up and take your clothes off," she said.

He stood, but he hesitated to strip for her.

Reaching out her hand, she swept the back of it over his fly. She grinned mischievously when his erection pulsed beneath the tight denim. "Now, Kip."

"Oh, what are you doin' to me, princess?" He sighed. Off came his shirt, and his hands hastily fumbled for the snap of his jeans.

She held up a hand. "Wait—"

His eyes shot to her; he scowled with impatience. "For God's sake, what?"

Her eyes traveled over his broad shoulders, to his sculpted chest and narrow hips. "Do it slowly," she ordered, her command uttered with confidence, though her insides twisted with anxiety. His chest rumbled in frustration, and she prayed she wasn't taking this pseudodominatrix role too far. He was a virile man. She'd bet he'd never let a woman have control during sex. That he was letting her do it was exhilarating, arousing.

He stared down at her, his common sense warring with his libido. She knew which one she wanted to win. She decided to better her odds. One of her hands slid seductively up her thigh, trailing in, the tips of her fingers just barely brushing against the nest of curls there.

"Oh, Christ," he choked out; his gaze pinned on her legs.

She'd learned the hard way that she had to go after what she wanted, and Kip was her reason for coming back to Martha's Vineyard. It was a dirty trick, using his arousal against him, but she couldn't give up on him. "Something wrong?" she asked innocently, crossing one leg over the other, trapping her hand between them.

Kip closed his eyes against her deliberate torment. "You're a witch. A siren," he whispered. When he opened them again, his stare was so intense, she felt singed.

His brow rose in question when she laughed lustily. "A siren is capable of seducing a man," she explained. "She weaves a spell, and she always gets what she wants. You know what I want, Kip."

His mouth formed a straight line of restraint; he swept his hand over the trail of hair that disappeared into the vee of his jeans. His voice was smooth as fine whiskey as he turned the tables on her, asking, "Do you know what I'm going to do to you when it's my turn, princess?"

Arden's legs squeezed tight on her hand. She licked her lips, feeling the shift of control as surely as that rail broke away and was taken by the wind. With just a look, and her own vivid imagination, she became the prey. Mutely, she shook her head.

Kip grinned, obviously accustomed to the role of aggressor. His gaze skimmed over her breasts, her belly, the juncture of her thighs, making every point of eye contact tingle. "I'm going to taste you. No," he amended, "I'm gonna devour you."

Only his eyes moved, locking with hers, bright with a wildness she wanted him to let loose on her. He toed off his deck shoes, one then the other. "I'm gonna hear you scream my name when you come for me. And then . . . oh, and then. I'm gonna start all over again."

Did she just hear herself whimper? It must've been her, but she was flushed, and it sounded like a freight train was roaring in her ears. She felt feverish all over, and her mouth was dry. Where she'd been chilled to the bone moments ago, now she was an inferno of heat and need.

She reached a shaking hand to the nightstand, pulling a condom from it as he lowered his jeans to his thighs. She was fascinated when his hard, thick sex came into view; it pulsed in time to his heartbeat.

Both of them were breathing hard, the game intensifying by the second. Arden's heart was pounding in her chest, so loud she'd swear he could hear it. She opened the packet, holding it in her hand as she bent forward and captured the head of his penis in her mouth.

"Oh, my God. Ah, Christ, Arden. You win," he rasped, throwing his head back, his legs shaking and his breath rushing through his clenched teeth. His hands cupped her head, fingers tangling in her already mussed tresses; it was all the encouragement she needed.

She licked the tip of his sex, tasting the salty wetness on the velvety smooth head. She looked up at him, waiting until his gaze lowered. When his eyes met hers, she wrapped her fist around the swollen shaft. "We both win," she murmured, and kissed the dark flared head before surrounding it again with her lips. Arden wondered fleetingly if it was sadistic to be wickedly aroused by his pleading expression.

His fingers tightened in her hair, but he didn't force her to take him deeper. He just gritted his teeth and endured the sweet torture.

She took him into the warm recesses of her mouth, and his body tensed, muscles solidifying under her ministrations. What they were doing was so intimate, yet it was the most natural thing in the world to be doing it with Kip. She wanted to give him the same exquisite bliss that just thinking of him made her feel. She wanted to show him love.

His knees bent slightly, and he slid her hair over her breasts, teasing her hard nipples with the silky strands, careful not to graze the scrapes she'd sustained. Even as immersed as he was in the pleasure she was giving him, he was mindful of her injuries. Arden loved that about him, but she didn't want him to think about anything. She only wanted him to feel, to give himself over to the sensations.

She stood, brushing her breasts against his chest. She gauged his reaction as she lifted one foot between his legs, and pushed his jeans to his ankles.

His eyes lit up with surprise and lust, but his chuckle was strained. And he didn't object when she reached a hand up into his short hair and brought his head down for her kiss.

Sighs and groans accompanied their panting breaths; his arms were manacles around her, crushing her naked body to the fiery heat of his. "Kip," she murmured between bone-melting kisses, needing to say his name.

His answering growl vitalized her.

She never realized how fun sex could be. When she was married, the coupling was quick, serious. It was more of an arranged marriage than anything else, and Arden hadn't wanted to do any of the things she was craving to do with this man. She took pleasure in arousing Kip, teasing him, tormenting him. She enjoyed his body, breathed in his scent, and relished his responses to her. She memorized every touch, every tingle, as his hands stroked along her back, trying to bring himself under control. She didn't care what it took, she was going to find a way to prove to Kip that they were meant to be. Nothing this good could be wrong.

She nuzzled his bare chest, circled his nipple with her tongue, and he gasped when she tugged at it with her teeth. His erection was hard as steel, branding hot as it pulsed against her belly. She shuddered as pre-come spilled onto her skin. She was turning him on so much, and she gloried in it, pressing closer still.

"Keep that up, honey, and you won't need that condom for a while," he warned.

She grinned, her hands wedging between them. She took his sex in one hand, rolling the condom over it with the other. She looked up at him again. "Now lie on the bed."

Arden was giddy with the power of commanding this man. He moved around her and sat where she'd been on the mattress, kicking off his jeans, and leaning back on his hands as she'd done earlier. *God, he was an amazingly attractive man,* she thought.

With a seductive smile, she approached the bed and began to straddle him, his sex brushing the heated folds of flesh.

His arm snaked around her, and with a speed she didn't even comprehend, she found herself under him, flat on her back in the middle of the mattress.

"We're not there *yet*, honey," he said, his hands capturing hers and his mouth crashing down on hers, his tongue demanding entrance.

She granted it, and arched her back, but he was careful still. He slid his lips lower to tantalize her throat; he nipped at her shoulder.

"Not nearly there," he said, avoiding the scrapes on her chest, licking from her ribs up.

Finally, to Arden's relief, he captured one aching nipple in his mouth and began to suckle, letting go of one hand to tease and stimulate the other swollen breast.

Arden couldn't think. Her brain was muddled by the sensations racing through her. Every tug of his teeth made her shiver and gasp. It felt so good! She'd never been attended to, healed like this, and she savored the pleasure.

Her hands sank into his hair, and she was only a little disappointed that he'd cut it. Then she did something she'd never dared; she pushed him lower, grinding her moist sex against his chest, letting him know without words what she desperately wanted.

Kip chuckled at her impatience, but he let her guide him until his lips kissed along the soft down between her thighs. He lowered his hand and petted her, parting the wet folds of her sex. With his fingers, he stroked the lips of her vagina, teasing the sensitive, slick flesh.

Her clitoris was swollen and distended; she could feel his breath fan over her, and she moaned incoherently. Her heels dug into the mattress, her hips tilted of their own volition, needing him like a drug.

She was beyond speech; she couldn't have uttered a word if she tried. But then his hands slid under her to cup her buttocks, his head lowered, his tongue entering her, his mouth closing around her opening, and he sucked.

Now she couldn't keep the words in. "Oh, oh . . . oh my God, Kip!" she screamed. One hand tangled in his hair, the other feeling for something, anything to grab onto as her body convulsed with the waves of pleasure that tore though her. His tongue flicked relentlessly at her clitoris, the center of her excitement, and she tumbled over again and again.

He finally let up, and she lay there, sated, exhausted from his exquisite torment. She caught her breath, and a smile drifted over her face when his appeared above her. A cocky grin curved his lips as he licked them as if savoring her taste. "Now we're there, princess," he informed her, his hand reaching down for his still-sheathed erection. He rubbed himself along her cleft, and her eyes met his as she bit her lip and nodded, wholeheartedly agreeing.

In one smooth, powerful thrust, he plunged inside her, eliciting a groan from them both. Arden gasped, arching her back, and her eyes rolled back in her head as she tipped her hips up, taking him deeper still.

Arden gazed up at Kip. The wonder in his eyes almost brought tears to hers. No matter what happened, he couldn't deny that this was special. A shadow of doubt still lurked, and she was determined to cast it out.

Her hands slid over his narrow hips, reaching to cup his tight buttocks. "Please. Now," was all she said, and she tightened her inner muscles around him.

It was enough. "Yeah. Now," he acquiesced, planting his hands near her shoulders. He stared down at her as he began to move, taking her slow and steady. His mouth crashed down on hers in a desperate kiss, and she tasted his desire. He dragged his lips from hers, lowering his head to her breast, his teeth tugging her nipple. He slid to the other, his tongue sending shivers over her skin as his sex stroked deliciously inside her, building her excitement.

Arden's guttural urgings went unheeded. "Harder," she pleaded, meeting his thrusts, but it wasn't enough. She needed more. She rolled her hips, digging her nails into his buttocks. Kip reared up, speeding his pace, his breathing becoming panting, and growls of need.

He ground against her clitoris with every driving thrust. "Come for me, Arden. Oh, yes. Come with me," he encouraged her. His hands reaching for hers, he linked their fingers together, and his eyes locked on hers as he took her higher and higher.

She *did* scream his name as she tumbled into the abyss, just like he said she would. Her pleasure was compounded as his own release gripped him, his body rigid, then shuddering above her. And he roared the words she'd longed to hear: he said he loved her.

Tears of joy and completion rolled down her temples. Kip kissed them away, his voice soothing her, assuring. He stayed inside her until she quieted and lay back, spent and blissfully sated.

She opened her mouth to tell him that she felt the same way; she loved him more than anything. But he kissed her slowly, seductively, and Arden couldn't rally this time. She'd been through a life-threatening ordeal, had the best sex of her life with the man she loved, and all in the last three hours. Her eyes closed with Kip's kiss, and stayed closed as exhaustion took her. She surrendered to it, a smile on her face, knowing that when she awoke, everything would be fine. Perfect.

Chapter Four

Kip sat naked on the edge of the bed as the morning light streamed into the room, his elbows on his knees and his head in his hands. "What the hell have I done?" he asked himself for the hundredth time since he awoke to find himself in Arden's attic, in her bed, her luscious body tucked to his side like she belonged there. What scared the shit out of him was that she did belong at his side, and he'd never sleep again without believing that faithfully.

He'd told her he loved her when he came. He winced, hating that he'd been so vulnerable that the words had slipped out. Not only that, but he meant them. He adored Arden, and seeing her again just proved for him that he always would.

"How am I gonna let her go?" he whispered, the lump in his throat threatening to choke him.

"You don't have to, Kip."

He spun around on the mattress to face Arden. God, she took his breath away. "I didn't know you were awake," he said, guilt lacing his voice. He didn't want her to know how hard this was for him.

"So I gathered. You've been sitting there talking to yourself for five minutes."

"A lady wouldn't eavesdrop," he chastised.

She chuckled. "We already had this discussion, Spencer. I'm

not always a lady. Which you kinda liked last night," she reminded him with a wink.

Kip couldn't keep the grin from forming. "Yeah, I did," he agreed. "Hell, I loved it."

She sat up, pulling the sheet over her breasts, but just barely. The scrapes on her chest were still fresh, and his guilt compounded as he stared at the red skin. "I'm sorry," he murmured, his fingers reaching out to trace around the wounds.

"You saved my life. I'm sorry I risked yours." She took his hand and kissed his palm. She let the sheet fall, and she pressed his warm hand to her breast. Her lids drifted closed and she sighed as he caressed it, making the mound swell, the nipple pucker.

She said his name like she had last night, and it was enough to yank him back to reality, out of the sexual tension swirling around them.

He dropped his hand to the mattress. "This can't happen again, Arden."

Her eyes snapped open. "Why not?"

He shook his head, "I can't do this again. I can't—" His hand raked through his hair. "Ah, damn it! To save myself, you're gonna make me hurt you, and I don't want to do that."

She pulled the sheet up again, this time not caring if she abraded the already chafed skin. "What the hell are you talking about?"

He didn't much like being naked while they were at odds, either. He pulled the rumpled bedspread from the end of the bed and covered himself. His cock had a mind of its own, and just looking at Arden was bringing his erection to life. "I don't think we should see each other again. *In* bed or out."

She scrambled closer to him. "What? Why?"

"It's not obvious? My life is here on the Vineyard. Yours isn't. I can't watch you walk away again." There. He said it. His pride took another hit, but at least she knew where he stood. And he did just that. He stood. Shucking the covers, he walked around the bed to retrieve his jeans.

"I wrote letters, Kip. You didn't answer them. You wouldn't

take my calls. You're the one who moved on, and I wasn't able to do a thing about it."

"You never came back," he accused, the bitterness welling again. He tugged his still-damp jeans up over his hips. Slipping into his shoes, he pulled on his shirt, but with no buttons, there wasn't anything else to do.

He looked over to her on the bed, then averted his gaze. The pain in her eyes was almost as bad as he felt. He nodded his head. "The first aid kit fell on the floor, but there's a bottle of peroxide in it. Take care of those scratches or they'll get infected."

Kip picked up his slicker by the door to the widow's walk. It was a good thing he was bent down. Her brush blew past him and hit the wall, dropping to the floor with a crashing thud. "What the hell?"

"Oh, you don't know what hell is, Kip." Her eyes shot fire at him, but they shined with unshed tears. "Hell is loving someone who pretends you don't exist. Hell is going on with your life, and realizing it's not much of one without that person." She shook her hair out of her face, but her sheet slipped. She didn't care. "Hell is finally having the courage to come home and realizing that you're not welcome there."

"Home?" he sneered. "Martha's Vineyard is your playground, Arden. It's *my* home." She was babbling things that he wanted her to explain, but if he got himself in deeper, he'd never get out. And he'd pay dearly later.

"No. It's my home now, too."

He cast her a sidelong glance. "Say again?"

She hit the mattress with her fist. "Damn it, Kip! I'm sitting here naked, but if you don't sit down, you'll get more outrageous behavior from me."

Curiosity got the best of him. "Say again?"

She glared up at him. "If you go home, I swear, I'll follow you. Without a stitch of clothing on. Every local, tourist, news crew, and reporter out surveying the storm damage in the harbor will look up and see me walking along the bluff to *your* house."

"You *have* changed," he admitted, struck again by her moxie.

"Yes. I have, and I want to explain some things to you, but I can't do that if I'm worried you'll leave. So please, will you just sit down and shut up for a little longer?"

Kip chuckled. The girl had spirit. For that alone, he lowered himself into the chair he'd tripped over the night before. "Talk," he said.

She took a deep breath. She had that deer-caught-in-headlights look again.

He helped her along. "Where the hell have you been for ten years, Arden?"

That seemed to provoke her into speech. "Well," she began, "I've been doing a bang-up job of screwing up my life."

This isn't going to work, he thought. She'd pulled the sheets up and she was covered, but he knew what lay beneath that cotton. If she didn't get to the point soon, he was getting the hell out before he took her again, and lost his soul in the process. "Get to it, princess," he ordered.

"Okay." She nodded, licking her lips. "The night before I left, I looked for you, but you didn't wanna be found. And we left early in the morning."

Kip groused, "I know. But I had an encounter with your mother, and she pretty much let me know that I wasn't good enough for you. I needed some time alone. But when I came up to see you in the morning, you'd left. I figured you agreed with her."

"You returned all my letters."

"I was still sore. If there's one thing we've got a lot of on this island, it's pride."

She grinned wistfully. "Don't I know it," she said. "But when you wouldn't write back or take my calls, I gave up. I figured you'd had it with me. I was so shy, Kip. I couldn't pursue you. Not then."

He nodded, conceding that her timidity had a hold on her then. "But you never came back." He pinned her in his stare, wanting to hear her explanation for that.

"My mother got sick right after we left that summer. Two years, and the cancer finally took her."

Kip lowered his gaze, unable to look at her. "I'm sorry," he rasped, knowing that as much as he didn't care for her mother, Arden had loved her very much. He wanted to go to her, hold her. But he couldn't.

"I went to college on the West Coast after that, and then my dad was diagnosed with cancer, too. Before he passed away, I married the man he'd chosen for me, and—"

"You're married?" *Oh, Jesus,* he thought. She'd changed, but when she said she wanted him, he at least thought she was legally able to act upon it.

"Divorced. He took all my money, but I wouldn't let him get his hands on this place."

"Ah, I see."

"No, Kip. You don't see at all," came her clipped response.

He felt like he was rolling with the storm from last night. Highs like a massive swell, and lows like the calm, still doldrums. "What was wrong with him?"

"Aside from the fact that he liked to gamble, he liked to put me down, and he liked other women, it's simple, really. He wasn't you."

He didn't know how to feel about that revelation. She was a product of her own making, after all. Just as he was. But the nagging fact was that, under her father's thumb, she'd been easily manipulated and coerced into doing his bidding. It wasn't hard to imagine Arden falling prey to the same kind of man. Especially one her father had handpicked for her.

The argument ten years ago, the one that had started this downward spiral was like that. She'd been too trusting, so innocent. And Kip had yelled at her for it.

Brody Jackson was an old family friend, and Kip had gotten his sea legs on Brody's trawler when he was barely old enough to walk. Kip was a young teen when Brody's wife ran off with some rich tourist, taking their kids with her. The betrayal broke the man, and he found his solace at the bottom of a whiskey bottle. Kip made sure his old friend got home safely two, three times a week by the time he was nineteen. He owed it to him.

Arden got her license when she was seventeen, and she had a car at her disposal on the island that summer. One night, she picked up Brody in his drunken stupor, and gave him a lift home. Kip remembered exploding with anger, railing at her for being so stupid. The man had a grudge against the wealthy, and she'd put herself in danger. Brody wasn't normally a violent man, but if he felt that he'd been wronged, he'd come out swinging. And the drink usually skewed reality enough so that he might have looked at Arden as one that had wronged him. She was petite compared to the big, burly man. If he'd had criminal intent, she'd have been defenseless against him.

She'd run home from the trail where they'd taken a walk, and Kip let her go, needing to calm his own rage, his own gripping fear of what *could* have happened. Maybe if he'd . . .

He shook his head of the memory. "Where did this new you come from?" He needed to keep his thoughts on the here and now. The past held too many regrets to count.

She smiled for the first time. "The prospect of losing this place. Never seeing you again."

He met her gaze, his body flooding with heat. She'd missed him. And from the look on her face, perhaps near as much as he'd missed her. "If he took all your money, how do you expect to afford this place?" He looked around the room. The attic was almost as big as his living room. Heating alone would cost her as much as he made in a month.

Excitement lit her eyes. "Prescott Manor is now Prescott House. It's a bed and breakfast. I'm officially a business owner, and new local. I got the permits, renovation plans, everything to prove it. Oh, and some hefty loans that'll take me a lifetime to pay off." She grinned sardonically.

Kip tamped down on the hope that swelled and threatened to take root. "You're really staying?"

"Forever. Spencer, I'm never leaving again. Unless you think we can't get over the past. Because as much as I love it here, Kip, you're the reason I'm back. Without you, paradise is just an island."

She bit her lip, and Kip almost groaned. Her excitement was contagious. He wanted nothing more than to keep her here with him forever. And she was right. He'd grown up here, on this beautiful island, where people came for pleasure and passed time. But since she'd left, it was just a place where he lived.

"I love you," he said, then held his breath, taking the biggest risk of his life.

Arden shrieked, her happiness so revealing, it was staggering. He stood up, and she launched off the bed, straight into his arms. Kip wrapped them around her, holding her tight, and he closed his eyes, fighting the emotions that squeezed his heart.

Her muffled, "I love you, too," choked his throat. She repeated it over and over as her arms nearly choked him for real, she held on so tight.

He swung them around until he was sitting on the bed, and she sat straddling his lap. His hands pulled her closer as she wiggled, her cleft grinding down on his aching cock. *God*, he thought. If he'd taken a two-by-four to the head in that storm, and he was knocked out, he hoped he never regained consciousness.

"I've got you naked on my lap," he growled. "I could come right now."

She giggled, and blushed prettily. She was embarrassed by his blunt language, but she didn't lower her gaze. Instead she gripped his waist with her thighs. "I can feel you throbbing. Right here," she said, and rolled her hips.

Kip sighed, his fingers digging into the soft, pliable flesh of her buttocks. He rocked with her, his jeans the only thing keeping him from being joined with her. "Marry me."

She stopped moving. Hell, Kip wasn't sure she was still breathing. She just stared at him with those sea green eyes he loved looking into. Her mouth opened in shock.

He reached up, gently combing his fingers through her hair. "A stupid fight, too much pride, and lack of communication took ten years from the happiness we could've had, Arden. We were so young."

Her head bobbed up and down, but she still didn't say a word.

He continued, "I'd see you up here on the widow's walk, and I always imagined you as a princess, looking down on her subjects." He shrugged. "Until I got to know you, that is. And I fell in love with you. I couldn't stop myself."

"I looked down at the harbor for you to dock every day." She smiled and ran her fingers through his hair. "With your long hair and that earring you used to wear, you looked like a pirate. I had so many fantasies about you."

He felt his cock responding to her wistful voice, her vivid words. He grinned. "Did you think I'd ravish you?"

She leaned forward, dragging a groan from his chest as she kissed his jaw, sending shivers up his spine as she nipped at his earlobe. "I hoped you would," she whispered, and her tongue flicked along his throat.

"Ah, God. You got it, princess," he promised, lowering his head, taking a nipple in his mouth, and sucking hard.

She cried out, and arched her back, her golden hair hanging down in the beams of sunlight. She shuddered in his lap, riding him, the rough denim of his jeans rubbing her swollen, sensitive flesh, bringing her to the edge. His hands caressed her spine, her buttocks, and slid up along her ribs to cup her shoulders. He sipped at her breasts, his tongue teasing, batting at the dark areolas, their coupling driving her hard and fast to completion.

She pulled his head up and covered his mouth with hers, but nothing could stop the scream of pleasure she uttered when he brought his hand down, his fingers entering her wet folds from behind, sliding into her with sureness and purpose.

"Ah, Kip! *Yeeees!*" Her body spasmed, quaking with the force of her rushed orgasm. He pushed in again, and curled his fingers, feeling her clamp down on them as she gasped and trembled again, more violent this time. He grinned painfully. His agony was her ecstasy. He wouldn't have it any other way.

When she slumped over him and caught her breath, her glorious hair draped over his shoulder, some even brushing over his chest. Kip tried to imagine something that would take his mind off of his still-dire state. He latched onto a thought and ignored her tremors of residual ripples of pleasure, asking, "What were you doing out on the widow's walk last night? You had to know it was so dangerous to be out there at the height of a violent storm. You could've gotten yourself killed."

"But you saved me," she qualified.

He grinned. "Ah. Buttering me up, eh? Seeing if you can get away with it? Hope I'll forget that I promised to yell at you?"

She shrugged.

"If you tell me why, I might let it slide. But only if you promise not to go back out there until I can get a sound walkway and rail put back on."

"I carved something in the wood a long time ago. I just needed to see if it was still there." Her tone was lazy, lethargic.

Kip wanted to chuckle. A little lovin' and the woman was as malleable as melted wax. But laughing would only cause him more pain. And he didn't want Arden to feel like she had to move, though soon it would be a necessity. He had to know. "What was it?"

She lifted her head, tears welling in her eyes. "It said, 'Arden Loves Kip.'"

Now he felt like *he* could melt. This woman tugged on his heartstrings like no one else. He cupped her cheek. "I love you, too," he said, kissing her with as much reverence as he felt. She took his breath away just by being herself. He wished for so many things; righting his wrong was one of them. He pulled away and made her look at him. "I'll carve you another one, sweetheart," he promised. "Besides," he reasoned, chucking her chin, "you've got me now. If you have a fantasy, I'll fulfill it."

"I have something for you," she said, slipping off his lap.

"I got something for you too, honey," he replied, his brows wagging, and she smacked his shoulder before jumping out of his grasp when he reached for her.

She wrapped the sheet around her and left the room, only to return with a piece of paper.

"What's this?" he asked as she handed it to him.

"The deed to this property."

"What? *This* property?"

"Uh-huh."

She sat next to him on the bed, decently covered by the sheet, much to Kip's disappointment. She wouldn't keep it on long, though, if he had his way. He looked up from the paper. "I don't understand."

"It's no secret that my great-grampa pretty much rooked your family out of this land during the Depression."

"That doesn't have anything to do with us, honey."

"Yes," she replied, "yes, it does. I came up here to make a new start, and part of that was making sure that at least one family squabble is put to rest. It's Spencer land. The manor is still mine, but the ground it sits on is now officially back in the hands of the rightful owner." She smiled, genuinely happy with her gift. "Of course," she shrugged, casually informing him, "now you're my *land*lord, and you better treat me good or I'll report you." She laughed, but her smile faded when she really looked at Kip. "What's the matter?"

He didn't know if he could talk; the lump in his throat felt huge. "It doesn't mean a thing to me," he said, "but I wish my father were still alive. He'd have loved you."

She smoothed her hand over his hair, nodding. "Because he felt cheated of his land?" she asked.

Kip couldn't keep it in. "No," he said, his voice breaking. "Because you love me, and want me to be happy. You're stronger than I ever gave you credit for." His chest hurt and his eyes burned, but he had to finish. "All I've ever wanted to do was protect you, shelter you. And you don't need that at all."

"I need you. That's where I get my strength."

"No, you—"

"Yes, Kip. You. It's always been you. Since the first time I saw you, I knew you were the one. It was wrong for me to marry a man I didn't love, but I paid for that sin. I came out of it praying that you'd be there on the other side." She sighed. "I didn't have the right to hope for that, but I did anyway."

He pulled her close, careful not to drag her onto his lap. He was still hard as steel, and he didn't want anything distracting him from his goal. Her face was tucked in the curve of his shoulder. "So, Arden. Will you marry me? Make a life with me here?"

She kissed his throat, nodding and snuggling into his warmth.

He chuckled. "I think I'm gonna have to compel a verbal response, Ms. Prescott, or whatever your name is now," he said, chagrined that he didn't even know it.

She lifted her head, looking him in the eye. "It doesn't matter what it is now. It'll be Spencer soon."

He pulled back when she tried to kiss him, his brow lifting. "Say it."

She slugged him in the arm. "Yes! I'll marry you!"

He let his smile have free rein now; he held her tight. "When?"

She giggled. "Labor Day?"

He considered it. "Hmmm. Sounds good to me. And I can look forward to it every year instead of dreading it as the day I lost you."

"Me, too," she agreed, turning and running her hands over his chest. "I've always looked forward to you."

"One thing," Kip said. "I'll mention it once, and then I won't nag you again."

Arden's hand slid down, stroking over his still-covered sex, but her voice was perfectly level when she said, "What's that?"

"If you kiss me like you did yesterday, and leave me hanging like that again—"

He wasn't even finished, and already she was laughing at

the memory. "Running naked across the bluff will be child's play."

His hand slid between her thighs, and she sighed, opening to him like a blooming flower. He stroked in and out of her wet passage, breathing in her scent as the tip of his finger circled that distended bud of nerves, toying with her until she was bucking against his hand, right on the brink of an explosive climax. He took his hand away, and held hers still.

"Kip, God, please—"

"That's what it feels like."

She writhed as he held her open, immobile, preventing her from crashing over the precipice.

"Don't tease me, princess," he murmured, kissing her brow, moist with perspiration. She used some of those colorful words she'd learned, swearing retribution. Kip delighted in her excitement, her promises that were meant to be threats.

When he knew she couldn't stand it anymore, he skimmed his hand back down over her belly to the juncture of her thighs, and he pushed two fingers into her, hard. He groaned right along with her as her tight passage gripped them like a vise, and her climax slammed into her, sending waves of sweet satiation through her. Her own hand covered his, keeping it there until the tremors subsided and she was liquid again.

"That's twice now you've come without me. And I'm still dressed," he said.

She turned and pressed her back to his chest. "You deserved that one," she informed him.

"True," Kip agreed, chuckling. "But you get me hard just watching you. I could do this all day."

Arden rolled over, onto her knees, and unbuttoned his jeans, tugging them down when he lifted his hips to help her get them off. He pulled his arms out of the sleeves of his shirt as she reached over and grabbed a condom from the drawer and tore it open.

She sheathed his aching sex and straddled him, sinking down on him. He'd been dying for this! He lifted his knees, and she leaned back, resting against them and taking him deep inside her. "I'd rather do this," she gasped.

"Oh, me, too," he said, repeating her words. "Stay with me, princess," he whispered, staring up into those eyes.

"Forever, Spencer," she promised. "Forever."

You won't want to miss
LARGER THAN LIFE
by Alison Kent,
available now from Brava . . .

He got up, dragged his chair around and positioned it behind hers. "I'm not going to give you reason to do anything but fall asleep."

Something she wouldn't be doing until she got to bed behind her locked door. "Just to clue you in, I'm not the type to fall asleep just anywhere. Not on a plane, never in a moving car. I even have trouble in hotel rooms."

"That's gotta be hell on your love life," he said, sitting and settling his palms on her shoulders, his thumbs at the base of her neck.

"I was talking about falling asleep. Not . . . other things." And dear Lord, but his thumbs felt good, rubbing pressure circles against her nape right where she most needed to be rubbed.

"I've slept in planes, trains, and automobiles," he said, and she smiled. "I've also slept in a Turkish mosque, a Russian freighter, on the ground in the Australian Outback, and underground in a Tuscan winery."

"A Turkish mosque?"

"Yeah. Don't mention that to anyone. I probably shouldn't have been there."

Funny man. Amazing hands. She was halfway asleep already. "In Turkey? Or in the mosque?"

He hesitated a moment then seemed to chuckle under his breath. "Both, now that you mention it."

Her head lolled forward as he massaged the tendons at the base of her skull. She closed her eyes. "If that's putting too much stress on your shoulder—"

"No worries, mate," he said, and she groaned.

"You don't have an accent. Did you pick up the vernacular while sleeping under the outback moon?"

"Actually, it was on the Russian freighter. I spent a bit of time there chained in the cargo hold with two blokes from Melbourne."

"What?" She tried to turn; he wouldn't let her, but held her head still while he worked his knuckles and fingertips along the slope to her shoulders. "Chained? You mean like a prisoner?"

"You could say. But being chained didn't make me the enemy."

The gun. The knife. "I guess these were your pre-engineering days?"

"About thirty of them, yeah."

"What were you hunting then? Sables? Minks? KGB informants?"

"Bad guys," he said, and left it at that.

She wasn't about to drop it that easily, no matter the fabulous magic of his hands. She shifted to the side, tucking one leg beneath her, and turned in the padded red seat. His gaze, when she met it, was indecipherable, though he did lift a brow.

He'd curled his hands around the padded top of her aluminum frame and red Naugahyde diner-style chair. She placed one of her hands atop his and shook her head slowly, thinking, wondering. "Who are you, Mick Savin? And don't give me that mule deer bullshit."

"What makes you so skeptical, Nevada Case?" he responded, hooking her fingers with his.

"Because I've been lied to by too many people in my life." She narrowed her gaze and her mouth. "And *don't* call me Nevada."

He didn't say anything in response. He didn't release her gaze or her hand. In fact, he seemed to tighten both holds. It was the only explanation for why she couldn't break away, because she wanted to break way. Of course she did; why wouldn't she?

"Then I'm not going to lie to you," he finally admitted. "I'm here on a hunt. And there are some men out there who don't want me to find what I'm looking for."

She didn't know why he'd told her that any more than she knew why she believed him. But she did. And she found herself twining her fingers tighter with his. "What are you looking for?"

"The truth?"

She nodded, unable this time to find her voice.

He smiled softly. "I can't tell you."

"Is that a lie by omission?"

"The lie is only in the lack of details. The truth is that I don't want you to get hurt."

"By you? Or by the men who caught you trespassing?"

"Both," he answered honestly, and she cringed.

"Am I putting myself in danger by having you here?"

"The truth?" he asked again.

And again, she nodded.

"I'm not a very nice man."

She looked down to where their hands were joined, said, "I guess that depends on the judge."

He said nothing, and she feared looking up. Not because he frightened her; he no longer did. And the only thing that had changed was the response of her intuition to the truth he'd told. He wasn't here for her. That much she trusted to be true.

What she didn't trust was the warmth of his skin, the secure hold of his fingers, his claim of not being a very nice man. But more than anything, she didn't trust what she was feeling. And she didn't like at all not trusting that about herself.

In the end, however, she was helpless against the pull of his gaze, and raised her eyes to meet his. The way he looked at her, the way he stared into her eyes searching for . . . she didn't know.

And so she asked, the ache in her chest subduing her voice. "What are you looking for?"

"I think I'm trying to decide if you mean it," he said.

"I don't make a habit of saying what I don't mean."

"What have I done that you would give me that benefit of a doubt?"

"You forget that I'm used to being lied to." Dear Lord, but her chest was aching, her heart hurting. "And I don't see anything but truth in your eyes."

"Even if it's a half truth?"

"If that's all you're able to tell . . ." She shrugged, looked back at their joined hands, admitting to herself that it wasn't so strange that they both had secrets. What was new here was that they both recognized—and respected—the same in the other.

"Neva?"

At his whisper of her name, she once again found her gaze drawn to his.

"If I could tell you more, I would."

"It doesn't matter." All that mattered was that she wanted to smile for absolutely no reason.

"It matters to me." He pulled one hand from beneath hers, reached up and drew the backs of his fingers along her hairline. "I've been involved in a lot of things no one could ever prove I knew a bloody thing about. Like I said, I'm not a very nice man. But that doesn't mean I'm an unfeeling ass."

"Ass." She paused, continued to fight the smile. "Is this that horse size thing again, because—"

He cut her off with a kiss. He cupped the back of her head, pulled her forward, and kissed her. For a minute, it didn't even occur to her to close her eyes. She watched his lashes flutter, felt the press of his tongue to the seam of her lips. She didn't give it another thought. She simply opened her mouth.

He tasted like the sandwich she'd made him, like she wanted him when she shouldn't, like a little bit more would never be enough, like he was hers. Hardly fair that he'd give her that after telling her that he wasn't a very nice man. She'd known her share of those, yet none of them had come close to offering her this.

His tongue slid over hers, tangled with hers, boldly stroked in and out of her mouth. She gripped his fingers tighter and slanted her head, giving him back the same. Oh, how she wanted this. How right it felt, he felt. How perfectly he kissed. How perfectly he fit. How soft were his lips. How strong his tongue.

Never in her life had she felt the pull of a man from a contact that was so simple while being so goddamn complex. And then he was gone. He abandoned her mouth, nuzzled his nose to hers, his breath warm as he sighed and said, "Go to bed, Neva. I'll clean up here."

His offer was so sweetly made and so welcome that she accepted. She left the kitchen, took his kiss with her to bed, and slept like she was somebody's baby.

Here's a hot sneak peek at
READY
by Lucy Monroe,
coming in July 2005 from Brava . . .

L ise sat on the porch swing, a throw around her shoulders to ward off the chill. Her white flannel nightgown wasn't warm enough for the winter weather, but she had needed to be outside. She'd spent so much time hiding in her apartment the last few months that the outdoors had called to her like the irresistible sirens of old.

The stars that were invisible in Seattle's light-polluted night sky glittered overhead and the fragrance of fresh air teased her nostrils. At three o'clock in the morning, the ranch yard was deserted. Even the dogs were sleeping. And she was thoroughly enjoying the solitude.

No stalker could see or hear her. Nemesis did not know where she was, and that would change tomorrow. So, for tonight she was determined to enjoy every nuance of the freedom she would not have again until her stalker was caught.

Being drawn to the swing could be attributed to having spent so many evenings of her childhood curled up on it, telling stories in her head and avoiding the coldness of the ranch house. Only she wasn't remembering her childhood, or telling herself a story in her mind, or even plotting her next book.

Instead, she was reliving the volatile feelings she'd had in Joshua's arms last year on this very swing before she'd come to her senses and rejected him. Those feelings had been so different from anything she'd experienced with Mike, she'd been terrified. And she'd run.

Just as Joshua had accused her of doing, but tonight she could not run from the memory. She didn't know why . . . perhaps because she'd realized today that Joshua still wanted her and while that desire frightened her, it also exhilarated her.

His wanting her confirmed her femininity in a way she was beginning to see she needed very badly, even if she didn't want to explore the ramifications of it.

But knowing he wanted her impacted her senses almost as much as the kiss had and she was filled with unwanted sexual excitement. If she closed her eyes, she could almost taste his lips again.

Remembering the moment when his mouth had laid claim to her own made her nipples pebble with a stinging sensation against her nightgown. Had she ever wanted Mike this way? She didn't remember it if she had. Pressing against her swollen breasts with the palms of her hands, she tried to alleviate the growing ache. It didn't do any good. Between her legs throbbed and she clamped her thighs together, moaning softly.

This was awful.

She was not an overly sexual being. The coupling of male and female flesh did very little for her. It was a pleasant way to connect on an emotional level, but that was all.

This consuming ache was not pleasant, nor did it feel particularly emotional.

She was a physical animal, in touch with primitive needs she'd been certain she didn't have.

In a reflexive move, her hands squeezed her breasts and she cried out softly, unbearably excited by the simple stimulation.

A harsh sound to her left caught her attention.

Her eyes flew open.

"Joshua . . ."

He stood a few feet away, sexual energy that matched her own vibrating off of him in physical waves that buffeted her already overstimulated body. He was just as he'd been on the night of the christening. Only this time he remained where he was, staring at her instead of joining her on the swing.

His face was cast in grim lines, his naked chest heaving with each breath of air he sucked in. The black curling hair on it tapered to the unbuttoned waistband on his jeans. The shadowy opening hinted at his maleness.

She wanted to lean forward and lower the zipper so she could see it all, which would be incredibly stupid.

Only right that very second, she could not quite remember why, not with her fingertips tingling with the need to act.

She watched in mesmerized fascination as a bulge grew in the front of his jeans. A large bulge.

"Lise . . ."

She looked up.

A gaze so hot it burned to her soul flamed her. They remained like that for several seconds of hushed silence, their eyes speaking intense messages of need while their lips remained silent.

The past ceased to exist.

The present consumed her.

Her reasons for caution melted away as her fear turned to a firestorm of desire. His presence devoured everything around them, leaving nothing but male and female communicating on the most basic level.

He took the steps that brought him within an inch of the swing. If she moved it, she would bump his legs.

She shivered at the thought of even that slight touch.

Dropping to his knees with a grace that spoke of leashed power, he knelt in front of her so they were eye level.

Neither of them spoke.

She couldn't.

He reached out and put his hands over hers where they pressed against now throbbing, turgid peaks. The heat of his skin seeped into hers, making her burn with unnamable longing.

When his head lowered to let their lips meet, she met him halfway. She wanted his kiss, desperately.

She concentrated on each individual sensation of his lips slanting over hers, his beard stubble prickly against her chin, his taste . . . like the most irresistible nectar, the heat of his mouth, the warmth of his breath fanning her face. She had never known the intense pleasure she found in his mouth, the conflagration of her senses she experienced when they touched.

Part of her was still cognizant enough to know she should stop him for the sake of her own sanity, but it was a tiny voice lost in a hurricane of physical sensations.

Joshua felt like he was going to explode in his jeans and he hadn't even touched her naked breasts, but he was going to.

Oh, yes . . . he was going to.

He began undoing the long row of buttons on her nightgown, until he could spread the opening wide, gently brushing her hands away from herself in the process. She would never know what it had done to him to come outside to check on her and find her sitting in the swing, moaning and touching herself.

And here's a first look at
Gemma Bruce's sexy whodunit
WHO'S BEEN SLEEPING IN MY BED?
coming in July 2005 from Brava . . .

Nan's heart skittered to a stop, seized up for a moment, then banged back to life, hammering at her rib cage. Okay, just one little backslide, just one night. She deserved it. And besides, Delia had eaten three donuts.

It didn't have to be a backslide. Damon Connelly might be the kind of man who liked to talk after sex. She could find out a lot of information that way.

Who was she kidding? She was rationalizing. She knew it and she wanted to ignore it, but she made a last-ditch effort to control herself.

"I'm not having casual sex these days."

Damon's eyebrows twitched. It was such a turn-on. "It won't be casual. I promise."

He stepped toward her. She stepped back against the table. His hands slipped around her waist. He lifted her up and sat her down on the top.

Nan reached back to steady herself. Her hand squashed into the baguette, but she was beyond caring.

He eased a hip bone between her thighs, then stepped between them. Pulled her forward until she was straddling him. Her skirt rolled up her thigh. She locked her ankles behind him and pulled him even closer.

He groaned as body parts came together in a teasing dance. Then his mouth covered hers so violently that she fell backwards. He grabbed her around the shoulders and held on, assaulting her mouth with thrusts of his tongue. Mashing his lips against hers, driving her teeth against her lip, drawing blood.

He eased up and ran his tongue along her teeth and lips, licking the blood away. "Sorry," he mumbled and went in for a second offensive.

This time he was gentler. It was even better, knowing that he was holding himself back. It gave her a chance to reciprocate.

She was vaguely aware of her cell phone ringing; a faint echo from inside her purse that she'd hung over a chair back. She briefly considered reaching for it, but couldn't let go of Damon.

His hair was soft and just the right length for wrapping around her fingers. She did and pulled. He groaned again and deepened the kiss. This time she fell backwards onto the tabletop, taking Damon with her.

The French bread went down for the count. Neither of them noticed. Damon's hands were everywhere, roaming at will, his touch hitting every spot but the one that needed it most.

"Not a table, either," he said against her ear. And suddenly she was lifted up. And being carried across the room, her legs still locked around his waist.

He shouldered the door open and stepped into the hall.

"Bedroom," he said.

"Yes," she answered. Didn't understand why he laughed.

He started down the hall with her clinging to him. Paused and threw the first door open. It was the closet. A muffled expletive and he started up again. The bathroom.

"And behind door number three . . ." she said breathlessly.

"Aha," said Damon as he opened the door to the bedroom.

Anticipation rushed through her. Just one little backslide, she promised. He'd be gone in twenty minutes—forty, max. But until then . . . Shit. He'd stopped just inside the door. Why was he just standing there?

"Hmm?" she asked.

Damon jerked. "Just looking." Then he moved again, across the room, and they fell on the bed together. He loomed over her, expression stark, eyes glittering with something scary.

A part of her brain, the part that was still trying to think rationally, was clamoring for her attention. She didn't know anything about Damon Connelly. She was nuts to let this man into her house, much less into her bed. And then the part of her that was responsible for her being sent to Camp Wilderness spoke up. *You'll get information this way. And have a hell of a ride along the way.*

She consigned her rational self as well as her good intentions to the bottom of Long Island Sound and reached for the buttons of Damon's shirt. It made the tussle in the parking lot look like an amateur sting. This was a fight to the finish. They groped for each other, getting in each other's way, but neither yielding ground.

Finally, Damon pushed her to her feet. His shirt hung by one arm. His trousers were halfway unzipped. Her dress was up by her waist. He steadied her on her heels, then pulled the dress over her head in one smooth movement. She stood before him in nothing but four-inch heels and a beige silk thong.

A sharp crack of sound, somewhere between a laugh and a cry, escaped from deep in his throat. He was breathing hard and taking her in.

He yanked the sleeve over his wrist and tossed his shirt past her. She started to reach for him.

"No," he said. "Stay right there. Just like that." His eyes were feasting on her. Scrutinizing every inch of her. While her insides were tugging with desire, with impatience, and with shear physical need. Her thong was wet with anticipation.

Damon shucked off his trousers, boxers, shoes and socks. Then he stood before her.

She licked dry lips and his cock jumped in response. What a sense of power. So why didn't he come to her or draw her toward him.

They stood facing each other, not more than four feet away,

discovering everything they could by sight, but Nan was eager to get to the touch and taste part. And so was Damon if she knew the signs. And she knew the signs.

Then he moved and she was in his arms, their bodies pressed together, sharing heat, exchanging desire. He didn't kiss her this time or suckle her, but scooped her off the ground and laid her gently across the bed. He lifted her leg, slipped off her shoe, and held her bare foot in his hand.

His tongue flicked across her toes. Nan wriggled. Jesus. The man even made feet erotic. He nibbled each toe, then slid his tongue up her instep leaving a heated wet trail to her ankle.

Oh, boy. She didn't think she could wait for him to make his way all the way up her leg. She reached for him again, but he pushed her hand away. Continued to lick and nibble his way up her calf and thigh. Exquisite torture. It was time to reel this baby in.

"Damon," she whispered.

"Soon." He nuzzled the crease at her hip, just inches from where he needed to go. She wondered if he needed a road map. She shifted under him, trying to give him a clue. His breath puffed out over her belly, making her shudder. He was teasing her.

Nan's whole body clenched in anticipation. Okay, she was going to die without ever getting to the really good part.

Finally, his tongue slipped beneath the tie of her thong. He followed the string to the triangle of fabric. She felt the rasp of his tongue on her skin, now just centimeters to the left of home.

"Damon."

He kept moving, bypassing where she needed him, then coming back a little closer and skirting off to the side again. She was squirming beneath him. Out of control, helpless to make him hurry.

Then his tongue slipped out of her thong and he moved away. Nan felt a wash of disappointment.

But he moved back to her, his mouth inches above the fabric. His head dipped, his teeth closed over the silk triangle, soaked from both their body fluids. He jerked his head. The fabric ripped as the thong came away in his mouth.

He tossed it to the side and dove to his final destination.

Nan whimpered. She never whimpered, simpered, or whined. But she felt like doing all three. She fell into a vortex of pleasure. The movements of his tongue, the nip of his teeth diffused waves of heat through the rest of her body; drove an acute tightening deep inside her.

She was caught up in the moment, yo-yoing between trying to guess what he would do next, and not caring at all as long as he kept going. She was turned on by the unpredictability of it all, and totally helpless to reciprocate. Finally giving up, she succumbed to the escalating rhythm of his tongue and her response to it.

She grabbed his hair, pulling him into her. He urged her toward the brink, winding her tighter and tighter, until the spring uncoiled and she rocketed through space. Damon hung on all the way, riding her until the last contraction subsided.

He followed his tongue up the center of her body.

"Can't wait," he said and thrust into her, before she could even say "condom."